BAD
SCENE

BAD SCENE

A COLLEEN HAYES MYSTERY

MAX TOMLINSON

OCEANVIEW PUBLISHING
SARASOTA, FLORIDA

ISBN 978-1-60809-500-1

Published in the United States of America by Oceanview Publishing

Sarasota, Florida

www.oceanviewpub.com

10 9 8 7 6 5 4 3 2

PRINTED IN THE UNITED STATES OF AMERICA

In Memoriam

To Floyd, the best four-legged writing coach an author ever had.
Rest in peace, good boy.

BAD SCENE

PROLOGUE

"It is time for the first volunteer," Brother Adem shouted to the 243 gathered along the cliff.

He sat on the broad shoulders of one of his followers, facing the crowd. His words, marked by a prominent Afrikaans accent, reverberated through the bullhorn he held to his lips. In the distance, the tip of the volcano glowed in the night sky, the reason for the church's long trek. Their ultimate destination.

"Time for the first volunteer."

In the darkness broken by the full moon, his followers' eyes sparkled as they connected with his.

Almost as one, they answered: "*Ja, Adem.*"

Brother Adem nodded with satisfaction. Haven, his personal guard, shifted beneath him. The big man's motorcycle jacket fit like a saddle.

Adem studied the dirty, hopeful faces. He wore his floppy hat over his long unwashed hair, along with the same filthy striped bell-bottoms he'd worn for weeks, traveling on the ship to South America with his children, hiking for days from the coast. His prison crucifix tattoo in the middle of his forehead, just slightly off-center, pointed at a long arched nose. His light green sunglasses hid pinpoint pupils.

"Who will be the first to reach perfection, children?"

"Me, Adem!"

There. A feminine hand shot up.

The volunteer was a pretty young American woman, her red hair long and wild. Her face was grubby but strikingly pale, hauntingly beautiful. Light eyes shone with faith. Her vulnerability stirred him. Adem had been with many of the females and couldn't recall if he had sampled her yet and wondered why he didn't remember her. She wore a thin, rumpled dress and her shapely breasts hung free underneath. His loins responded.

He would know her better before she reached perfection. She would not be a volunteer just yet.

He moved the bullhorn away from his chapped lips, spoke to Haven quietly. "The auburn-haired woman of approximately twenty years? Her name?"

Haven jostled underneath him, the smell of his unwashed body ripe and fragrant.

"Pamela Hayes," Haven said. "She joined us in San Francisco."

"And her perfect name?"

"Fenna."

Adem raised the bullhorn. "Why do you wish to be the first, Fenna?"

"Perfection, Adem. I want perfection."

Perfection in death. Adem nodded slowly, making a show of it, for he already had a volunteer selected, one of the extras brought along to ensure that the perfect number of 242—eleven times twenty-two—survived the journey. He had started with 245. Two were already gone. That left one more before the day of surrender, and it would not be Fenna. He would savor her first. He lifted the bullhorn and spoke. "And you shall reach perfection, my child. But today is not your day." He looked at the rest of the crowd in a theatrical sweep. "Who has today selected, children? This eleventh day of the month, a sacred day."

Two more hands. *Good.*

Adem's knees shifted Haven around like a horse as he gestured at the night sky over Tungurahua—the Throat of Fire—across the canyon. The cobalt blue space prickled with early stars, pulsing in the halo of light from the volcano.

"Eleven days from now we will make our first ascent. Molten rock from the bowels of Mother Earth will cleanse us. Tomorrow we march to our sanctuary to prepare."

The 243 answered: "*Ja, Adem.*"

"She knows. That mankind has ruined her domain. And she knows we understand. For we have come all this way. Many miles, children. And we are stronger as we reach perfection. She knows. But she needs a token of our understanding."

Ja, Adem.

Torches were being lit here and there, and their flames cast dancing light across his unwashed flock.

"For only in death is there a new life."

Ja, Adem.

"And we do not fear death."

Nee, Adem.

"And for this moon, this rare moon, and her throat of fire, we thank her."

Ja, Adem.

"So who will be the first?" Adem scanned the faces. He found the glassy eyes and bulbous cheeks he was searching for. An unfortunate-looking young man, ugly, with mental deficiencies. Godfried was his perfect name. The last extra brought along to ensure 242.

"You," he said, pointing. "Godfried. I feel your perfection rising."

Godfried's face dropped with surprise. "Me, Adem?"

"Yes, you. You will be the first."

A moment of hesitation. "I will?"

"Yes. You."

Godfried flinched. "I am not sure I am ready, Adem."

"Yes, child, you are."

"But . . . I'm frightened."

Now this was not good.

"*For only in death is there a new life,*" Adem repeated. "*And we do not fear death.*"

Godfried blinked quickly, unsure.

"Bring him here," Adem said, jostling on Haven's shoulders. "Bring my child here."

Two of the male members grabbed Godfried, one arm apiece.

The crowd parted and they pulled him forward.

He stood before Adem, looking up, his eyes flickering.

He was an awkward shape, with an underdeveloped torso and short, heavy legs.

Tungurahua flashed behind them.

"See?" Adem said. "Mother Earth understands your fear. And tells you this is normal. But that you will transcend."

It wouldn't do to throw him over. Not so early. The others would only think twice.

Adem narrowed his eyes at Godfried, the two men holding him.

"Do you want assistance, Godfried?"

Godfried eyed Adem, doubtful.

Adem raised his bullhorn, spoke to the 242. "Give your brother the encouragement he needs to reach perfection, children!"

The 242 shouted as one. "*Perfeksie!*"

Godfried stood upright, full of uncertain pride as he shook with nerves.

"Go, child."

Tears streamed down the young man's protruding cheeks.

"*Perfeksie!*" Adem said. "Now, brother."

"*Ja, Adem,*" Godfried whispered. He reared back and took off in a sprint, heading for the cliff.

And then he was gone.

His scream echoed through the canyon.

Unfortunate, Adem thought.

There was a collective silence by the 242. They had not witnessed perfection before. Then another cheer. Then the wind rushing through the trees.

Adem kneed Haven, turned to his children.

"We are renewed."

Ja, Adem.

"We will rest here for the night before we head to Verligting. Our sanctuary. To prepare for the day. The twenty-second." Another sacred day, a multiple of eleven.

The crowd dispersed into smaller groups.

Adem dismounted. Turned to Haven, big, bearded, and wild.

"The redheaded one? Fenna? Pamela? Bring her to my tent."

Haven gave a shrewd smile. "Yes, Adem."

CHAPTER ONE

"You left a message, Lucky?" Colleen asked, squeezing in at the bar where space was at a premium. San Franciscans took their drinking seriously, especially after ten a.m.

Maybe it was about her runaway daughter. Luck was the last one to see Pam.

Colleen had found Lucky in Spec's on Columbus, amidst the North Beach literati, standing next to an exotic dancer in a turquoise satin robe taking a break from the clandestine strip club upstairs. The jukebox thumped with "Miss You" and Colleen figured the end of the world was nigh if the Rolling Stones were pushing disco. Lucky wore his scruffy blue down jacket on top of his *Chronicle* newspaper apron, and was bent over a fresh vodka screwdriver, preparing to take the first sip without spilling any precious nectar. Stage Two Parkinson's made that a challenge, but Lucky was up to the task.

Heaped next to his cocktail was a pile of nickels, dimes, and quarters that would have filled a large collection plate. Part of the morning's take selling papers.

He took a sip, stood upright, lifting the drink in his palsied hands. It vibrated.

"So I did. So I did." Lucky was in his forties, most likely, although his lifestyle made him look older, and his disease even more so. His shock of gray hair was still thick but ragged. He brandished an infectious grin offset by a missing front tooth before he sucked booze through a red straw. He hadn't shaved in some time, possibly hadn't bathed since then, either. But like a shaggy old dog that slept in the yard, it was no big deal; Lucky was good company. He set his drink down gingerly, most of it already gone. He dug into the front pocket of his apron, rattling change. "Would a pretty lady like a drink?"

"Not right now," Colleen said, putting her hand on his arm. "And you make sure you leave enough coin for a room tonight."

"Sure, sure," he said. His thoughts seemed to wander as he bobbed to the music, his head loose on his neck.

"You left a message with my answering service, Luck?" Colleen asked again.

"So I did," he said, looking for the bartender, a young man in a white thermal shirt and tight jeans. "So I did."

"Allow me," she said, getting her money clip out of her new black leather car coat, recently purchased at Macy's on Union Square after a client had finally paid off his bill. A shotgun blast had taken her treasured bomber jacket. But the new coat was classier and went well with her faded wide bell-bottoms.

"Not too much OJ, Colleen. It gives me indigestion."

Buying a drink for Lucky felt like giving a kid a family-size bag of candy. She ordered a screwdriver and quietly instructed the bartender to make it weak. He nodded.

Soon, Lucky was positioned over another cocktail, Colleen lighting a Virginia Slim and brushing her chestnut-colored feather-cut back while he drank off the top and got upright again. Lucky smacked his lips, bopping to disco Stones.

"Luck?" she said, tapping ash. "Did you have some news?" She didn't want to ask about Pamela directly and put suggestions into his mind.

"Did you get your hair cut?" Lucky said. "You look like one of Charlie's Angels."

Patience was one thing Colleen had learned during her nine years in prison. "I did, Luck. And flattery will get you everywhere. But the reason for your phone call will make me truly happy." Lucky had spotted Pamela two months ago, hanging out with members of Moon Ranch near his flop hotel. Since then, Pam had gone missing. Again. Colleen was ecstatic that Pamela had finally split with the cult, and would give just about anything to reconnect. But Pamela continued to shun her.

Pamela was the reason Colleen came to California last year. Pamela had taken off shortly before Colleen's release from Denver Women's Correctional Facility.

Pamela had never forgiven her for killing her father.

"Lucky?" she said.

"Oh, right," Lucky said, setting his drink down sloppily. "Shuggy."

"And who might that be?"

"Shuggy Johnston," he said. "Room next to mine. The biker den."

"The Thunderbird?"

Lucky slurped his screwdriver and gave a shaky nod.

Colleen knew all about the Thunderbird, a seedy residence hotel in the Tenderloin. She'd had the dubious privilege of renting a room there when she needed a verifiable address to satisfy parole.

"This Shuggy's a biker, I take it?" she said.

"Room 312. Biker den."

"Why is it a 'den'?"

"He's always talking about a 'den.' Rides a chopper with a swastika eyeball painted on the tank. His friends ride too. They come to see him. Yes they do. To buy."

"Shuggy deals?"

"Isn't that what they do?"

"Is that what you wanted to tell me, Luck? That this Shuggy's a dope dealer?" With Lucky, one had to be sure what he was getting at.

Shook his head *no*. "I was trying to sleep. Toilet paper in my ears. Newspapers don't sell themselves, you know." He thumbed his own chest. "I work for a living."

"I know you do, Luck, and you are to be commended for it. So, it's sounding like this Shuggy Johnston had some questionable visitors? Who woke you up?"

"Came up to the third floor, they did—the biker den. Heard them talking. Yes. Saw them too. Through the crack in the door."

"You need to be careful, Luck."

He frowned. "I know. I know. They already caught me once."

Not good. "And?"

He gave her a solemn look before his eyes darted to a 1940s wartime poster on the wall with a ship going down: *Loose Lips Sink Ships*.

"Ah," she said quietly. "It's confidential."

He tapped the side of his nose.

She tapped hers, too, then signaled the barman to let him know they were leaving and to settle up. The barman scooped up Lucky's pile of change, converted it to bills, which Lucky stuffed haphazardly into his jeans. "Let's go outside," Colleen said. "You need to get out of here anyway." She tipped the barman, patted the bar to let him know she appreciated him looking after Lucky. They left, not a moment too soon. "Stayin' Alive" had just come on the jukebox.

Outside, in the alley leading up to Specs, the gray morning that was often San Francisco cast a pale glow over their heads.

"So, what's this all about already, Luck?" Colleen asked.

"You're a cop, right, Colleen?"

"Not in the slightest. But I know a couple of good ones."

Lucky's unsteady neck shook as he looked this way and that, then back at Colleen. He put his hands into the pocket of his apron, rattled the change that was left.

"Somebody's gonna shoot the mayor," he said.

Colleen experienced a mild jolt. But Lucky was full of stories.

"You sure about that, Lucky?"

He nodded, a rickety headshake.

"Why?"

"Because he likes the gays."

"The mayor likes a lot of people."

"Yeah, but this particular guy has a beef with him."

"*What* particular guy?"

"A government guy who doesn't like the gays either."

"At City Hall? On Van Ness?"

Another conspiratorial nod.

"Does he have a name, Luck? This shooter? You can tell me."

Lucky scrutinized her. "The bikers scare me. If they catch me again, I'm toasted."

"They scare me too. And if I pass your information along, your name will never come up."

He gave her a squint. "Solid?"

"Solid. I am the owner and proprietor of Hayes Confidential, Luck. *Confidentiality* is so important that I put it right there in the name, see?"

He nodded.

Then he said, "Jordan Kray."

That knocked her a little further to one side. Jordan Kray was a city district supervisor and a former cop.

"Are you absolutely sure about that, Luck?"

"Sure as shinola."

"And you heard this outside the biker den," she said. "Where you were listening at the door?"

"Through the walls. And the crack. They're loud, Shuggy and his dudes. They went to some Nazi Klucker meeting."

"Klucker?"

"Ku Klucker Klan."

Neo-Nazi bikers. Nothing new. "How many in this biker den?"

He held up three fingers.

"And you're absolutely sure they were discussing how Supervisor you-know-who is going to shoot the mayor?"

"Because 'he loves those fags,' they said."

The current mayor was on record for supporting gay rights. And, despite being the People's Republic of San Francisco where everything progressive was eagerly received with open arms, there were still plenty of good old-fashioned bigots lurking.

"When is this shooting supposed to take place?" she asked.

Lucky shrugged.

"Have you told anybody else about this?"

Shook his head.

"Good. Then let's just keep it between you and me."

"No *problemo.*"

"And do me another favor, Luck, and stay somewhere else for a while. No Thunderbird. I don't like you being so close to Shuggy and his Nazi Klucker pals."

"Where am I supposed to stay?"

"The Hugo, Sixth and Mission. Or the Falcon, one block away. They're closer to the *Chronicle* anyway. Less of a trip for you in the a.m."

"Yeah, but those places don't always have a room for me."

She got out her clip, peeled off a couple of twenties. She got one of her business cards out, jotted her personal phone number on the back, futzed with the broken zipper on the top pocket of Lucky's down jacket, tucked her business card in with the money folded around it. Zipped it up as best she could, which was halfway. "With what you have here, you can rent a room for the better part of a week. Do it today and make me happy. In fact, do it right now. Before you even go back to work."

He looked down in the direction of his pocket. "How am I going to pay you back that much money?"

She gave his cheek an affectionate pinch. "With all the good info you give me, mister. You are my eyes and ears on the street."

"Aww." He looked down, blushing.

Her voice croaked slightly before she spoke. "Lucky, you haven't heard or seen anything new about Pamela, have you?"

"Your little girl."

"She's nineteen now. But yes, I suppose you could still say that. You saw her a couple of months back, with some Moon Ranchers. Remember?"

"So I did. Near the Thunderbird."

"And if you ever hear anything about her again, or the people from Moon Ranch, you're going to let me know again, right away, correct?"

"I'm your eyes and ears."

She smiled. Straightened his collar.

"What about the mayor thing?" he asked.

"I'm going to talk to someone," she said. "You, however, are *not*. Loose lips, remember?" She made a zipper motion over her mouth.

Lucky made the same zipper motion.

"Good man," she said. "No more biker den for you. Hugo. Sixth and Mission. If they give you any guff, you tell them to call me and I will set them straight."

"Hugo," he said. "Six and Mission. Hugo. Six and Mission." He turned around and marched off down Columbus, mumbling the words to himself.

She watched him, swinging his arms like a big kid, his apron flapping over his baggy jeans, his down jacket puffing out his skinny torso, talking to himself. He looked so vulnerable. He *was* vulnerable.

The mayor story might be drunken biker BS. But she'd check it out. Because the world was going to hell.

CHAPTER TWO

The Thunderbird was a three-story flop hotel on O'Farrell in the heart of the Tenderloin, one of the city's "non-touristy" areas. Built of brick and stone shortly after the 1906 quake in what had once been the ritzy part of town, not much had transpired since in the way of upgrades. A non-functioning neon sign in the shape of a stylized thunderbird, black with dirt, hung over the doorway, where a couple of residents sat on the steps with a boom box thumping Earth, Wind & Fire. A window was boarded up. Another had a sign advertising rooms available, by the day, week, month. Section 8 accepted.

Little parking was to be had. O'Farrell was one-way so Colleen circled the block, parked near the Mitchell Brothers Theater, where the marquee proudly proclaimed the club to be the home of the country's first lap dance. Locking up the red Torino, she headed down to the Thunderbird. A working girl in gold hot pants with platforms to match her shiny blond wig was hunkered down outside the corner store, smoking a cigarette to keep warm. It didn't appear to be helping. In her skimpy black tank top, her skin bore a blueish tint.

Colleen did not recognize the stoop dwellers from her time at the Thunderbird. But residents came and went. One grizzled young guy wore a long sleeved Mad Dog T-shirt. His friend was a heavyset Latino in a pink hair net and sunglasses. Both seemed to lack facial expressions. The music pulsated.

"How're the rooms?" she asked.

"Like shit," Mad Dog said.

"Hey, you guys wouldn't happen to know if Shuggy Johnston is home, would you?"

Hair Net examined her. "Out. Why?"

"Just in the neighborhood and thought I'd say 'hi.'"

A stare. Plus one from his friend.

Did she look like a narc? Maybe she was bathing too often. But Shuggy Johnston did indeed live there. She could always ask the manager, Lawrence, from her residence period, but then she would be giving the game away. Low key was king.

She thanked them, strolled back up O'Farrell, stopping at a payphone near the Mitchell Brothers, where she called SFPD's anonymous tip line, said there was a rumor that Jordan Kray was going to shoot the mayor. The woman manning the hotline seemed barely interested but made note of it.

Colleen hung up, dissatisfied with SFPD's response. This called out for a little more due diligence.

*   *   *

It was late evening when the motorcycles came roaring down O'Farrell towards the Thunderbird. Colleen was dozing at the wheel of the Torino, parked across from the liquor store. She sat up, rubbing her eyes as the bikers curbed their rides. She readied her Canon SLR from under the *Chronicle* on the passenger seat.

Two choppers had raked front ends and the other was a big black Harley motor trike, like something a kid might find under the tree. A big kid in this case. Not that big actually, a fireplug in leathers with a sprig of frizzy hair. He climbed off, stepping down, having to reach. A Confederate flag was painted on the trunk door on the back of his trike. If he was over five foot tall, she'd have been surprised.

Using the newspaper as a partial shield, she snapped a photo.

The other two were more typical biker specimens, one a tall bean-pole with sunglasses on at night and a sweep of black hair that he flipped to one side as he climbed off a beige Harley Police Special. He stood, hunched over like Nosferatu in black leather.

She snapped a photo.

The last guy rode a matte black Frankenstein bike of no determinate year or style. He was late thirties—early forties, built like a football player who had stopped exercising but was still plenty intimidating. He wore a faded sleeveless denim jacket over a motorcycle jacket so old the leather was worn down to dirty white skin in places. Long greasy dark hair was held in place, more or less, by a black paisley bandanna. Through the telephoto lens she saw his face was hard and gray, like cement, pocked with ancient acne scars. He'd been good-looking at one time, but that had been a long time ago. The years had etched sharp grooves around a sneer. Thick eyebrows protruded above deep-set, hooded eyes. A brutish intelligence lurked but *mean* was the prevailing feature.

Colleen could read his face like a book.

That was because he looked a lot like her ex, another guy who'd had *badass* down to a T. It repulsed her that she had ever been that foolish, but she'd been sixteen and he'd been in his twenties. And she'd ended his life long ago.

She took a photo.

He shut off the bike, clambered off, spit as he hitched up his faded jeans.

The three men mounted the half dozen stairs to the Thunderbird.

Colleen stashed the camera, slipped on a pair of sunglasses, pulled her hair up, stuffed it under a black ball cap.

Out of the car she flipped up the collar of her leather coat, jammed her hands in the pockets, scooted down, across O'Farrell, up to the Thunderbird. Archie Bunker was yelling at Edith at high volume from a TV in a ground floor room. Colleen wandered by, checking out the bikes as if out of casual interest.

On the black gas tank was painted a swastika with a white eyeball in the center, like a third eye. As Lucky had said. The big brute was Shuggy Johnston.

A classy bunch. Guys who might well sit around and brag about someone going to shoot the mayor. And this crowd might know what they were talking about.

She was about to turn back when she noticed, on the corner by the liquor store, the girl in the shiny blond wig in her mini and platform shoes, wearing a short jacket now, looking at Colleen looking at the bikes. A snitch? Colleen headed back to her car, taking a circuitous path.

She drove home to Potrero Hill, an old Edwardian top floor flat with big white rooms, sparsely furnished, and high ceilings that reverberated with the rush of the freeway up the hill. The place was shabby chic and the view from her many windows most days was fog, but she liked it just fine. After her stint sleeping in a defunct warehouse she had guarded for a client, broke, it was heaven. One bedroom had a bed made up for her daughter, Pamela, if—*when*—Colleen found her.

In her office overlooking downtown and a Bay Bridge swirling in vapor, she called Inspector Owens at work. She knew he wouldn't be there this late so she left a message, saying she needed to talk to him as soon as possible. She didn't want to get ahead of herself, but Lucky's story was seeming less of a story and more of a possibility.

Colleen turned in, lay there on the warm, undulating, water-filled mattress. Thinking about Pamela. And where she might be. Hoping she was safe. Hoping she wasn't in some kind of trouble again.

CHAPTER THREE

"Sorry to drag you away from the bad guys," Colleen said.

She and Inspector Owens were sitting in Red's Java House on Pier 30. The view of the early morning Bay Bridge looming overhead was worth the cold drafts that blew in through gaps in old doors and windows. The lunch crowd hadn't arrived yet and they almost had the place to themselves, save for a couple of longshoremen sitting at the counter, lamenting the decline of San Francisco's waterfront. What was left was moving over to Oakland.

"Fucking containers," one said, slurping coffee.

"Your call sounded important," Owens said to Colleen, as he sipped a cup of black coffee. Owens was heading into middle age, with the beginnings of jowls on a face paled by too many nights under the fluorescent lights at 850 Bryant, and a body thickening around the middle. The disco look had invaded his wardrobe, however, today with a checked jacket and a shiny wide tie of iridescent blue. His graying hair had been blasted by some formula for men, rendering it an unnatural-looking reddish-brown, and was blow-dried, touching his collar. Colleen had to give him credit for trying. A lot of guys his age were giving up. And that was something Owens didn't do. Plus, he had a young wife he was trying to keep, if the rumors were true.

Owens was one cop she could trust.

But, as reassuring as his presence was in general, today something was off. A tenseness around the eyes. But she didn't know him well enough to ask. Maybe it was Colleen, worrying about the biker den.

"I think it might well be," she said, pushing her cup of coffee away. She hadn't really wanted it in the first place. Unlike Owens, her outfit was basic, a floral polyester top tucked into her faded bell-bottoms under a suede sheepskin coat she had not taken off, trying to keep warm.

She told him what she knew about one of the supervisors scheming to shoot the mayor.

Owens sat for a moment, set his cup down, licked his lower lip. "And where did you get this little gem of information, Colleen?"

She shook her head. "Hayes *Confidential?*"

"Thought so. Well, I wish I had a dollar for every assassination rumor that came along."

"You'd have a few dollars," she said. "But not that many, surely." She got out her envelope from One-Hour Photo and splayed out the shots of the three bikers. "Neo-Nazi/KKK biker types. The big guy is Shuggy Johnston. Lives at the Thunderbird Hotel on O'Farrell. He's the one to watch. He's also rumored to deal dope. I checked around. LSD is his specialty."

Owens studied the photos. "And you're sure your source is telling you the truth?"

"As much as he knows. It could all be a drinking story, but you and I both know one or two supervisors who hang with a—*ah*—less tolerant crowd."

"Did you think of calling the hotline?" It was clear Owens had better things to do.

"I did call. But the operator I spoke to seemed about as interested as if I was reporting skateboarders in my driveway."

"It would've been logged. Someone will get to it."

"Maybe. But I think it might need closer scrutiny sooner."

"I'll see someone gets these," he said, gathering up the photos, looking at his wristwatch.

She was a little disappointed. "I know you're busy, but I guess I was hoping . . ."

"It's not my department. It's not really anyone's department. These things are handled ad hoc. If it warrants attention, a team will be formed."

She looked him in the eye. "Okay, tell me if I'm out of line, but is everything okay?"

"With me, you mean?"

They really didn't know each other personally.

"No, the guy posing as Inspector Owens."

He looked at her for a long moment. "Busy. Getting ready to take some time off work."

"The holidays and all that," she said.

"Right."

He sure didn't sound very jovial about holidays and time off. But it was none of her business. She thanked him, wished him a happy Thanksgiving, and they parted ways.

A busy morning so far but she still had to get some real work done, meaning paid work. She drove over to the Marina where she parked kitty-corner to an imposing 1920s stucco house facing the yacht club. The Golden Gate Bridge was fighting its way through the fog. Eventually the garage door opened and a new baby-blue Dodge Magnum backed out, sporting rakish rear side windows with decorative louvers. A little bald man in glasses sat at the wheel. Colleen followed at a distance to an address on Polk Street where he parked, plugged the meter with quite a few coins, and went into an apartment above a dry cleaners. She got a photo of that. An hour later he came out with a furtive, self-satisfied look on his face, look-ing either way. She got photos of that too. She smoked a cigarette, listened to KGO *Newstalk* carry on about gay bathhouses, waited some more. Just over half an hour later, a young woman left the apartment. She was statuesque, with long blond hair that looked great with her dark one-piece jumpsuit and short red leather jacket. Red platform wedge sandals made her seem even taller. She wore sunglasses even though it was overcast. She was clearly out of Mr. Philanderer's price range. Colleen got a picture of her, too, and wished she could have gotten the two of them together. She made notes in her file and sighed at what it took to pay the bills. But di-vorce work was plentiful.

CHAPTER FOUR

Middle of the night, the white princess phone by Colleen's bed rang. She blinked herself awake, checked the clock. 2:05 a.m. The bars had just shut. She suspected it might be her friend Alex, in her cups again. Ever since Alex's father had died of lung cancer, she had taken her drinking to a new level, barhopping with friends in the city and then driving down the coast late at night to the mansion she'd been left. Colleen had urged Alex to stay over in the future, not go up against the cliffs of Highway 1 when she was seeing twice as many guardrails.

Colleen rolled over, picked up the phone. Rain pattered on the windows. She croaked a hello.

"Ms. Hayes?"

Not Alex. Hurried voices in the background. Sounds of activity. Not a bar.

"Speaking," Colleen said.

"This is SF General Hospital Emergency Room. We have a patient in serious condition, a Mr. Herman Waddell." The woman's voice was calm, professional, but distressed. "We found your business card in his pocket."

Colleen's heart thumped unpleasantly. "Is he a middle-aged guy, gray hair, a little weathered-looking?"

"That's him. We thought he might be a vagrant."

Lucky. She had never known his real name.

"He's a friend," she said. "How bad is he?"

"Unconscious. Badly beaten."

She felt the breaths coming fast and quick. The irony of Lucky's nickname hit her like a sucker punch. "And he's in the ER?"

"On his way to surgery most likely. They're doing a CAT scan first."

"I'm on my way," she said. "By the way, he's got Parkinson's."

"That's good to know."

Colleen hung up, pulled on jeans and a white T-shirt as she stepped sockless into her white leather Pony Topstars. Threw on her leather coat, grabbed purse and keys, exited out the back, taking the stairs down to the rear parking yard two at a time. Wondering who the hell beat poor Lucky up. But she already had a pretty good idea.

CHAPTER FIVE

"Subdural hematoma," the surgeon said, pulling off his green surgical cap. He was a tall, slender man with flecks of gray in his beard. It was almost three a.m., but in the stark fluorescent hallway of SF General, it could have been any time of day, except for the relative silence of what would normally be a busy public hospital.

"That doesn't sound good at all," Colleen said. "What exactly is a 'subdural hematoma'?"

"Bleeding in the brain," the doc said. "The best we could do was relieve some of the pressure by draining blood. Are you a family member?"

"A friend. I don't think he has any family."

"Well, if he does, this would be a good time to notify them."

Colleen fought a palpitation. "Are you saying he's not going to make it?"

"Never say *never*." The doctor frowned. "But someone went to town on him. His skull is fractured. Blunt-force injury."

If the attack wasn't random, she could only think of Shuggy Johnston and the bikers Lucky had spied on. The story about shooting the mayor.

But she needed proof.

"Have the police been notified?" she asked.

"The ER would've done that once they triaged him and suspected a crime. But, being as General is the San Francisco Knife and Gun Club, SFPD don't always show up right away. Sometimes they bundle multiple reports into one call."

"Can I see him?"

The doc pursed his lips. "Not sure what good it would do."

"I would just really appreciate it." And if she could find out how Lucky got to SF General, it would help nail down any evidence.

"I'll get one of the nurses to take you back there. But give it a little while. They'll need to discharge him from the Recovery Room and move him to Intensive Care."

Colleen thanked him. More than troubled, she headed down to the ER, asked the desk nurse where the EMTs might have found Herman Waddell. It felt odd to be using Lucky's real name. But Lucky wasn't an appropriate name for him today.

The ER nurse, a black woman with a short Afro, said, "That would be on the ambulance report."

"Which ambulance service brought him in?"

The nurse gave her a squint. "How about you tell me who *you* are first?"

"A friend," Colleen said, introducing herself. "I'm almost certain he's got no family."

"DPH," she said. Department of Public Health. She dug through an admittance log on a clipboard, showed Colleen: M. Donaldson, H003 EMT/Paramedic, Truck 41.

"Mickey Donaldson," the nurse said. "Mickey D."

"You don't have the phone number of his station, do you?"

"Nope."

"It would really help if I knew whether Herman was conscious, said anything."

"I can't give you his number. Sorry."

"What happened to Herman's things? His clothes? His wallet?"

"Why don't you let SFPD handle that?"

"Right, but the surgeon said that might take a while."

"Leave your number. I'll put a call in to DPH. But you might not hear anything right away. I can also have SFPD contact you. They'll have to write it up."

Eventually. Colleen thanked her, left. In the hallway by the ER she found a payphone, called directory services, asked for the number of Central Emergency on Grove Street. There were half a dozen city DPH ambulance stations. Central would be the place to start.

A clerk at Central told her truck 41 was dispatched out of Mission Emergency. They gave her the phone number. She called Mission Emergency. EMT Mickey Donaldson was out on a call. She asked about an emergency he worked concerning a man picked up probably around one a.m. They couldn't give that information out. She asked what time Mickey Donaldson went off shift. They said seven a.m. She left her numbers.

Back in the hospital, Lucky had been moved to Intensive Care. They balked at letting Colleen into the ICU at first but Colleen pushed and was shown to a room where, behind a blue plastic curtain, she recoiled when she got a look at him.

A thick bandage covered the top of his head and one side of his face. What skin was visible was bruised and swollen, purple in places, crimson in others. His observable eyelid was a puffy slit. A ventilator tube snaked into the side of his mouth, the hiss of oxygen like a deflating tire. An IV hung from a bracket on a stand, feeding a clear fluid into his arm. A high-tech computer device that seemed to be reading his cardiac state was connected to him with wires. An inconsistent green line on a dark screen hobbled from left to right. Lucky's pulse rate was displayed in changing red letters: 45, up to 90, then back down to 55, and so on. Even to a medical novice like Colleen, that didn't seem good.

The head nurse stood by. She was a matronly woman with dark features.

"Can he talk?" Colleen whispered.

"He mumbles now and again," the nurse said. "Nothing intelligible."

Colleen turned. "Well, that's a good sign, isn't it? Talking?"

The nurse frowned. "Possibly."

"Where are his effects?"

"Bedside table." She nodded at it.

"Okay if I take a look?"

The nurse grimaced.

"I'm trying to find out what happened to him," Colleen said. "It would really help."

"Be quick." She opened the bedside cabinet, removed a large paper sack, handed it to Colleen. Colleen rested it on the corner of the bed, next to Lucky's blanketed foot.

She went through the items. Shoes, socks, underwear. Lucky's jeans. A plaid shirt he'd worn almost every time she'd seen him, still damp with the blood that saturated the collar. No down jacket.

She handed the bag back to the nurse. "I'm guessing his jacket's a goner?"

The nurse nodded. "We took whatever was in the pockets and put it to one side. Along with his wallet."

"Where would that be?"

She squinted. "At the nursing station. We hold them until he's discharged. Or give them to SFPD."

"If I could just go through it quickly," Colleen said. "You can watch."

"I don't have time for that."

"Then maybe you can just find out one thing for me. Is there any money in his wallet?"

"Why?"

"I'm trying to determine if he might have been robbed." A robbery meant a possible random event. No robbery pointed at Shuggy Johnston.

"Wait here." The nurse padded out of the room. Colleen turned to Lucky, put her hand on the back of his. It felt cool and waxy, which sent a chill through her. Suddenly, his head turned. He murmured around the tube in the corner of his mouth.

"Luck, it's me—Colleen. You're in the hospital. You've been in an accident. But you're going to be okay." One could only hope. "Can you hear me?"

Lucky's one visible eye split open a millimeter.

"*Coh?*" he tried to say, but it was almost without sound. She was doing her best to read his lips, not easy with the breathing tube. And painful to watch.

Colleen squeezed his hand.

"Don't try to talk," she said. "Can you feel my hand?"

Lucky returned a feeble clasp.

"Good. I'm going to ask you some *yes* or *no* questions, and you nod, or squeeze my hand. Whatever works—got it?"

Small hand squeeze.

"Do you have any idea who did this to you, Lucky?"

Shook his head *no.*

"Can't remember?" she asked.

Shook his head.

"Remember *anything* about it, Luck?"

Miniscule headshake.

"Were you at the Hugo?" That was the hotel Colleen had directed Lucky to.

Headshake.

A jolt of alarm caught her. "Not the Thunderbird?"

He nodded.

So Lucky had stayed at the Thunderbird after all.

"Were you in your usual room?" she asked. "313?"

Head nod.

"Next to Shuggy Johnston in 312? The biker den?"

Nod.

Colleen's heart sank. "Did Shuggy have his biker friends over last night?"

Head nod.

"Were you spying on them?"

There was a delay before he responded. Then, a single sad nod.

A wave of nausea washed over her. "Did they catch you spying, Luck?"

Now there was a longer delay. He looked away. The ventilator hissed.

"Luck?"

Nod.

"Oh, Luck," she said, squeezing his hand. But there was no point reprimanding him. The damage had been done. "I'm so sorry."

He looked back. His one visible eye glistened.

"Is your stuff at the Thunderbird?" she asked.

Nod.

"I'll get it, keep it at my place until you're out of here. I'll call the *Chronicle*, let them know you won't be selling papers for a while." If ever, she thought.

Nod.

She saw him try to speak around the ventilator tube. The word "thanks" formed on his lips. She squeezed his hand. "I'll be back later to check on you. Don't go anywhere without me, okay?"

Hs tried to smile at the joke. He squeezed her hand. He was trying to form a word on his lips around the hissing ventilator tube. It seemed important.

"What is it, Luck?"

It looked like he was saying "Pap." *Pah*.

"What about your pop? You want me to call your pop? Where is he? I don't have his number. Where is it?"

Shook his head.

"Pah," he gasped, his one eye wide open, glassy, but alert. He was trying to tell her something.

Her heart leapt at the possibility.

"Did you say *Pam,* Luck?"

Painful nod.

"Excuse me," a woman's cold voice said behind Colleen.

Colleen spun, not realizing how focused she had been on the conversation. The head nurse had a black wallet in her hand.

"What on earth do you think you're doing?" she said. "This man is in critical condition."

"I'm sorry. I didn't mean anything by it."

"Well, you're going to have to leave—right now."

"If I could just have another moment . . ."

The nurse turned her head and shouted. "Security!"

Colleen put her hands up in appeasement. "That's not necessary. I'm gone."

The door to the ICU opened and a heavyset guard in black pants and gray uniform shirt came charging in, his belt jangling.

"Show this woman out," the nurse said.

He took Colleen's arm. "Let's go."

"Got it," Colleen said. "*Got it.*"

She stifled a sigh as she was led out of the ICU. Lucky had wanted to tell her more. But he'd told her enough. If he wasn't delirious, he knew something about Pamela.

Did Pam have something to do with Shuggy? Colleen shuddered at the thought.

Outside, Colleen lit up a Slim, blew smoke into the wet night air.

Finally, a trace of Pam—maybe. But, once again, associated with the wrong people.

CHAPTER SIX

Outside the emergency room a sharp wind blew up 22nd Street as Colleen stepped out her cigarette. The images of Lucky's swollen and bruised face lingered. Pam's possible involvement didn't help. The next step was Shuggy Johnston. But how?

Colleen went back inside, blinking away the fluorescence, called her answering service from a payphone in the hall outside the ER. No new messages.

Commotion outside alerted her to the fact that a fresh emergency had arrived.

Back in the emergency room, paramedics were hustling in a woman on a gurney that reeked of smoke. She was chattering away deliriously in Spanish and one of the paramedics, a Latina with black hair in a braided ponytail, consoled her as she pulled the gurney. The man doing most of the pushing was compact and muscular, with a sculpted, swept-back jet-black pompadour. His powerful arms bulged out of a short-sleeved blue shirt with a blue Department of Public Health Paramedic patch on one arm.

Colleen looked for a name tag. None.

"'Scuse me," he said as they rushed past.

Colleen went through the receiving door to where the white DPH ambulance was parked, its doors still open. The truck number was 41, the same one that brought Lucky in earlier that night.

Not long after, the paramedics returned, wheeling the gurney back out, heaving it back into the rear of the ambulance. Colleen waited for them to finish.

Then she caught the man's eye.

"I think you brought my friend in earlier," she said. "Around one thirty a.m."

He stopped. "The guy beaten up pretty bad?"

"'Pretty bad' is a nice way to put it," she said. "You must be Mickey D."

"I am he." He gave a broad grin, which quickly faded. "How's your friend doing?"

"Still alive—barely. Just got out of surgery. Where'd you pick him up?"

He stood for a moment, rubbed his cheek with a finger, obviously thinking about divulging information.

"I'm a friend," Colleen said. "I'm trying to retrace his steps."

He nodded. "We got a call from a payphone at the Shell station on Sixth and Mission, after someone heard moaning from a dumpster."

"You found Lucky in a *dumpster*?"

Mickey shook his head and grimaced. "Hard to believe, isn't it?"

There would also have to be more than one person to throw Lucky in a dumpster.

"Lucky for your buddy he was groaning," the EMT said.

Colleen called SFPD from the payphone, reported the crime. 911 said they would follow up.

She waited for close to an hour, then went back inside to check in on Lucky. No change, which wasn't bad, considering, but they wouldn't let her in the ICU. SFPD didn't stop by.

She waited outside the ER until her bones chilled, then headed home, swinging by the Thunderbird. No bikes parked outside. The third-floor rooms, where Shuggy stayed, were dark.

CHAPTER SEVEN

"And you heard nothing unusual last night?" Colleen asked Lawrence, the manager of the Thunderbird.

It was evening, the next day.

"Define *unusual*," Lawrence said in a weary monotone, a cigarette dangling from his mouth. "You know how it gets around here."

That she did. It was like that right now: TVs, stereos, residents laughing and shouting.

Colleen knew Lawrence from her short occupancy when she needed a verifiable address to satisfy parole. For a man in his thirties, he did not look well. He was too thin, face too drawn, dark rings under his eyes. His lanky blond hair hung over his forehead in an unkempt swoop. Colleen wasn't sure if drugs were the culprit, or some illness.

"Yeah, I know how it gets around here," Colleen said. "I used to live here, remember?"

"Last night wasn't any different."

"Lucky might not live," she said, in the hopes of triggering a response.

Lawrence took the cigarette out of his mouth, flicked the filter with his thumb, knocking ash onto the beat-up hardwood floor of the hall.

"That's a bad scene," he muttered.

"You don't recall *anything*? It would've been late."

"I zoned out early." He pointed at his ear. "Headphones."

"See Shuggy at all last night?" she said with a side look.

Lawrence's face turned to stone before he shook his head.

"His room was right next to Lucky's," Colleen reminded him.

"Yeah, I know that."

"I know you know. Because it's the room you always give Lucky. Because no one else wants it."

"Beggars can't be choosers."

"I'm pretty sure Lucky paid for his room," she said. "But the police are going to be following up. So, if you know something . . ."

Lawrence tapped more ash onto the floor. "You don't have to tell me how it works."

"Shuggy have friends over last night?" she asked.

Lawrence gave an irritated shrug. "I mind my own business, Colleen."

"I couldn't care less about the fact that he deals. But if you know something that is evidence in a crime, especially something this serious, it's unlawful to keep it to yourself."

"You think I don't know that?"

He probably wouldn't tell the police anything anyway.

"I need to pick up Lucky's stuff," she said. "I'm going to hold it for him."

They looked at each other. Upstairs someone called someone an asshole at volume. Somewhere else, a man brayed with laughter.

"I can't let you do that," Lawrence said.

"Sure you can. You know Lucky knows me."

"I'll put it in storage. Check back tomorrow."

She wanted to check out Lucky's room. "I don't want his stuff to disappear, Lawrence. And I don't have time to come back tomorrow."

Lawrence huffed, disappeared down the hall, returned with a key on a yellow plastic diamond. "Knock yourself out."

She flashed a plastic smile, took the key, went up to the third floor, unlocked 313. 312, Shuggy's room next door, was silent. The rest of the floor was relatively quiet, if you ignored a TV down the hall blaring *One Day at a Time*.

In Lucky's room, the bed was unmade. She found his backpack leaning against the wall. She gathered his stray clothes, his *Chronicle* apron from the arm of a chair. She folded it, put it in the backpack, hoping he'd make use of it again. In the bathroom, she found a pair of drugstore readers, a toothbrush, comb, and stick of deodorant. She took the glasses, decided to forgo the other items and buy fresh for Lucky.

Next to the john sat a small stack of *Chronicle* newspapers. Yesterday's unsold papers were Lucky's TP supply. Sections of pages had been torn off.

She was about to turn away when she saw an almost illegible scrawl on the top corner of one paper, next to the weather prediction.

joly ranchers 312 10 pm monday pamila

She froze. The Jolly Ranchers were what Lucky called members of Moon Ranch, the orange-robed, head-shaved, baseball bat–wielding spiritualists who practiced their faith up at Point Arenas—where Pamela had once been a member, until she ran off almost two months ago. Lucky'd spotted her once, nearby. Colleen wasn't allowed up at Moon Ranch as they had taken out a restraining order against her, and a parole violation would be the end result if she did.

This scrap of paper looked like a note Lucky had written to himself. He had mentioned—or tried to mention—something about Pam before Colleen was tossed out of SF General ICU. Had he overhead Shuggy talking about Pam? Colleen checked the date of the paper. Tuesday. Yesterday. So what was Monday about? Next Monday?

She tore off the pertinent part, folded it, slipped it in her pocket. She checked the rest of the papers for notes. Nothing. She tossed them in the trash can.

Pam. Monday.

How in hell did her daughter get connected with all of this?

She exited Lucky's room with his few extra belongings. A Hertz commercial with O.J. Simpson thundered down the hall. She went next door to Shuggy's, 312. Still silent. She knocked anyway. No answer. She didn't bother to rattle the doorknob because there was a serious combination padlock on a heavy-duty bracket on the door.

Downstairs on the first floor, a door opened.

"How's it going up there, Colleen?" she heard Lawrence say. "You about done?"

"Just finished."

Downstairs, backpack over one shoulder, she handed Lucky's key back. Lawrence had a fresh cigarette going. "If you hear anything, give me a call," she said. "And I'd appreciate it if you kept this visit between the two of us."

He flicked more ash. "Don't feel the need to rush back here, Colleen."

"Have a wonderful evening, Lawrence."

Lawrence didn't bother her as much as wondering about the connection between her daughter and Shuggy Johnston. And what *Monday* meant. And if it had anything to do with shooting the mayor.

Colleen went out onto O'Farrell, up the block, heaved Lucky's backpack into the trunk of her car. The working girl in the gold hot pants was coming out of a liquor store with a pack of cigarettes. They traded stares as Colleen took off.

CHAPTER EIGHT

In her kitchen overlooking a rainy Potrero Hill the next morning, Colleen made extra strong coffee, took it into her office where she sat down, turned on the desk lamp against the gray skies. She pulled her most recent photos from an envelope and flipped them over as she sipped coffee. There was her client's husband leaving his Polk Street liaison with a self-satisfied smirk on his face. Mr. Philanderer had no idea his world was about to come crashing down. Despite Lucky, and Pam, and the rumor about the mayor, Colleen still had paying clients and work to do.

She called her client, who lived in the Marina. The woman was furious, but at the same time, darkly satisfied to know her suspicions about her husband had been correct. Colleen experienced a swell of relief. An adulterer wasn't worth getting your heart broken over and it made her job easier if her client wasn't a teary mess. Colleen arranged a time to meet with her that day.

She went through her older photos. There was Shuggy Johnston, getting off his chopper in front of the Thunderbird, along with his two compadres. She had little doubt Shuggy and his pals had a hand in Lucky's savage beating. But she needed hard proof. Lawrence wasn't going to be any help.

She made a phone call to Owens at work on the off chance he was in, even though he said he was taking time off. He wasn't in. With Luck's recent development, it seemed critical to look into the mayor rumor sooner, if it hadn't been done so already. Owens said he'd take care of things and was good to his word, but, with Pam in the mix, it added a level of anxiety. She didn't know Owens well, but she called his house anyway. He lived in West Portal, a middle-class neighborhood by the Muni tunnel.

A young woman answered, and Colleen recalled hearing that Owens had robbed the cradle. This babe in arms had a harsh tone. Colleen told her she was a colleague and got a simple "he's not here," followed by a hang-up before she could leave a message.

So much for that. For now.

Colleen threw on her gray rain jacket and drove over to the Marina, met her client in a fancy little coffee shop, gave her photos of her beloved and his dalliance, and went on to explain that although the photos confirmed her husband's affair, they would most likely be considered hearsay in court, since the two parties were not together in any of them. She suggested that her client mull things over, giving her the standard *think-twice* speech. Sometimes marriages were worth saving, etcetera. Her client laughed out loud at that, set her cup down with a clank, and said what she wanted was a shot of Mr. Philanderer and his blond squeeze together so she could nail the bastard but good.

"You say he's got her stashed over the dry cleaners? Great— because that's exactly where I'm going to take him—the cleaners. I want that photo."

More paid work. Colleen had bills, although her mind was on Lucky, neo-Nazi bikers, and Pam especially. And the curious scrap of newspaper Colleen had found in Lucky's room. *Monday. Ten p.m.*

So she motored over to Polk Street, windshield wipers streaking away rain, and idled across from the dry cleaners for a moment. The apartment upstairs was dark.

Patience.

She drove to a bus stop where she parked in the red zone long enough to use a payphone. Parking in San Francisco was not getting any easier. She slipped in a dime, called SF General, learned that Lucky was still in the ICU. She was put through to Nurse Stevens, the head nurse who'd kicked her out. There was minor improvement. Lucky had even mumbled that he was hungry. Good, Colleen thought. *Great*, in fact.

"I'd like to stop by," she asked.

"The answer is *no*," Nurse Stevens said. "He needs his rest. Tomorrow—*maybe*."

"Was there any money in his wallet, by the way?" She'd had to leave before she found out.

"Twenty-seven dollars."

So Lucky hadn't been robbed. But Colleen already suspected that. Colleen thanked her.

The puttering of an SPFD meter maid motor cart broke her thoughts. It drew up behind the Torino. Colleen hung up the pay phone, dashed to the car, waving her arms. She managed to talk herself out of a ticket and headed home. It was when she turned left on Gough that she saw the car following her.

CHAPTER NINE

It wasn't always easy in a city like San Francisco to tell if someone was following you in a vehicle, especially in the rain. Traffic was a given so someone behind you was a given as well. But an unmarked police car stood out, particularly a new white boxy LTD the size of an aircraft carrier. Everything about this one was as generic as could be, with plain wheels and hubcaps, which she had spotted in the rearview mirror when it turned behind her on Gough. It stayed two cars behind, standard tail procedure. With the rain it was hard to make out who was at the wheel. There might have been two people.

She turned right on Geary, the main east-west artery out to the beach, even though she wasn't going that way. The sedan turned as well, hiding in a block of cars.

She swung over to the left of four lanes, as if heading out to the avenues. Dialed in KSAN, the Jive 95, studying the rearview mirror.

Big White was a few car lengths behind, one lane over.

At a yellow light she gunned it, the Torino lifting, leaving most of the traffic behind. Big White picked up enough speed to follow through.

Up the hill approaching the Geary underpass, where two of four lanes split to the right, she waited until the very last moment, shot over, exited the main thoroughfare, up the hill towards Masonic.

Stopped at a green light, briefly, checked the rearview. There was Big White, dawdling along behind, killing time. Following for sure.

Something to do with her warning about the mayor? Owens wouldn't have her tailed, but whoever the case had been handed to might. Supervisor Jordan Kray was an ex-cop and SFPD might be checking her out.

On Masonic she turned left, skidding slightly on wet asphalt, and drove into the upper Sears parking lot, full enough early in the day. She drove around the upper lot, crawled toward the exit, lurking by the wall with the engine running, tucked away.

And here came the white Ford, bouncing into the lot. With the rain she couldn't get a good look inside. The car headed back towards the Sears entrance, no doubt looking for her.

Colleen flew out of the lot, headed home.

The cops were following her.

The Jive 95 started playing "Miss You" by the Stones. Colleen changed the station.

CHAPTER TEN

Later that morning, Colleen sat at her new, used IBM Selectric, typing up a report for a client. She'd bought a refurbished model, cheaper than paying someone to do her typing, plus no waiting. The typewriter had a correction feature, a white ribbon that was a pain to change but a boon for her typing skills. Right now, she was hunting and pecking.

Kind of how most of her cases went.

She finished the report, pulled it from the typewriter, gave it a quick once-over, started on the invoice. She needed to stay solvent so she could chase down Pamela, her reason for coming to California in the first place, fresh out of prison, just over a year ago.

She still had to check in on Luck at SF General.

The doorbell rang, pulling her out of her thoughts.

Colleen pushed her roller chair back, went out to the long front room, pulled the window blind back an inch. It had stopped raining and the street glistened. Down on Vermont, double parked, was a white Ford LTD sedan. An unmarked cop cruiser, the second one today. Or perhaps the same one that had followed her earlier.

At the intercom in the hallway, Colleen asked who it was.

A man's voice, nice, belonging to Sergeant Dwight, who said he was referred to her by Inspector Owens. About time. She buzzed him in, waited at the top of the third-floor landing. She brushed her hair out with her fingers, realized she was slumming it in her chamois-soft denim bell-bottoms, bare feet, and a yellow Smiley Face *Have a Nice Day* T-shirt Alex had given her because Alex said she needed to smile more. No bra but it was too late to do anything about that.

A youngish guy came smartly up the stairs in a slight jog, about thirty, athletic, dressed conservatively in gray slacks, herringbone tweed jacket. He turned at the top of the stairwell and she noticed his steely blue eyes right away, contrasting his brown layered cut, long for a cop, but neat, just off the collar. Understated but hip. Slim blue button-down shirt and dark blue tie. Well-defined facial features, handsome in a supporting actor kind of way. Good-looking but downplaying it, most likely angling for an older look to climb the career ladder.

But she sure noticed. It had been a while since she'd been out on a date, or whatever they were calling them these days.

He smiled at *Have a Nice Day*. "Ms. Hayes?"

"Colleen."

Got his badge out.

Most people didn't look twice at a badge, but Colleen wasn't one of them. Matthew Dwight was an SFPD sergeant, Special Operations.

She showed him in. He chose to stand, his back to her, looking out the kitchen window at the fog breaking over her deck facing an invisible Potrero Hill.

"Nice old place," he said.

"I like it."

"Just you, is it?"

Professional or personal? He wasn't wearing a wedding ring.

"I just moved in," she said.

He turned from the window, giving her a smile to possibly make up for the nosy question. "Inspector Owens passed along some information," he said, putting his hands in his pockets. There was the telltale bulge of a gun under his right arm. A lefty.

"That's right," she said. She wanted to hear him say it first. Due diligence.

"An alleged threat to a member of city government. The mayor, to be exact."

She nodded.

"Supervisor Jordan Kray's name was mentioned," he continued.

"And you've been assigned."

"Unofficially."

"Just *unofficially*?"

"These kinds of investigations are kept under the radar—unless they go somewhere."

"And what makes them go somewhere?"

He rubbed his chin. "The first step is establishing the validity of the tip."

She leaned back against the kitchen counter, crossed her arms. She had promised Lucky anonymity, even if that didn't mean too much to him now. But she still had a responsibility to protect him and he'd gotten into enough trouble already. She never quite trusted SFPD. Especially when unmarked cars followed her around. "I wouldn't have mentioned it to Owens if I didn't think it was serious."

"I'm sure you might think that, but it's my job."

"Didn't Owens give you the photos? Shuggy Johnston and his two blood brothers?"

"He did."

"My source heard them talking about the mayor. Those are the ones to look at first."

"But your guidelines and mine might be different," he said, raising his eyebrows.

"Which is a nice way of saying you don't quite believe me."

"With all due respect," he said, "you've got a history."

"You looked into my record."

"I like to know who I'm dealing with."

"Same here," she said. "But I'm sure Owens vouched for me."

"He did."

"Then let me ask you this," she said. "If I wasn't a woman, with *a history*, would you still want to talk to my source?"

"I need *all* the information before I can proceed."

She took a breath. How to handle this? "What I can say is that my source is in the hospital right now and might not make it. And the reason he's there is that those bikers throwing Jordan Kray's name around in connection with shooting the mayor put him there."

He frowned. "You have proof they beat up your friend?"

"Ninety-nine percent."

"So, give me his name."

"You've got plenty to go on—if you want to pursue it."

He let it go. "The assertion is that these bikers have a connection to neo-Nazis and the Ku Klux Klan."

"Swastikas and Confederate flags on their bikes." She mentioned Shuggy Johnston's drug dealing.

"Okay," he said.

"And what does 'okay' mean?"

"It means I look into it," he said.

"Excellent. Look into it, *how*?"

"I thank you for coming forward, Colleen, but this is where your involvement stops. It's our case from now on." He got out a business card, a gold cross pen, and jotted a number on the back of the card. He handed it to her. "My home number is on the back. If you have any more information, give me a call. In the meantime, you're done with this case. Owens told me that you're hands on—and that doesn't work with me."

She took the card. "I want to be kept in the loop. I'm the one who brought it to your attention. And my client paid for it with a beating."

He put his pen away. "I can't promise anything."

She wanted to ask him about SFPD following her that afternoon. It might have even been him. She trusted Owens but Sergeant Dwight she didn't know.

"*Have a nice day.*" He smiled at her shirt.

She showed Dwight out, sat back down at her typewriter.

Screw this. She could leave the mayor thing alone—maybe—if Pamela wasn't in the picture.

She got up, went to her closet, slid hangers, looking for an outfit that might bait a biker.

CHAPTER ELEVEN

It wasn't until early evening that Shuggy's Harley came roaring down O'Farrell. Colleen was parked across the street, a few car-lengths up, smoking a Virginia Slim, the window half open. Decked out in a black leather mini and platform sling-back heels, the SF cold goose-bumped her bare legs after a day of stakeout, in between checking Mr. Philanderer's love nest and calling SF General. Lucky was still in the ICU and she wasn't allowed to visit. She had her leather car coat on, which looked great, but wasn't exactly warm.

She sat up as Shuggy backed his chopper into a spot in front of the Thunderbird.

On his own.

Colleen tossed her cig out the window, rolled it up, hopped out of the car, clumped across O'Farrell, dodging a Yellow cab blaring its horn. Shuggy stood at the top of the half dozen stairs to the Thunderbird, his keys out.

"Hey, Shuggy!"

He turned, his unblinking eyes scouring Colleen in her tight white lace stretch top under her leather coat. No bra. Not too subtle, but she hadn't figured Shuggy for the subtle type.

"Hey there," he said in a gravelly voice, reminding her of her ex, taking her back to darker days for a moment. "I don't know you, do I? I sure think I would have remembered."

She looked away coyly, then back, meeting his gaze with a come-hither smirk. She introduced herself as Carol Anne, a variation of her go-to alias. "I used to live here a while back."

"Well, all I can say is that it's too bad I wasn't around at the time, Carol Anne. What can I do you for?"

She dropped her voice. "I heard you might have a little Lucy." Lucy in the Sky with Diamonds—LSD.

"Oh, yeah?" He squinted a smile. "Where'd you hear that?"

She was fishing. Shuggy was known for dealing acid and Moon Ranch were known for making same. And Lucky's note had mentioned them. *Monday. 10 p.m.* "Oh, word gets around."

"I wish." He dropped his voice, too. "Waiting on a shipment."

"Oh, that's too bad," she said, one platform on the next step up, exposing some side thigh. Nine years of working out in Denver Women's Correctional Facility gym hadn't hurt her legs. "But I'm up for anything else you got." She laid the innuendo on with a trowel.

His eyes darted to her bare thigh. "Got some wicked Jamaican if you care to smoke a Jay."

"You don't say."

"I do say."

"Sure—why not?"

A minute later, they were on the third floor, Shuggy unlocking the combination padlock to room 312. She was able to only get two of the three numbers.

Shuggy's room didn't disappoint as a biker drug-dealing lair, with an American flag as a bedspread and at least a thousand dollars' worth of stereo equipment stacked up against one wall. The turntable sat on top of a huge Pioneer speaker cabinet. A dorm fridge buzzed by the bathroom door. A 17" RCA color TV teetered on a dresser. On a mirrored mantelpiece she noticed a set of scales and a bong. Tools of the trade. The place reeked of stale dope.

"Park your tush," Shuggy said, tearing off his biker jacket within its sleeveless denim jacket as a single item of clothing, revealing a muscular torso and big arms. He unplugged the phone. He had his own phone, in a place like this. But it made sense for a dope dealer.

Colleen adjusted her miniskirt and sat perched on a grimy green love seat under the window. One arm was torn and tufted. While Shuggy got a couple of tall cans of Schlitz Malt Liquor out of the dorm fridge, she studied the posters on the wall: from psychedelic optical eye play to R. Crumb's *Stoned Again* with the melting face, to a reproduction Waffen SS recruiting poster, a stoic German soldier in a Stahlhelm helmet looking off into the distance.

Shuggy flicked off the overhead light, leaving the two of them in semi darkness for a moment, making Colleen wonder before he flipped on a black light over a psychedelic poster that began to move with waves of electric color. He handed Colleen a beer, turned, dropped a tonearm on a record already on the turntable. She was able to make out a spider web tattoo on one elbow. If it was legit, he had killed someone. Her concern for Pam only grew. The Stooges came on. "Search and Destroy." Standard biker fare. Shuggy came over, sat right next to her on the sofa, the rough denim of his big leg not quite touching hers. She waited a sec, gave him a tight smile, moved as if he might be on the right track but perhaps moving a little too fast. He smelled like motor oil. He tore the pop top off his beer, gave the unopened can in her hand a questioning look.

She pulled her ring top with a *pop* and they clinked cans. She took a sip of bitter malt liquor while he gulped a good third of his. The whites of his eyes glowed under the black light.

"Cool pad," she said.

"Works for me." He drank, took her in with an appreciative nod, making no bones about it. She remembered, as a sixteen-year-old, being flattered by such stuff.

"That's a kick in the ass," she said, nodding at *Stoned Again*.

He grinned. "Which reminds me." He set his beer down on the floor, pulled something out from under the sofa. Placed it on his lap.

An MC5 album cover with a pack of rolling papers and a bag of weed on it.

"All right," she said, but not too excited. Smoking dope was never her thing. A glass of Chardonnay was.

He sat back down, brushing her leg, pulled a rolling paper out of the pack.

"Who told you I had acid to sell?" he asked casually, tipping weed from the baggie onto the rolling paper.

"Oh—some guy at Winterland."

"Winterland? Who did you see?"

"Queen."

"Seriously?"

"Oh yeah," she said.

Shuggy lined up fine green weed on the rolling paper. "What guy?"

"What guy *what*?"

"Told you I had some Lucy."

She'd hit a nerve. "Chuck, I think it was. I honestly didn't listen. Why—do I look like a narc or something?"

"You can't be too careful."

She turned as she sat, put a hand playfully on her hip, jutting out her boobs. Keep the fish on the line. "Seriously?"

"Well, if you are, it might just be worth it."

She play-slapped his arm.

"I don't sell to just anybody," he said.

"Well, ex*cuse* me," she said, doing her best Steve Martin. "I'm not just *anybody*."

"I can see that. Otherwise you wouldn't be here. But I'm not some fucking street dealer either. I don't mess with dime bags and loose joints."

"No offense, dude. So, what are you? More of a middleman?"

"I got specific clients. I only deal one-on-one in special cases. Like you."

Maybe he was bigger than she'd thought. That might help to take him down. "Well, I appreciate you inviting me up, Shuggy."

"Take your coat off," he said. "Stay a while."

"I'm cold."

He eyed her, licking the cigarette paper.

She remembered being sixteen years old, a dumb kid seduced by a guy just like him. Roger had been ten years her senior at the time, rode a Harley, always had dope, and she had been a complete and utter moron, thinking he was paying her special attention and might be her ticket to freedom. But shortly after, she had become pregnant with Pam, and the rest was history.

She shook the thought off, stood up with her beer, walked over to the SS poster. "My ex used to have this in the garage," she said.

"Yeah? Where was that?"

"Denver."

"What happened to your ex?"

"Got sent down. At Arrowhead Correctional as we speak." Actually, he was dead, but the rest of it was true enough.

"No shit?" Shuggy said.

"No shit, Sherlock."

"What for?"

"This and that," she said, tiny-sipping her beer, studying the items on the mantelpiece in the dark. Roach clip. Razor blade and a length of straw on a mirror. She turned, looked at Shuggy twisting up the end of the joint.

"Then what *did* he go to prison for?" Getting impatient. She could imagine him very impatient. Just like her ex. It gave her pause, even with the Bersa in her jacket pocket. She needed to manage this guy, draw him out.

She frowned. "I'm not sure I should say. He used to ride, too. '58 Hydra Glide."

Shuggy whistled a low whistle. "Nice."

"We had some times on it."

"I just bet."

"Had to sell it to pay the lawyer. Didn't do a damn bit of good. Damn Hebrew took our money and my ex still got ten years." More fiction but it was dipping into a life she had lived.

"What do you expect from a kike?" Shuggy said. "But *ten* years? Babe, you don't get a dime for nothing. Your old man wax somebody?"

"Some *nobody*," she said. "Some spook who jumped a friend, coming out of a bar in West Denver. Put him in a wheelchair. Well, Rog and a couple from his den took care of that burrhead but good. But, wouldn't you know? Someone squealed and Rog got busted for it."

"Your old man was in a den?"

She turned away. "Why are we talking about him, anyway?"

"Because if he's what you say, then he's a brother," Shuggy said.

She turned back. "Are you shitting me?"

"Do I look like a shitter?"

"AYAK?" Colleen said. *Are you a Klansman?*

"AKIA," Shuggy said somberly, meeting her gaze. *A Klansman I Am.*

Her visit to SF Public Library had paid off. But her back shuddered all the same.

"Well, well," she said. "Small world. Who would have thought the Klan would prevail in the People's Republic of San Francisco?"

"We do our bit, Carol Anne. There's a lot of scum here."

Wasn't that the truth? She toasted him with her nearly full beer. "Respect." *You sick bastard.*

She left her barely touched beer on the mantelpiece.

"You gonna smoke this thing or what?" he said, holding up the unlit joint.

"If you ever get around to lighting it."

"I'm waiting for you." He patted the empty seat beside him.

She strolled over, like a model on a runway, sat down casually next to him, six inches away, knees together. He was eating it up but he was cool, patting himself down for matches, found some, sat back, splaying his big legs wide, brushing her knee again, accidentally on purpose. This time she didn't move hers.

"You'll have to try out the Bull," he said, tearing off a paper match.

"The Bull would be your hog out front."

"'74 hardtail. Almost as hot as a Hydra Glide." He lit up the reefer. It had an acrid smell. "How much longer is your ex in for?" He held out the smoldering joint.

She took it, gave it a small hit. It tasted sharp. Chemicals. She blew out the smoke before too much went down, handed it back. "Three more years until he's eligible for parole. And he's not really my ex—but I am waiting for him. That's what you're asking, right?"

He took a miniscule hit on the joint. Handed it back to her. "Your old man and I have a lot in common."

She took the J, took a play hit. It tasted awful. Handed it back. "You wish." The words seemed to echo. Something wasn't right. Her head, even on a small puff, was buzzing. Shuggy wasn't smoking. He tried to hand the joint back to her. She shook her head. It kept shaking even after she stopped.

"What the hell was in that spliff?" she said.

He gave a crooked grin as he put a hand on her leg casually. His fingers were rough and calloused. "Just a little dust."

Angel dust. PCP. Elephant tranquilizer. The kind of stuff that made people boil their babies.

"Jesus H." She smacked his hand away. "You dusted me?" Roger got her drunk as a skunk when she was sixteen. Took her virginity the same night.

"You're the one who wanted to get high, Carol Anne." Shuggy set the dead joint on the album cover on the arm of the chair. "What am I supposed to think?"

"I did *not* say I wanted to get fucking ambushed." She rubbed her forehead. Lordy.

She stood up, wobbly, with her legs apart, letting him get another long look. On the hook. She was going to reel him in. Club him like a fish on the deck. She turned away. "I was just looking for a little Lucy." She turned back. "And you try to fucking *hit* on me? You just got done saying my old man is your brother."

"Come on, Carol Anne. You came up here. Jesus."

She gave him the eye and a little smirk to go with it. "I'm not saying I wouldn't think about it if my old man wasn't inside . . ." She looked away.

"Cool. C'mon. Sit down."

She sat down, next to him. Wiggled her butt into position as she straightened her legs out in front of her. "We take things at my speed. Got that?"

"Cool. Your old man is one lucky motherfucker. That's all I can say."

He was. Until she stabbed him in the neck with a screwdriver, left him to die on the kitchen floor. Went to prison for it.

She stood up, head still spinning. "I got to jet. I got to feed the cat where I'm house-sitting. When are you getting some Lucy?"

"Monday. Give me your phone number. I'll call you."

Lucky's note had said Monday.

"What kind?" she asked.

"Arenas Light."

Moon Ranch's specialty. Was she getting closer to Pam? It was good news, she told herself, even as it was bad news. Her nerves tightened.

"I can come by Monday," she said.

"Monday's no good. Tuesday. Gimme your number."

"Don't have one."

"You don't have a fucking phone number where you're house-sitting?"

"She doesn't want me using the phone." Colleen strutted over to his phone, saw the number. She grabbed a ballpoint off the mantel-piece, scribbled it down on a loose rolling paper. Tucked it in her jacket pocket, gave it a pat. "I'll call you."

"Call even if you don't want to score." A sly smile.

"Hey, I know," she said, as if just thinking of it, "I could meet some of your den brothers." Maybe she'd nail the other dirtbags who beat Lucky half to death. Even a dude Shuggy's size couldn't have thrown Lucky into a dumpster single-handed.

"You want to go to a meeting?"

And if the deal on shooting the mayor held any water, she could pass that on to Matt Dwight as well.

"Sure," she said. "I'm overdue."

"Call me tomorrow."

"You got a meeting tomorrow?"

"More like a gathering of the tribes," he said. "Be here around seven."

"Deal." She winked goodbye, left, the Stooges hammering away. She did her best to get down two flights of stairs, holding the ban-ister to keep her wobbly legs in check, leaning over at one point to see if Lawrence the manager was in the hallway. He wasn't.

Outside, the San Francisco cold had manifested in wet fog, stick-ing to her bare legs like moist hands, and she thought of Shuggy's. Too much like her ex. The fog was better.

She got into the Torino, fired it up, relieved to get away, even as she planned how to handle tomorrow's meeting. She wouldn't tell Matt Dwight about her plans just yet, or her progress with Shuggy, since she'd been sworn to staying on the sidelines. She would just have to be careful. More careful than driving after smoking dust.

She swung by Mr. Philanderer's love pad on Polk. No activity. She dialed in the Jive 95, her head still warm and fuzzy. They were playing Wings. "With a Little Luck."

Luck. Lucky. She needed to check in on him.

She didn't feel like calling SF General, being told she couldn't visit.

So she turned on Sutter, headed over to SF General.

Luck could use a little luck.

At SF General, outside the ICU, still in her short skirt and her black leather coat, Colleen used the wall phone and asked for Nurse Stevens.

Nurse Stevens said she would meet Colleen at the door.

She appeared, hands folded, a subdued look, one of regret. Colleen startled, fearing the worst.

"I'm afraid I have some bad news," Nurse Stevens said quietly.

CHAPTER TWELVE

"Dead?" Colleen said, her head ringing with the news of Lucky's demise.

The overhead lights in the hallway seemed to buzz louder. Hadn't Lucky been improving? Wasn't he communicating?

"I'm very sorry," Nurse Stevens said. "Your friend stroked out. He didn't really have much of a chance to begin with, to be perfectly honest. But, please know that we did our best."

"I know you did," Colleen said. And here she was, thinking she might even find Lucky sitting up, perhaps smiling, her magical thinking playing a sick joke.

On Lucky most of all.

"I have to get back to work," Nurse Stevens said.

She thanked Nurse Stevens, who had given her a hard time at first, but was only doing her job. She stopped at the ER on the way out, asked if SFPD had looked into Lucky's beating yet. The ER nurse didn't think they had. Colleen went out to 22nd Street, feeling about as gray as the evening sky.

She got into the Torino, stared at the fuzzy lights of Potrero, thought about a cigarette, decided Lucky deserved a moment of her silence instead.

She stopped at a payphone on Potrero outside a convenience store, called Sergeant Dwight at 850 Bryant. He wasn't in. She called him at home. He answered.

"Herman Waddell," she said.

"Your source?" She heard the TV murmuring in the background.

"That's right," she said. "But everyone called him Lucky."

"*Called?*"

"He's dead." She started to choke up.

There was a pause. The TV in the background went silent. Matt must have turned the volume down.

"I'm very sorry to hear that, Colleen."

She could tell he meant it.

"Thanks," she said. "Maybe you'll take that mayor thing seriously, now."

"How long had Lucky been at SF General?"

"Two days," she said. "And, as far as I know, SFPD haven't followed up yet."

"Communication between General and SFPD isn't always as smooth as it ought to be. But now it's a homicide."

"So maybe Owens."

"I wouldn't count on it."

"Because he's taking time off," she said. "Which means they're backed up."

"I'll make sure Homicide knows about it," he said.

"Thank you," she said. "Lucky died for this."

"I hear you," he said. "But I need to remind you to stay out of it. And the mayor thing. *Everything.*"

She didn't respond.

"Did you hear me?"

She fought a cigarette out of the pack, stuck it between her lips. "I hear you."

"I need you to do more than just hear me. I need you to promise me you'll back off."

"I'll stay away from the mayor thing," she said. "And Lucky." For now. "But I have some business with Shuggy Johnston."

"Some business *how*?" he said with some irritation.

She lit up her Slim, took a drag, blew smoke into the wet night air. "I found out that I know someone who might be involved with Shuggy. I need to stop her."

"Someone like *who*?"

Pam was personal territory.

"Just someone I know."

She heard him take a breath. "I don't care. Stay well away. Are we clear on that?"

She had a Klan date with Shuggy tomorrow. She didn't like to lie to someone like Matt. But right now, what mattered was Pam.

"We're good," she said.

CHAPTER THIRTEEN

"You're going to a party," Alex said, "without *me*?"

Alex was sitting on Colleen's sleek leather sofa with the chrome arms, her feet tucked up underneath her, still wearing Colleen's kimono. Hadn't even gotten dressed. She had stayed over last night, too drunk to drive home to Half Moon Bay from San Francisco. Again. Her day had been spent nursing a wicked hangover. She sipped a cup of tea. Colleen stood in front of the mirror over the Edwardian fireplace, putting on mascara.

"It's not your kind of party, Alex," she said, working the curled lashes of one eye with the wand.

"I beg to differ. Every party's my kind of party."

"Not this one," Colleen said. "This is work."

"Something to do with your friend Lucky?"

"Yes."

Alex drank tea. "Feel like talking about it?"

Colleen started on the other eye. "You know how I feel about discussing working cases."

"Now I *really* want to know," Alex said, setting her cup down on the glass coffee table. "Especially since your friend died over it."

Wand in hand, Colleen turned. She was keeping her look relatively conservative tonight: good jeans, dry-cleaned, black pumps, burgundy blouse with the buttons done up. Now that she had Shuggy's attention, the *Fuck Me* outfit could go.

She brought Alex up to speed with Shuggy Johnston and her suspicions.

Alex blinked in disbelief. "You're going to a fucking Klan rally?"

Colleen went back to work in the mirror. "It's just a meeting of some of the local crazies, the local den being one of them."

"Well, that sounds cozy. Any activities planned? Like a lynching? Or are you just going to burn a cross on some poor bastard's front lawn?"

"Don't be ridiculous." Colleen finished the upper lashes. "You know San Franciscans don't have front lawns."

"That settles it." Alex stood up, cinching the robe together. "I'm coming with you. Give me a moment to change."

Colleen turned. "No, Alex, you are most certainly *not* coming."

"I don't want to read about you in the morning paper."

"This is precisely why I didn't want to tell you."

"For good reason, Coll. What part of the term *racist maniacs* don't you understand?"

"I'm going to keep my eyes open. But I need to confirm who killed Lucky. And these knuckle-draggers are prime." She wasn't going to tell Alex about the mayor rumor. Or Pam. "Don't worry."

"*Don't worry*, she says. Are you taking Little Bersalina with you?"

Little Bersalina was Alex's nickname for Colleen's Bersa Piccola, her 22-caliber pistol that was small but effective.

"No need to, Alex," she said. "These Klanners are more bark than bite."

Alex squeezed out a doubtful look. "Over four thousand black Americans were hung during Reconstruction, almost all of them by the Ku Klux Klan. In 1920, over eight million Americans—four percent of the population at the time—were card-carrying members."

"Really?" Colleen said. "I had no idea. How do you know all that?"

"I majored in history. In case you thought all I did was go to keggers. Our nation's true past will haunt you."

Colleen put the applicator back in the bottle, set the bottle on the mantelpiece. She went over, put a hand on each of Alex's shoulders. "You're sweet to worry. But there's nothing to worry about." She gave Alex a reassuring smile. "What are you going to do tonight?"

"I think I'll go down to Peg's Place for a drink."

"*One* drink. And no nose candy."

"Yeah, yeah."

"I mean it, Alex. You're not the only one who worries."

"Same goes for you. Those nutjobs are probably breaking out the moonshine and nooses as we speak."

Colleen threw on her oversized leather jacket, waived bye, headed downstairs to the Torino. Starting it up, she feathered the throttle while she reached down under the dash and got the Bersa hanging in the gym sock. She slipped it into the pocket of her coat and set off. No need for Alex to worry.

*   *   *

"Nice ride," Shuggy said when Colleen pulled up in front of the Thunderbird. The V8 engine rumbled in idle.

"Hop in."

"You too chicken to ride the Bull?" Shuggy stood by his motorcycle, wearing pretty much what he'd been wearing yesterday: beat-up leather jacket, torn sleeveless denim jacket on top of it.

"It's got to be fifty degrees out there," she said. And it was. A San Francisco winter wasn't a Midwest winter, but the cold bit in a way the latter didn't. Besides, she wanted to be able to leave the festivities when she chose to. "Another time. Get in, already."

Shuggy took another appreciative look at the muscle car, climbed in.

"Get on the freeway," he said. "Hunter's Point."

CHAPTER FOURTEEN

"Is it safe to park here?"

Colleen pulled the Torino up in front of an isolated warehouse in Hunter's Point. Vehicles were parked everywhere in the near darkness, up on the curb, back behind the fence. A lot of pickup trucks. Confederate flags prevailed. Across the bay, the distant lights of Oakland shone in the mist. The muffled sounds of primitive rock 'n' roll boomed from within the building.

The neighborhood, ironically, was mostly black, despite KKK meetings and the like. Poor, forgotten, neglected. The naval shipyard had closed a few years ago.

"Over there," Shuggy said, pointing Colleen to a loading bay where a big open dock door cast an oblong of light into the night. A large man in camouflage stood by, wearing a matching fatigue cap. His arms hung by his side, as if he might be hoping for trouble. "Jimbo'll watch your car."

Colleen motored through the open gates, tires crunching over rough asphalt, pulled up next to a shipping container. Two bikes were parked to one side, the same ones Shuggy's compadres had ridden up to the Thunderbird the other day. She killed the engine. She and Shuggy got out, headed for the door. The music was louder, hard-edged rock with a dirge-like feel. The singer had a ragged growl of a voice as he sang about a tree where justice was delivered with a rope.

"And who do we have here?" the guy at the door said, eyeing Colleen. His coquettish voice didn't go with the camouflage and Klan armband, a white cross on a red background, drop of blood in the center. His rubbery face slid into a grin.

"This is Carol Anne, Jimbo," Shuggy said. "She's with me."

You wish, Colleen thought.

"Well, hello there, Carol Anne," Jimbo said, drawing out the *hello*.

"Watch my car, will you?" she said.

"You got it," Jimbo said, "but I still got to pat you down."

Wanted to pat her down, more like it. Colleen was getting nervous with the Bersa in her pocket.

She turned to Shuggy. "You didn't say I was gonna get groped."

"Don't worry, Carol Anne," Jimbo snickered. "I'll be gentle."

"This is total bullshit," she said. "I'm a white female. My old man is doing a dime for you people."

"She's cool, Jimbo," Shuggy said.

"She's not a member though, is she, Shuggy?"

"Fuck it," Colleen said. "No one touches me without my say-so. See you later, Shuggy. You'll have to find your own way home." She turned to go.

She walked slowly.

"Whoa!" Jimbo shouted after her. "You're good, Carol Anne."

She turned back. "That's more like it."

Jimbo stood back with a shit-eating grin. "You guys have a good meeting. Dr. Lange is going to talk soon."

"The lady don't take shit," Shuggy said as they headed in.

"Make a note," Colleen said.

Inside the drafty old warehouse, the music became a direct aural assault. Sparse fluorescent lights in the high ceiling, many burned

out, cast a pall over several hundred shadows milling about. Remarkably silent for such a large crowd. Much of the throng was
gathered around a low stage where the band thudded away. A row
of kegs on one side attracted others. Construction lamps on metal
tripods glared either side of the stage, like pseudo torches. A white
cross banner hung on the wall behind the band next to a red flag
with a swastika in a white circle.

An emaciated singer scowled at the audience. He sported a dark
buzz cut, long sideburns, and workpants held up by black suspend-
ers under a plain white T.

Now that her eyes had adjusted, Colleen saw that the crowd was
made up of skinheads and punks, but the bulk were faceless white
men wearing clothes straight from the Sears catalog. Short hair,
lacking style, was the norm. Facial hair was not. They might have
faded into nothingness were it not for the preponderance of arm-
bands with white crosses, Confederate flags, the odd swastika. Dotted throughout the crowd were white Klan robes, but without
facemasks. A friendly event, no need for anonymity. Several men
in fatigues stood guard around the edges, pistols on their hips in
plain view.

To the right, a chunky woman and a preteen girl in matching
Klan robes manned a table where they doled out scoops of sloppy
casserole to a line of men gripping paper plates. It was obvious the
two were mother and daughter. They were also the only ones who
appeared to be smiling.

"You all enjoy that!" the woman said, slapping a pile onto a plate.

"This way." Shuggy pushed through to the front of the stage and
Colleen followed. With Shuggy's size and garb, people immediately
gave him room. As they got closer, she saw the words *Fist of Vengeance* on the band's bass drum, fashioned out of lightning bolts.

There were few women and Colleen was getting furtive looks.

Two biker types in leather showed up and Colleen recognized them as the two who'd stopped at the Thunderbird with Shuggy, the tall beanpole and the fireplug.

"I got to talk to someone," Shuggy said to Colleen. He marched off.

She was left with Ace, the little guy on the Harley trike, who had a pinched face, fuzzy hair, and a sullen leer, and Stan, the lanky guy with a pointed nose and hair combed over in an unmistakably Hitleresque affectation. He was well spoken while Ace fought with a stutter and ogled her over his beer cup.

Off to one side of the stage, Colleen saw Shuggy heading for an important-looking guy in a gray suit that was definitely not off the rack. He sported a tie and a stylish Burt Reynolds haircut and mustache. A group of underlings hovered around him. A tall, skinny woman in a black skirt suit, short pixie hair. A portly man in a blue Klan robe, wearing thick glasses, looking like an insurance salesman out trick-or-treating. Two bodyguards, dark suits, no ties. The important guy looked at his watch. Dr. Lange, Colleen suspected. He might well be a source in unraveling the mayor rumor. Shuggy went up to him, everybody else moving away, and stood with his hands on his hips, talking close.

"That's Dr. Lange?" Colleen asked Stan.

Stan confirmed. "He's going to speak soon."

"You guys know him, too?"

"Oh, yeah," Stan said, puffing up.

"You S-Shuggy's old lady?" Ace asked her, staring over his cup.

"I'm not anyone's old lady. But I've got an old man."

"S-so w-where is he?"

"Doing ten to fourteen."

"You don't say," Stan said. "What did your old man do to earn such a lengthy stay?"

Trying to impress her. "Dealing out justice for his brothers while this crowd drinks beer and shakes their fists at the kiddie music," she said.

"There might be some of that," Stan said. "But we're not like them, Carol Anne."

"I guess I'll have to take your word for it," she said. "There sure are a lot of vigilantes lining up for casserole." She shook her head. "Some den."

"We're n-not like t-them!" Ace blurted out, his face turning red.

"What do you do, Ace? Scold them if they ask for seconds?"

His face reddened. "We s-stand up and t-take n-names."

She gave a grin. Draw these guys out. "I see."

"S-straight up. We k-kicked some dude's ass the other night." He nodded with satisfaction and slurped beer.

"What dude?"

"S-some s-snitch."

Stan glared at Ace. "Maybe cool it, little brother?"

"What *dude* got his ass kicked?" Colleen asked Ace.

Ace blinked rapidly. "S-some r-retard."

"You guys beat up a *gimp*? Whoa. Big time."

Stan interjected while Ace turned red with verbal frustration. "Ace shouldn't be talking out of school, Carol Anne, but he's telling it like it is. We don't play at it like these other guys." He thumbed his chest with pride. "When it counts, we can be *counted on*."

"So what exactly did you guys do?" Colleen asked, wanting details.

"Only threw his f-fuckin' ass in a d-dumpster!" Ace spat.

"That's enough, Ace," Stan said.

Colleen suppressed a shudder of disgust, even as she welcomed the admission.

"Shuggy, too?" she asked casually.

"You th-think he'd miss a p-party like that? It w-was his idea."

So it was official: Shuggy and his pals beat Lucky to death.

"Why?" she asked.

"Something big is going down, Carol Anne," Stan said, tapping his nose. "And we caught some weasel listening in. So he really did it to himself."

"What's going down?"

"You'll find out."

"I hate surprises," she said. "Come on, Stan. Quit playin' hard to get."

Stan blushed and shook his head. "All in good time."

She couldn't push too hard without raising suspicion.

"Well, I guess I stand corrected." Colleen nodded with feigned respect, while inside, she roiled. "I take it back. I'm glad to know you guys." And she was, because these two, along with Shuggy, were going to pay. She'd hand them over to Owens, or Sergeant Dwight.

The singer snarled into the mic: "This one is called 'Justice Is My Name.'"

Fist of Vengeance pounded into a song that sounded similar to the previous one, filling the air with angry noise. This one featured the tale of Joe, a hardworking white man trying to feed his family while immigrants squatting in his building steal from him when they are not cat-calling his wife and underage daughter. Joe loses his job when a "mongrel" siphons gas out of his truck and he's late for work. If the message of Joe's plight wasn't clear enough, his Jewish landlord won't do anything about the squatters either. The overworked police are too busy fighting crime in the ghetto to help. Then, while looking for work, Joe's wife and daughter are raped by the squatters. Joe is obviously going to have to take matters into his own hands. He loads up the shotgun and heads downstairs.

The crowd was eating it up, those at the front of the stage shouting along, fists raised and shaking in unison.

No longer will I turn my cheek!
No longer will I live in shame!
The time has come for vengeance!
Justice is my name!

Colleen looked over at Dr. Lange across the room. Shuggy was gone. She caught Dr. Lange's eye. He gave her a timid smile. She returned a long, sleepy one, the kind men liked.

He liked it.

Another lead she might be able to pass on.

She flashed Stan and Ace a smile and pushed off toward Dr. Lange and his crew.

"We got one more before Dr. Lange speaks," the singer said into the mic. "This one is called 'Final Solution.'"

Oh joy, Colleen thought.

The band plowed into another major offensive. The action at the front of the stage was beginning to resemble a football game without helmets.

Dr. Lange was going over papers, his speech most likely. Colleen approached.

The tall woman in black blocked Colleen's way.

"Can I help you?" She had to shout over the music.

"I just wanted to introduce myself to Dr. Lange," Colleen yelled back. "I'm an admirer of his work."

"He's about to talk."

"Real quick."

"I'm sorry."

"Maybe afterwards."

"He's got a red-eye to Los Angeles."

Damn. "He's a busy man," Colleen said.

"Yes, he is. Who are you with?"

"I'm a friend of Shuggy's," she said.

The woman's eyes narrowed. "I see."

Colleen caught Dr. Lange's eye again. He came over, his hand out.

"I'm Dr. Lange," he said in a high voice. "I don't believe we've met."

"Carol Anne Aird."

"Thanks for coming. How do you like it so far?"

"Well, to be honest, my ears are bleeding, but then I came to hear your speech."

"I know this music isn't for everybody."

"It's the price we pay to reach people," she said.

"Exactly. *Exactly.* You're a smart woman."

"I'd love to get involved," she said, with another one of those looks, before she added, "with the organization."

"That would be splendid. I'm thinking of running for office. And I can use all the help I can get."

"What office would that be?"

He gave her a knowing look. "When you know, you'll know. But let's just say that this city is long past due its spring cleaning."

Colleen wondered if one of those cleaning tasks was shooting the mayor.

"Well," she said. "Sign me up."

"Excellent. You do understand you'll have to be vetted first?"

"I don't have a problem with that," she said. "Can I get a business card?"

The tall woman interrupted. "Your speech, Dr. Lange?" She shot Colleen a squint.

"Doris," he said to the tall woman. "Get this woman's contact info."

Dr. Lange was introduced onstage by the clown in the purple Klan robe. "And now, let's give a warm welcome to the man whose book, *The Plight of the White Race*, has earned him continued respect and given a voice to the silent majority."

Dr. Lange stepped up and spoke in a squealed monotone about the reasons white people were in dire trouble: racial interbreeding, liberals, communists, the Soviet Union, sexual permissiveness, Africa, Latin America, Israel, foreigners, weather patterns, government subsidies to minorities, the breakup of the nuclear family, birth control, and more. He never once mentioned a race by name, but you knew exactly who he was talking about. Nothing about a call to shoot the mayor. But if anyone had a hand in such a thing, he would be a fit.

"I need to get your contact info," Doris said to Colleen.

Colleen had her phony business cards for Pacific All Risk, but she didn't want any exposure at all with this crowd. And she honestly didn't think Doris would see that her info got to Dr. Lange. The green-eyed monster was lurking behind her beady eyes.

"Doesn't Dr. Lange have a business card?" she asked.

"Dr. Lange needs to be careful who he gives his contact information to."

Colleen returned an artificial smile. "I see."

All Colleen wanted to do was leave, but she needed to get hold of Dr. Lange after his speech. She looked over at the kegs, the crowd, saw Shuggy watching her. No smile.

The speech was only ten minutes but it was a long speech.

Dr. Lange stood down to moderate applause, came back over.

Colleen got in front of Doris.

"Excellent speech, Dr. Lange."

"Why, thank you, Carol Anne."

"Can I get your card?" Colleen said, blocking Doris as she hovered about.

"Didn't Doris give you one?"

Colleen dropped her voice. "I think there might have been a misunderstanding."

"I see." Dr. Lange reached into his jacket pocket, came out with a gold business card case. He extracted a card, got out a pen, jotted a number on the back.

"That's my direct line," he said. "Maybe you and I can get together over dinner and discuss a potential role." Raised one eyebrow.

"I'd like that," she said, taking the card. "I'd like that *a lot.*"

Doris couldn't take it any longer. She barged in. "You're going to be late for your red-eye, Dr. Lange."

"Yes, Doris."

Colleen bid adieu, trading looks with Doris who, surprisingly, hadn't pulled a knife on her.

Fist of Vengeance got back onstage to raucous cheers.

"Let's have another hand for a really smart man who fucking tells it like it is."

Another smattering of applause was followed by drum rolls and screeching guitars. Drunken young men jumped up and down. Colleen reminded herself to pack earplugs next time.

Shuggy was talking to Stan and Ace. She took the long way around, headed for the exit as the band thumped away.

Outside, the air was fog wet and pleasantly bereft of racket. She ignored Jimbo, headed to her car. The big trike and Stan's Police Special were still there.

"Carol Anne!" she heard Shuggy roar across the lot. "Where do you think you're going?"

Jesus. Colleen stopped, turned.

Shuggy was striding across the parking area, shoulders tight.

"Home," she said. "I think that casserole did a number on me."

"Not without me, babe. And I'm not ready to leave yet. Got that?"

So it was going to be like that. "Well, *babe,* I got to boogie so you'll just have to catch a ride with one of your biker buddies. Hope people don't think you're some kind of sissy, sitting on the back. Maybe you can ride on the big tricycle, huh?"

Shuggy plodded up, eyes blazing.

"What did you fucking say to me?"

Shuggy was two feet away now, his hands twitching, about to become fists. Just like her ex. Colleen's hand was over her pocket flap, ready to pull the Bersa. But she didn't need Shuggy for an enemy. Not just yet.

She broke out into a big grin. "Jesus, Shug. Can't you take a fucking joke?"

Shuggy blinked. "What?"

"I'm messin' with you, dude."

He stared for a moment. "Hilarious," he said, not smiling.

"But it has been a long night, Shug. That freaking noise in there gave me a mother of a headache. I need to get home. I can take you back now if you like. Otherwise, it's Yellow Cab. But I'll make it up to you." She winked.

"Run hot and cold, don't you?"

"Hey, I know," she said. "I can come by Monday. You said you'd have some of that kinky-poo Arenas Light by then, anyway, right?"

Shuggy shook his head. "I already told you: Monday's not good."

She'd see about that. Monday was the day that Pam might show.

"Tuesday." He looked at her with narrowed eyes. "What were you and Dr. Lange talking about in there?"

"Oh, this and that." She gave his big arm a squeeze. "See you on the flip side."

"Next time, don't leave me without a fucking ride."

She gave him another wink.

He stared, as if trying to make her out, backed away a few steps, turned, strode back to the warehouse.

She got her car keys out, got into the Torino, fired it up. Smoke belched out of the twin pipes. She headed off toward the gates.

In the rearview mirror, she saw Shuggy watching her, motionless.

What part did Pam play in this mess?

She'd find out. Monday.

CHAPTER FIFTEEN

Colleen found Sergeant Matt Dwight sitting on a barstool at a high table in Henry Africa's where the Tiffany lamps cast soft light on the hanging ferns that gave the bar its jungle-themed name. The model train whirring around on the suspended track overhead was audible over the gently volumed disco music as tiny wheels clacked away.

It was early evening the day after the KKK pageant and the bar was a distinct contrast. It was also relatively empty. The pretty people tended not to go out until later.

Matt Dwight wore a suede sport coat, purple shirt with big collar, wide brown knit tie. His just-shy-of-regulation haircut had been freshly blow-dried. Off duty. But a man like Sergeant Dwight was never truly off duty.

And maybe just trying to impress? Under different circumstances she might not have minded.

Colleen had donned long black polyester flares, a soft white cashmere sweater with a big floppy collar, and a checked, draped blazer, topped off with pointed Frye ankle boots. The kind of outfit one wore to stay warm on a stakeout like Mr. Philanderer's trysting place, which was around the corner on Polk.

Matt Dwight was nursing a beer. Colleen ordered soda water.

"Thanks for coming," she said.

"We'll see about that," he said. "What did you want to talk about?"

Her soda water arrived. She took a sip.

"How's the investigation going?" she asked.

Matt frowned. "No comment."

"Sounds like *no progress*."

He drank some beer. "No comment. And"—he drank another sip—"you know better than to ask, right?" He set his pilsner glass down on a beer matt.

She placed Dr. Lange's business card on the table.

Lecturer. Writer. Activist. America First.

"Dr. Lange," she said. "The voice of the Aryan Alliance." She had spent the morning at SF Public Library on Van Ness, at the microfiche machine. "He gave a talk last night at a neo-Nazi, KKK, neighborhood racist get-together in Hunter's Point—in between Nazi punk tunes by Fist of Vengeance. Shuggy Johnston was there, as well as his two biker buddies. Ace and Stan admitted to beating up Lucky and throwing him in a dumpster, along with Shuggy. Stan—the tall one—also hinted that something big is coming." She took a sip of soda water. "Dr. Lange talked about running for office, but didn't say what office. He'll elaborate when he and I get together"—she raised her eyebrows—"but he did mention 'cleaning up San Francisco.' So it makes the mayor threat look a little more serious." She nodded at the card. "That's his direct number on the back."

When she was done, Matt Dwight pursed his lips with apparent respect. "You have covered a lot of ground since I last saw you. But it's ground you were *not* supposed to cover. You assured me you'd stay well away."

"I'm sorry," she said. "But Lucky was murdered." She wasn't going to mention her concern for Pamela. That was private. "And I feel responsible. I still haven't heard from SFPD regarding Lucky. They normally follow up on suspicious hospital admissions. The time after a homicide is crucial. Every day the trail grows colder."

"I know. Homicide has a lot on their plates."

"I've called—or tried to call—Owens," she said. "But can't get hold of him."

"He's out of the office."

That she knew. What she didn't know was the reason. His wife had been distinctly unfriendly when she had called. Marriage problems? "So, do I contact Homicide myself? I'm not sure where Lucky stands with SFPD at the moment."

"No," Matt said. "This is connected to the mayor thing and I need to make it very clear *one more time* that you back off, Colleen—and do *not* discuss any of this with anyone else, either. We can't afford to scare off a key suspect we've got our eye on."

"That suspect being Supervisor Jordan Kray?"

He gave a sigh of exasperation. "That doesn't concern you, Colleen."

"I have time to work on it." She sipped fizzy soda water. It was not in any way like a glass of Chardonnay.

He shook his head. "Owens said you were a pain in the ass."

"One that has helped Owens solve more than one case—at no cost to the City of San Francisco."

"Look, Colleen, I really appreciate this new info—really—and I'm going to make good use of it. But the mayor case is being triaged with the chief. There are reasons—good reasons—why you're not privy to them. Okay? This is not a job for Jane Citizen."

Jane Citizen. "I'm the one who alerted SFPD to this, bub. You might have all been living in blissful ignorance if I hadn't."

He drank some beer. "I'm sorry about your friend. Really. And I appreciate the leads. Owens says a lot of good things about you, too.

I can see why. But you need to do as you're asked. You don't want the chief coming down on you, do you? Not while you're on parole."

She did not. She drank soda water. "Got it," she said.

"Good." He smiled. He had a nice smile. "Now that that's out of the way, can I buy you a drink? Something stronger than club soda?"

They sat there a moment, looking at each other. *Voulez-vous coucher avec moi* oozed over the sound system. She suppressed a smile at the timing.

"I'm actually working a case tonight," she said. "So, it'll have to be some other time. Maybe I'll even tell you my sign."

He laughed.

But if he thought she was going to stay away from Shuggy and his crew, with Pam in the mix, he was mistaken. Colleen had passed on the info from last night, taken care of her civic duty.

Now she'd take care of Pamela.

* * *

Outside Henry Africa's, Colleen got her camera bag back out of the trunk, got into the Torino, started her up. Mr. Philanderer's wife was pushing for a photo of the two lovebirds together so she could sue the pants off him. Colleen had never felt such a desire to finish a crummy investigation, get paid, focus on what mattered.

Down Polk Street, past the Palms Café, the lights were on upstairs over the dry cleaners. *Yes.* There was no street parking to be had so she drove around the block. San Francisco was getting to be New York. She was just about to head home when she saw Mr. Philanderer's blue Dodge Magnum parked near Sukkers Likkers. She drove back up to Van Ness where she finally found a spot. She got out, camera bag hoisted over her shoulder, jogged back down to Polk.

She passed the spot where the blue Dodge Magnum had been parked.

Gone. Damn!

At Sukkers Likkers she picked up a pack of Virginia Slims and a book of matches. In the car, she tore open the pack, ripped off a paper match, lit up, blew smoke and frustration out the window. It started to spit rain. She turned on the windshield wipers.

At Gough she got on the freeway, headed south but didn't turn off at her exit.

She stopped at a Union 76 on Ocean, near the 280 Freeway, where gas was now up to seventy-one cents a gallon. While the attendant filled up the car, she used the payphone. Called Boom, her sometimes helper, roadie for a local band a former client of hers sang with, and a Vietnam vet working his way through college.

Boom was home, studying. Finals week was approaching.

"I hate to drag you away, Boom," she said. "But I can really use a little backup Monday night. Staking out the Thunderbird Hotel on O'Farrell."

"I always need the work, Chief," Boom said in his deep, easy voice.

"Around ten. We'll be done in a couple of hours and you can get back to the books. Bring a little persuasion."

"Think I'll have to use it?"

"No. Just something to wave around in case things go south. Use rock salt."

She told him about Shuggy, possibly meeting with Moon Ranch. And Pam.

"You found Pamela, Chief? But that's great."

"*Maybe* I've found her." Then, "I'll pay you a bonus."

"Deal. Grandma's eightieth is coming up. I'm taking her to The Tonga Room. Sip Blue Hawaiians while the indoor rain comes down on the little thatched raft floating in the pool." Boom's grandmother had raised him single-handed in the projects.

"I'll pick you up around nine. I need you to rent a room for me at the Thunderbird Monday night. Second floor if you can. And use an alias."

"I've got one or two of those," Boom said.

CHAPTER SIXTEEN

"Are they finally here?" Boom said, looking up from his textbook.

The bare overhead bulb reflected off his glasses, stark light over room 201 in the Thunderbird Hotel where Boom, an imposing black Vietnam vet, sat on a sagging bed while Colleen waited by the window for Moon Ranch to show. It was past eleven p.m. They were over an hour late.

The room had peeling wallpaper and reeked of disinfectant, not quite masking the other odors lurking underneath. Elsewhere in the hotel, TVs and stereos railed, punctuated by the occasional shout or laugh.

"Just a pizza delivery," Colleen said with a sigh, watching a Chevy Vega take off. She let the curtain fall back into place. Lucky's cryptic note had implied Moon Ranch would be here at ten. More to the point, it suggested that Pam might be somehow involved. Shuggy, upstairs in 312 with AC/DC blasting, had said he was getting some acid tonight. Colleen had tiptoed up there when Boom and she first arrived, smelled the weed from outside Shuggy's door.

It had been months since Colleen had seen Pamela, and then only from a distance.

Boom pushed his glasses into place, went back to studying macroeconomics. He wore his camouflage USMC jacket to ward off the cold.

Elsewhere the noise was standard Thunderbird Hotel. You could set off a bomb and people might not notice.

"Looks like the Ranchers are no-show, Boom," she said with a sigh. "And you've got a final tomorrow."

"No sweat." Boom flipped a page. "We can give it a little longer."

"I appreciate it." Colleen remained by the window, peering out the gap in the curtains. She wore a black ball cap and her gray rain jacket. Little Bersalina was nestled in the right pocket. She had her Canon SLR camera ready.

Pamela had taken up with Moon Ranch, a sect based up in Point Arenas, last year. Shunned Colleen. Worse, Moon Ranch took out a restraining order against Colleen when Colleen went up and tried to talk some sense into her daughter.

Her split from Pamela began over a decade ago, when Pam was still a child. Colleen had come home from the rubber plant in Denver one evening, found Pamela crouching in the corner of her bedroom in just a T-shirt. Her father's physical abuse had always been an issue in terms of punishment, but that night, for the first time, his unhealthy interest in his daughter finally reared its ugly head. Colleen recalled the sparks of anger that stippled her vision. Mostly at herself for not seeing it sooner. Back downstairs, she found her ex in the kitchen, frying eggs in a pan. Avoiding eye contact. When confronted, he said Pam was making up stories to get attention. *She's like that.* Pam had always been inward, and now Colleen saw why she'd been even more so.

The handle of the screwdriver sticking out of the tool bucket in the corner of the kitchen caught her eye like a magnet.

She remembered her vision shaking, her neck tightening.

It was over in a flash.

Seconds later, her ex was writhing on the linoleum, grasping at the screwdriver buried in his neck. Colleen stood on his arm as she turned the flame off under the eggs, moved the pan. When he stopped moving, she went upstairs, tried to console Pamela, but it was like holding a giant stone. She called her mother to come take care of Pam, then called Denver PD, turned herself in.

Colleen spent nine years and four months in Denver Women's Correctional Facility, the brunt of a fourteen-year sentence. The worst part? Not Roger, her ex, struggling as his life blood drained away on black-and-white linoleum. He'd gotten what he deserved. No. Colleen's regret was that she had lost Pamela. Going to prison widened that divide.

Pamela never seemed to forgive her. Colleen hadn't considered that. A father so contemptible was not worth grieving for, surely. It was one of the more baffling questions that plagued her most days. She just could not get her head around it, even after all this time.

Her thoughts were broken by a beat-up white van pulling up.

The van looked familiar. She raised her camera to one eye, zeroed in on the license plate through the telephoto lens.

The same van that had been parked outside her apartment a couple of months ago. That belonged to Moon Ranch. Here to make a delivery of Arenas Light, she bet.

Was Pam in that van?

Two figures sat in front. Colleen eyed them through the viewfinder. Two men. Colleen sighed, snapped a photo.

The van's hazard lights flicked on, flashing. Both front doors flipped open. The men got out, in orange robes, one man stocky, with a black watch cap and a daypack slung over one shoulder. The other wore a puffy down jacket over his robe and had the customary shaved head. The man in the watch cap looked around.

The two men came for the Thunderbird.

If two cult members visiting a drug dealer could be called elation, that's what Colleen felt. Because Lucky had been right enough. Although there was no trace of Pamela. Yet. Maybe she was in the back of the van.

"Looks like Shuggy's delivery has finally arrived," she said to Boom, snapping the lens cap on her camera, slipping the SLR into her shoulder bag on the chair. "Two guys. The taller one without a jacket looks like he might have the goods in a daypack. But Pam might be in the van, too. Go downstairs, let those two in before they ring Shuggy's doorbell. Take a quick look in the van. If Pam's not there, give me a sign, and we'll stop these two on the landing—find out where she might be." It was hard to control the anticipation.

Boom dog-eared the page of his textbook, shut it, reached down to the side of the bed, picked up his satchel, put the book away, and pulled a sawed-off shotgun. He stood up. He filled the little room. He tucked the gun inside his partially zipped-up camouflage jacket.

She nodded at the shotgun. "What do you have the cartridges loaded with?"

"Rock salt," he said. "I heard what you said."

Someone shot with a cartridge full of rock salt would suffer, to be sure, but not fatally. "Better hurry. Let them in before they ring Shuggy's bell."

Boom made a *right-on* fist, went out into the hall, then quickly downstairs. She followed Boom out into the hall, flipping off the room light, the hall light too.

AC/DC blasted in 312. "Hell Ain't a Bad Place to Be." Elsewhere the noise was standard Thunderbird: TVs, people shouting.

Downstairs, Boom opened the front door.

"You guys are late," she heard him say to the two Ranchers who'd arrived. "Shuggy's upstairs waiting for you." Colleen pulled a washcloth from her back pocket, one she'd borrowed from the bathroom, went over to the light bulb hanging on the landing, unscrewed the hot bulb. There was ambient light from upstairs and downstairs, but this floor was nicely darkened. She stepped back into the room, closed the door partially, watched through the crack.

"Go ahead," she heard Boom say to the two visitors.

One Rancher thanked him and Colleen heard two pair of feet enter the house. Boom went out into the street.

Colleen darted over to the window, checked the street. Boom was peering into the van. He turned, looked up, gave her a shake of the head and a thumbs-down.

No Pam.

Spit, she thought. She had gotten ahead of herself.

Plan B.

She hurried over to the door, and, through the crack, saw the two men in orange robes on the darkened landing, the guy in the down jacket in front, the other guy with the bag behind him. They were looking around, possibly wondering why no lights were on.

Colleen pulled the Bersa, flipped the safety off, tucked the gun behind her butt, opened the door.

"Oh, hi," she said.

Down Jacket actually smiled. A woman always generated interest from men.

She heard Boom coming in the front door downstairs, ready to back her up.

"Damn light's burned out again," she said to Down Jacket. Shook her head. "Or someone swiped the bulb again. Wouldn't you know it?"

She came up with the Bersa, fast, saw the man flinch. His hand went inside his jacket, but she already had the gun on him. She shook her head.

"'Freeze,' as they say on TV."

He did, hand in his jacket.

The taller guy behind him with the pack turned quickly. Boom was coming up the stairs evenly, sawed-off shotgun out.

"That will be enough of that," he said.

"Take your hand slowly out of your jacket," Colleen said to the guy in front. "And it best be empty when you do." She raised her eyebrows.

"Are you a cop?"

"No," she said. "Lucky for you, by the looks of things."

He slowly brought his hand out, empty.

"Gimme the bag," she heard Boom say to the tall guy.

"They're ripping us off," the guy in front said to Colleen in disbelief.

"Kinda," Colleen said, gun on him.

He gritted his teeth.

"What's the verdict?" Colleen asked Boom as he went through the bag.

"My guess is a few thousand tabs of acid."

"Wow," Colleen said, reaching inside the man's jacket. She came out with an old .38 compact with a duct-taped grip. "This doesn't look very legal. I better hang onto it."

He glared at her. If looks could kill.

"Where's Pamela?" she asked him.

"Who?"

"Aadhya," Colleen said. Pamela's Moon Ranch name.

"Aadhya took off. Couple of months ago."

"I thought she was coming tonight."

"You heard wrong."

Colleen's mind was spinning. "Okay, you two, on your way. Tell your boss he gets this bag of goodies back when I find out what happened to Pamela Hayes—Aadhya."

"I told you, Aadhya took off."

"Not to be rude, but I need to hear what your boss has to say."

He looked at her for a long moment, clearly not happy. But happy enough to get out of there unhurt. But not too thrilled at being robbed.

Colleen said to Boom: "Show these two out, will you? Make sure they leave."

"You got it, Chief."

The two men shuffled off downstairs, Boom behind them, just as a door upstairs on the third floor opened, AC/DC loud through the opening. Shuggy emerged.

"Hey, guys?" he said over the banister. "Is that you?"

"Pizza delivery," Colleen shouted back in a deep voice.

There was a pause. "What?"

"Pizza," she said, gun behind her back.

The van started up outside.

Shuggy's heavy footsteps came thumping down the stairs.

Shuggy appeared shirtless on the landing. Muscular but with a gut and tattoos. He squinted in the dark.

His mouth dropped when he saw Colleen. Outside, the van squealed off.

"What the fuck? Carol Anne?"

"Hey, Shuggy," she said. "How's it going, dude?"

"What are you doing here?"

She shrugged.

Boom came back in, up the stairs.

"Who the fuck're you?" Shuggy said to Boom. He turned back to Colleen, mouth agape.

"I'm so glad you didn't use a racial epithet, Shuggy," she said.

"What the fuck are you doing here, Carol Anne?"

"You should have just stayed in your room, Shuggy." Colleen came out with the gun, waved Shuggy into the darkened room with it. "C'mon, c'mon."

Boom followed, bag over his shoulder.

"That's why you wanted to know about Monday," Shuggy said, putting it together. "You wanted to fucking rip me off."

"Not you specifically," she said. "Moon Ranch." She smiled. "This has nothing to do with you, right now. If you want to keep it that way, you best pretend nothing happened. C'mon. Get in here already."

Shuggy came into the room, looked at her, then Boom, then back at Colleen, shook his head. "You think you're actually gonna get away with this?"

"You know, I really do, Shug. Where's Pamela?"

"What?" Shuggy squinted. "Pamela?"

"Pamela Hayes. Aadhya. She delivers for Moon Ranch. Where is she?"

"How the hell should I know? Why do you even care?"

"Shuggy, as a rule, the person with the gun asks the questions. When did you last see her?"

Shuggy thought. "Couple of months?"

"So why did someone tell me she was going to be here tonight?" Colleen wasn't going to mention Lucky by name, even though he was dead. There was—or should be—an active murder investigation over Lucky and she wasn't going to interfere with that.

Shuggy's eyes shifted. "I don't know."

A queasy feeling juiced Colleen's stomach, the thought of Pamela and Shuggy together. She pushed it aside.

"Okay, Shug, time to get in the closet. And I don't mean your sexual preference."

"Just leave the bag of stuff and I'll forget all about this, Carol Anne."

"Nice try, Shug," she said. "Thanks, but no thanks. I think I'll hang onto it. And no games. You don't want Moon Ranch thinking you had something to do with ripping them off, do you?" She gave a light switch smile.

Shuggy was shaking with rage. "You are truly fucked up if you think this is the end of it."

"Probably. But get in the closet, already. I'm getting tired of this conversation."

He complied, squeezing his big frame to get in. She pushed the closet door shut. Went and got a straight-backed chair, propped it against the doorknob, locking him in.

"You are going to be one sorry bitch," Shuggy muttered through the door.

"Let's go up to Shuggy's place," she said to Boom. "See what we can find."

Downstairs they heard a door open, movement, someone coming out into the hall.

"What's going on up there?" Lawrence the manager shouted. "Who left the front door open? How many times do I have to say it?"

"Damn," Colleen said to Boom. "The manager." She nodded at the window. "Fire escape. Let's get out of here. You've got a final tomorrow."

"So I do." Boom went over to the window, heaved it up, held the curtain for her. "You first, madam."

She climbed out onto the fire escape. Boom followed.

Soon they were back down on O'Farrell, hurrying for the Torino. And Colleen wondering where Pamela might be.

CHAPTER SEVENTEEN

Back home, Colleen poured herself a glass of Chardonnay, kicked off her shoes, lit up a Virginia Slim. Sat down at her desk in her office where she hefted the clear plastic bag of LSD tabs. A good couple of pounds. Each tab was white, about an eighth of an inch wide and half as tall. A single hit could go for a couple of bucks, up to ten, so this bag was worth a fair amount. But acid had a shelf life. That would work in her favor.

If Shuggy was telling the truth, Pam had last been seen with Moon Ranch a couple of months ago. Moon Ranch would be making contact once they found their delivery had been diverted.

Almost two a.m. She got a sheet of paper out, wrote "Moon Ranch Arenas Light LSD confiscated at the Thunderbird Hotel, November 13, 1978" across the top, spilled a few tabs out on the sheet next to the heading, set the bag of tabs next to it. Got her Polaroid camera out, set up the shot, photographed the prize. She wrote down the van information, along with the license number. She folded the sheet of paper, slipped it and the Polaroid into an envelope, addressed to her lawyer, along with a note.

"If anything should happen to me, contact Inspector Owens at SFPD. Douglas Fletcher of Moon Ranch is the one to question first."

She put a thirteen-cent stamp on the envelope, set the envelope by the front door in the alcove, finished her wine, took a shower, went to bed.

She lay back on the warmth of the water-filled mattress, thinking of her daughter.

CHAPTER EIGHTEEN

The next morning, a shred of blue broke through the clouds as Colleen looked down at Vermont Street. No white Moon Ranch van. No suspicious vehicles. She checked the back of the flat, peering over the third-story railing down to the yard, which had parking for the building's tenants. Safe.

Shortly after, she left in a pair of high-waisted bell-bottom jeans and her white leather Pony Topstars with the red stripes, and the letter to her lawyer and the bag of acid inside a paper bag. She'd called Gus Pedersen, her lawyer, earlier, brought him up to speed, told him to expect the letter. Gus was on his way out to go surfing, but was customarily unphased with the development, which was why he was the perfect lawyer for Colleen. The bag of LSD was going to a safe place. In addition, she carried her Bersa in her hollowed-out hardback copy of *Pride and Prejudice*.

Messing with Moon Ranch meant she would have to be extra vigilant in watching her back. Shuggy didn't know her true identity, or where she lived. For now. She drove down to the Transbay Terminal in rush-hour traffic, keeping one eye on the rearview mirror.

At the Transbay Terminal she parked on 1st Street, recalling a recent case she had worked here. She got out amidst the inane racket of video games wafting out of the Fun Terminal, fed the meter, took her paper bag of acid and letter.

The Transbay Terminal buzzed with commuters, which was fine—hectic and anonymous. Back by the snack counter she placed the bag of LSD in a locker, inserted three quarters, pulled the key. On the way out of the terminal, she mailed the letter to her lawyer.

On the way home she swung by Mr. Philanderer's love pad above the dry cleaners on Polk, did not see his car parked anywhere. Ten minutes later, Mr. Philanderer's blond left the apartment, alone, in jeans, dark glasses, and a floppy hat.

Colleen decided to wait. She needed that photo of the two of them together.

Twenty minutes later, Blondie returned with a sack of groceries.

Fifteen minutes later, a tall young man with sculpted brown hair, sprayed to a fare-thee-well, wearing a snug blue leisure suit that showed off his bodybuilder physique, stopped by. He checked the street both ways before he rang her doorbell.

Blondie answered the door, gave him a peck on the cheek as she let him in.

Colleen got a photo of that.

Well, well.

It looked like Mr. Philanderer was being philandered on.

All in a day's work for Hayes Confidential.

Feeling slightly grubby, she drove home.

At the top of Potrero Hill, the community garden and elevated freeway across the way, she turned right on Vermont, past her building, kept going. Circled the block before she went in.

On the corner she spotted two men parked in a beige Mercedes sedan where she wouldn't have seen them if she hadn't been looking. She drove past, turned right on 19th, headed downhill. One eye in the rearview.

The sedan appeared in the rearview mirror. Following her. She needed the safety of a crowd.

Ten minutes later, she was driving up to Twin Peaks, one of the highest points in the city. The Mercedes was not far behind and making no real effort to remain hidden. At the top of Twin Peaks, the sun was punching its way through clouds and there were plenty of cars parked and people out snapping photos and taking in the view.

She pulled up to a vista of downtown San Francisco and shut off the engine. She plucked her Bersa from *Pride and Prejudice* and tucked it into the pocket of her black leather coat. She lit up a cigarette and got out of the car, strolled over to a view of Market Street below leading to the Ferry Building and the Bay Bridge beyond that. With all the sightseers, she wasn't alone.

The Mercedes pulled up next to her red Torino and parked. The doors opened; two men got out. One young man with a shaved head wore an orange robe under a beat-up leather jacket. The hint of a shoulder strap was visible under his arm. The other man wore a pastel green polyester suit and white loafers with no socks. He was middle-aged, lean, with raw features and wiry gray hair raked over to the side. Sunglasses hid his eyes.

They sauntered over.

"Where's your orange robe?" Colleen said to the older man, tapping ash into the air.

"Let's just dispense with the small talk." His voice was as rough as his exterior.

"Sorry, Mr. Fletcher. I'll keep it simple. Just for you."

"You know my name."

"It's on the restraining order you guys took out against me. You're the head honcho up at Moon Ranch."

"Then you know you're not supposed to have any contact with us."

"Seems you just contacted *me*," she said, smoking. "And if you think that interaction down at the Thunderbird last night counts as a violation of the restraining order, I'm more than happy to let SFPD deal with it."

He turned to the younger man. "Wait in the car." It was like ordering a dog around. The young man headed back to the Mercedes, got in, sat, and stared straight ahead. If he had any emotional reaction to anything, it was beyond Colleen.

"I want my package back," Fletcher said.

"And get it you shall. Once I know where Pamela is."

"She's gone."

"Yes, I know. You guys were hovering around my place a couple of months back, looking for her. She'd run off. You thought maybe she'd come to me." How Colleen had wished. "But she hadn't."

"So how would we know where she is now?"

"Because it was rumored she was going to be at the Thunderbird last night."

Fletcher raised his stiff eyebrows.

"And no," she said. "I'm not going to tell you how I knew that."

He nodded. "She used to help make the drop. No more. Like I said, she's gone."

"So she came back? After she ran away? Or someone found her? Brought her back to Moon Ranch?"

"No. She's well and truly gone."

"When?"

"Two months ago, as I said. More or less."

"So why did I hear that she was going to be part of the festivities last night?"

Fletcher sighed, obviously weighing his words.

"How bad do you want your acid back?" Colleen said.

"When I spoke to Shuggy about setting up the drop, he requested Pamela be there," Fletcher said.

"Why?"

Fletcher gave a nasty smile. "Why do you think?"

Her heart dropped. Just what she didn't need to hear.

"How well does Shuggy know Pam?" Colleen said, her voice taut with emotion.

"Not as well as he would probably have liked." Fletcher gave a quick smile. "Feel better?"

She actually did. "Shuggy was hitting on her."

"When she used to help with deliveries, Shuggy always asked for her. He liked her, trusted her. When we spoke on the phone last week, he asked for her again."

"And what did you say?"

"That I would see what I could do."

"Even though she was gone."

Fletcher shrugged. "Just trying to keep the customer satisfied."

Lucky must have overheard that phone call.

"Even though she couldn't be there," Colleen said.

Fletcher shrugged. "She didn't drive the van last night. That's all you need to know. She's gone."

"So, where is she now?"

"How should I know?"

"Because Moon Ranch doesn't like it when people leave without permission. You do your best to track them down, convince them to come back. So you surely tried. I need to know where you last saw a trace of her. In exchange for that, I might be able to return your little tabs of joy. Before they go stale."

"I hope you're keeping them out of direct sunlight."

"Of course. I care deeply about your drug-running operation."

"Are you aware of the risk you're taking?"

She puffed on her cigarette, exhaled. "I've sent details of the interrupted transaction to my lawyer. Anything happens to me, he takes that info, goes straight to SFPD. SFPD might not care too much about dope in our fair city, but if evidence of drug dealing is put right under their nose, even they have to do something about it. So there goes your acid. And your client Shuggy. And a lot of lucrative, repeat business. And for what? A little info? Pamela is gone. You got everything you were going to get out of her, what little money she had, money she finagled out of her grandmother. Whatever hold you had over her is finished. Focus on some new gullible kids. Not my daughter. Just let me know where she went, and I'll get you the locker key to your product."

Douglas Fletcher put his hands in the front pockets of his Polyester pants partway, chewed his lip.

"Five-fifty-five Fillmore," he said. "She was there shortly after she took off. Last place we know of."

"Two months ago?"

Fletcher blinked in thought. "Early October. The second week."

About six weeks.

"And you couldn't persuade her to come back?" Colleen asked.

"Pamela is incapable of true enlightenment."

Colleen ignored that. "And what is five-fifty-five Fillmore?"

"You wanted to know where we last saw her. Now you do. The rest you can find out for yourself. Although you may not want to."

A chill of apprehension trembled through Colleen. "Don't think you're getting your package back until I check things out."

"Then it better be soon."

"One more thing: if I see you or any of your people hanging around my place again, I'll get upset."

He stared at her through his sunglasses. "Your daughter detests you. You know that, don't you?"

Colleen flinched. "Thanks to you."

"No," he said. "Her damage is all your doing. She hates you—more than you'll ever know." He smiled an ugly smile, turned and left.

Colleen stood there, heart pounding like a piston about to break, smoking the last of her cigarette with shaky fingers. Thinking of Pamela. And all she had done wrong as a mother.

CHAPTER NINETEEN

At one time, 555 Fillmore had been an imposing church of light brick with embedded carved sandstone crosses and tall stained-glass windows. Built just after the 1906 quake, it had changed hands more than once, was converted into a roller rink in the early part of this decade, and fallen on hard times, recently taken over by a "church" from South Africa by the name of *Die Kerk van die Volmaakte*, which translated from Afrikaans to "The Church of the Perfect." Colleen had spent a couple of hours in front of a microfiche machine at the public library on Van Ness and learned that the faith seemed to believe that its founder, a charismatic young man with long oily hair and a crucifix tattoo in the center of his forehead, by the name of Adem Lea, or Angel 22, was the reincarnation of Jesus, biblical Adam, and a few other people as well, including Tsar Nicholas and Brian Jones of The Rolling Stones. Adem Lea had brought the church over from Johannesburg when he fled the country to avoid a prison term for tax evasion and human trafficking.

The building had suffered its share of distress, from boarded-up windows to graffiti to crumbling mortar between its bricks, to handbills posted on its once stately columns, which held up a tall portico. Despite that, a sizable congregation was gathering outside. Colleen stood across the street in the light drizzle of early evening, watching, wondering what Pamela had gotten herself into now.

All ages and races were represented, all shapes and sizes, with one common physical trait: a vacant expression. Most were dressed in a mishmash of thrift shop clothing, except for the two men on the door who wore heavy off-white robes and were checking ID cards as people funneled in. The run-down look was by design, Colleen had learned, austerity being one of the eleven tenants. Eleven was a significant number, as was twenty-two—Adem Lea's angel designation. Multiples of eleven were important. The church exacted a hefty tithing from their working members—their entire salary in many cases—which was the reason for a labor law investigation by several members' families. Die Kerk also had a few high-profile supporters in its ranks, but much was shrouded in secrecy, although people who got on their wrong side did not tend to fare well. One man who filed charges against Die Kerk for holding his daughter had his house burned down. Parents who made inquiries about their son were run off the road in Napa. Colleen wasn't surprised. Moon Ranch had a similar MO. It was standard cult operating procedure.

She didn't see anyone who looked like Pamela in the crowd.

First Moon Ranch, now this. Out of the frying pan into the fire.

Colleen crossed the street, feeling overdressed in a smart beige raincoat over a dark knee-length dress, stockings, and black high heels. Her idea of going to church was obviously different than Die Kerk's.

Beginning with a policy of invitation only, it seemed.

She got in line behind a group of women, doing her best to blend in. No one seemed to be talking. No one seemed to smell very good either. One of the eleven "reëls"—rules—advocated bathing no more than once a week, the day after the Sabbath. God's protective layer of oils was negated by soaps and fragrances.

The robed guards were busy verifying blue ID cards. When her turn came, Colleen tried to squeeze behind a large Samoan woman.

"Wait, woman," a swarthy guard said to her. "Where is your docket?"

"I left it at home this morning. I just came from work."

The big man put a hand on her shoulder, left it there, something she didn't particularly care for. "You need a docket."

"Where would I get a temporary one?"

"Your guardian." He shifted Colleen to one side with his big hand. "You're holding up the line." He looked over her shoulder. "Next."

Colleen stood back, wondering how to get in. From inside the hall, the squeal of a Farsi organ announced the beginning of an eerie dirge.

Hands in the pockets of her raincoat, she scanned the lost faces. None with Pamela's haunted, angry countenance.

"Do you need a docket, woman?"

Don't we all, Colleen thought, turning to see a large bear of a man in a run-down pin-striped double-breasted suit that looked vintage '40s. A frilly blue ruffle collar stuck out incongruously. Wild hair sprung out of a beret pulled down tight on his melon head. A long wispy goatee completed the oddball look. He smelled like he'd run a marathon, which, judging by his physique, he hadn't. His eyes stared down at her hungrily.

Colleen fought the shudder of repulsion. He might be her ticket in.

"That would be perfect," she said.

He put a meaty hand on her waist, a little too friendly, guided her back toward the door.

"This woman is my guest," he told one big guard.

"Amen, Brother Arno."

Soon they were in the dark, airy church, lit by the flickering lights of the former roller rink, in a gutted hall with no seats. A couple hundred people milled about, no one speaking much. Stained-glass windows added a suggestion of spirituality. The air echoed with off-key electronic music. Guards in robes and sandals wandered about, keeping watch. Onstage, behind an empty podium, a large white screen fluttered with a draft of air, projecting a larger-than-life full-length photo of Adem Lea, Angel 22. He was a slender man in his forties with a piercing stare, made even more so by the tattoo of a crucifix in the middle of his forehead, just off center. He was also completely naked, from head to toe. Below the photo was an inscription in what Colleen assumed was Afrikaans: *God het niks om weg te steek nie,* and English: *God has nothing to hide.*

It took a moment for her eyes to adjust. Once they did, she jumped when she noticed a plump middle-aged woman standing naked on one side of the stage, a black hood over her head. A sign around her neck read: *vir skaamte.* On the other side of the stage a young black woman stood in a similar situation.

"What on earth is that?" Colleen asked Brother Arno.

"They are cleansing their shame," Brother Arno said. He stood close to her, his body touching. Her quills were up even as she knew she must use her attraction to her advantage.

"No men?" Colleen asked.

"Men shame themselves in different ways."

Colleen just bet they did with this crowd. If Pamela was involved, it needed to be brought to a stop. Moon Ranch were starting to look like Cub Scouts.

"Your first time with Die Kerk?" Brother Arno said with an air of suspicion.

"My first service here." Colleen introduced herself as Carol Aird. She scoured the room, looking for Pamela. No luck.

"What drew you to our church, Carol?"

"I guess I'm looking for something," she said. More like *someone.*

"Aren't we all," Brother Arno said sagely, stroking his goatee.

"I'm looking forward to the sermon," she said. "Where is Brother Adem?"

Brother Arno gave her a curious look. "Brother Adem won't be preaching tonight. He's on a journey. A search for perfection. With 242 of his chosen ones."

More numerology. She had read something about mysterious pilgrimages to far-flung places, but there were scant details.

"Really?" she asked. "Where to?"

"That is not for me to share."

"When did they leave?"

Brother Arno looked her over before he answered. "Over a month ago, now."

"I see," she said, watching people siphon in. Still no Pamela.

"Are you looking for someone in particular, Carol?"

"Yes, as a matter of fact."

"Who would that be?"

"A friend," Colleen said, not sure how to proceed. "Her name is Pamela. Pamela Hayes. Would you know her? Have you met her?"

"I don't think so. What is her perfect name?"

She had no idea. But she worried about exposing herself as a Grade A phony. "Good question. To be honest, I don't really know her all that well. She was a friend of my brother's before she came to Die Kerk, and he told me how much it had done for her. She couldn't stop talking about it."

"I see." Brother Arno was growing suspicious.

She didn't need to be thrown out. "I've been intrigued with Die Kerk ever since." She gave him an intimate smile, pushing back her feelings of disgust. He had to be close to three hundred pounds.

"So you don't have a guardian, Carol?"

"Not yet," she said, giving him the eye. "I hope that's not a problem." She parted her lips, stared into his eyes.

He returned a furtive smile. "Well, we were all new once."

"Exactly." She turned. "Just look at these people. They seem so . . . content." They didn't. "So alive." Not really. "So . . ."

"*Perfect*," Brother Arno said.

"Yes," she said, turning back to him. "*That's* the word."

His hand rested on her lower back, just above her rear. "It takes time and the ultimate sacrifice to reach true perfection. And a commitment."

The ultimate sacrifice made her shiver. "If something is worth having," she said, "the price is never too high."

"How true." Brother Arno began stroking her lower back. He leaned over. "I could help," he said. "I could be your guardian."

She clasped her hands together. "Would you? Would you be my guardian, Arno?"

"*Brother* Arno. And yes, I would. But there are conditions."

Ugh.

"We can go upstairs," he said matter-of-factly.

She jumped. His rubbing hand formed a larger arc, touching her butt. She moved away.

He continued: "I see you are alarmed, Carol. Don't be. Attitudes toward fornication are merely society's conditioning. Fornicating is a way to break those conventions and enable your search for perfection. To shorten your path to all Die Kerk has to offer."

She moved away again. "I think I'm going to say 'no thanks to the fornicating' for the moment." She laughed, tried to pass it off as a joke.

He came in again, his words hot in her ear. "Why? Are you menstruating?"

She turned, glared at him. "Please tell me you didn't just say that."

"There is nothing shameful about bodily functions, Carol."

"Agreed. But it's *my* body. And I don't feel like discussing it."

"Do you believe you need to be in love to fornicate? Die Kerk does not promote romantic liaisons."

She moved again. "What time does the sermon start?"

He came in again, breathing hard. His breath was rank. "I understand your nervousness. But physical intimacy is a shackle that must be broken between guardian and neophyte. In order to overcome your anxiety, and your woman's shame, and the physical attraction that exists between us, which is shallow and fleeting and only impedes perfection, we fornicate, so that the act doesn't overshadow the true bond we will build."

"What—no dinner and a movie first?"

He laughed. "I must admit, your teasing excites me."

Lucky her. She moved yet again. "Look, I don't want to hurt your feelings, Brother Arno, but I'm a gentle slope kind of person as far as the old fornicating goes. I really need to take my time."

"All women must pass this step. We can go upstairs now, where it's more private." He was rubbing her back again. "It won't take long and I can get you an application. I can even introduce you to Brother Adem."

"I thought he was on a pilgrimage."

"When he returns."

"When will that be?"

"A few weeks."

Did that mean Pamela would be back in a few weeks? "Let me think about it, Arno."

"*Brother* Arno."

"*Brother* Arno."

He breathed heavily as he moved in yet again. Grimaced. "Then I'm afraid I'll have to have you removed, Carol. I'm the one who authorized your temporary docket. I can just as easily unauthorize it."

"Well, that's not much of a date, is it?"

"'Dating' is an antiquated concept propagated by a collapsing world. It's also forbidden. Reël number seven. Don't you want to find your friend? What was her name? Pamela?"

She had come this far. She'd have to endure a little more of stink man.

"Well, yes, Arno . . ."

"*Brother* Arno."

"*Brother* Arno," she said. "But I really want to hear the sermon, too." *And see if Pam shows.* "Then we can go upstairs—maybe." She put her hands on his big shoulders, pushed him back a foot. "How's that?"

Brother Arno huffed his disappointment, crossed his arms over his chest.

More people arrived. Still, they were remarkably quiet for such a large crowd.

A man got up onstage and went behind the large screen. The nude women with hoods stood on either side with heads hung. Not long after, lights dimmed, and the projected picture of Adem Lea disappeared. Colleen used the opportunity to move away from Brother Arno into the crowd. A tinny gong sounded over the loudspeakers.

Rousing music boomed as a grainy black-and-white film flickered on the screen.

A hush fell over the already subdued crowd when Brother Adem Lea appeared on-screen. Mercifully he was dressed, wearing his floppy hat. He appeared to be in a forested setting. Trees loomed. Birds called.

The first words he spoke were in Afrikaans, a language Colleen had no sense of. But he was solemn, delivering some sort of prayer that the crowd mumbled along with.

When the recitation was over, Colleen leaned over to a young man. "What was that about, please?" she whispered.

"Silence," the man said. "It is the *gebed van die volmaakte dood*." Whatever that was.

Thankfully, Brother Adem Lea switched to English, spoken with a strong South African accent.

"Blessings, children. I regret I cannot be with you but know that I am with you in spirit. I and 242 other brothers and sisters destined for perfection are on a sacred pilgrimage, in a place far from nuclear attack by our corrupt and immoral government. Please keep us in your prayers and understand that if you continue to follow the eleven principles, you too will join me on the path to perfection."

He went on to say how there would be no miracles performed this week, but that he knew which members had cancers and illnesses, and would heal them from afar. He praised members for their tithings, in particular one woman who had recently joined from Indianapolis, who was feeding her children birdseed in order to save money to construct Die Kerk's sanctuary, Verligting, at the Throat of Fire. Colleen wondered what the Throat of Fire was. Something to do with his current location?

"Our mission is so important, children, I cannot stress it enough. Aided by our corrupt and immoral government, we humans have destroyed our world, and only one solution exists to appease God. We all know what that is, and it is blessed. Rest assured that *you* are blessed for having recognized what so many others haven't and for taking the only action."

The finality of his words chilled Colleen.

He spoke in Afrikaans again, and when he was done, he gave a two-fingered peace sign. The film flickered off. Pulsating psychedelic blobs appeared on the screen. The organ music resumed. Subdued conversation followed.

"Ah, there you are."

Colleen turned to see Brother Arno. Not looking too pleased.

"What is the 'Throat of Fire,' Brother Arno?" she asked.

Brother Arno eyed her. He wasn't about to answer.

"What's this solution Brother Adem is talking about?"

"Reaching perfection, woman."

"And how does one do that?"

"By not asking so many questions—especially when one is new. One follows. One learns."

Colleen just needed to learn how to manage Brother Arno's horny expectations.

He reached out. "Take my hand."

Christ in a hammock. "Where are we going?"

"To the office—upstairs."

She took a deep breath. She had to find her daughter. "For an application, right?" she said. "An *application.* That's it?"

"Yes."

She took his hand. It was clammy, soft, moist.

Brother Arno led her across the crowded floor. Rank-and-file members stepped out of their way. He guided Colleen to a dark wooden stairwell, up a creaking flight of stairs that he labored to mount. The smell of must prevailed. The Farsi organ wailed in the hall downstairs.

Upstairs, down a hallway, he stopped at a door. Got out some keys. Unlocked the door.

Into a windowless room. A storeroom. Stacks of boxes. Cleaning supplies. He left the light off. The room was dusty, close, and barely lit by weak ambient light from the hallway.

She made out a mattress on the floor by a radiator.

"This doesn't look like much of an office, Brother Arno."

He steered her in, pulled the chain on a single overhead bulb, shut the door behind her. "It's quite comfortable." He took off his jacket, hung it on the hook behind the door. His body odor was sharp and sour.

He turned to her, gave her an oily smile. "You are a very agreeable woman, Carol. Your body is quite a distraction to the goal of perfection."

"I get that a lot. But you said you were going to get me an application."

"All in good time." He unbuckled his belt, smiled, thrust his big pelvis out. "Would you care to do the rest . . ."

The hairs rose on the back of her neck.

"Brother Arno," she said, putting her hands together again. "After my husband died, I took a vow of celibacy. To honor his memory." Kind of true. A decade in prison had certainly helped. And she had been the one responsible for his death. But ever since, her involvement with men had taken a backseat. A select one or two. "I really need time to adjust to the—ah—commitment."

"Understood," Brother Arno said, biting his lip at the prospect. "There are alternatives."

"I bet."

"If you're not comfortable with full penetration, we can substitute. You may simply fellate me."

He dropped his pants to the floor. His legs were fat and hairy. He stepped out of his shoes. His black socks came up to his pudgy knees.

"Sorry." She shook her head. "Not my thing."

"I only need what any man needs."

"I'm not saying 'no,'" she said. "But I want to find my friend Pamela first." She got the photo out of her pocket. A black-and-white picture-booth print of Pamela, taken a couple of years back before Colleen got out of prison. Pamela's face was desolate and angry, lined by her descent into drugs at the time. Colleen held the photo up.

Brother Arno's eyes narrowed on the picture. Colleen wasn't sure but she thought she saw a glimmer of recognition.

"You've seen her, haven't you, Brother Arno?"

"I'm not sure."

"Yes, you have." She held the photo closer. "Take another look."

"I will. After you service me."

He stood there in his silly ruffled shirt, threadbare at the collar, his pants around his ankles. Fetching.

"Answer the question, first," she said, holding the photo up.

"Then, will you do as I say?"

She took a deep breath through her mouth, so as not to breathe his body odor in the confined room.

"Yes," she said.

She saw his eyes light up with desire in the pall of the single bulb. "You know what I think, Carol? I think you enjoy toying with me."

"Why would I want to do that?"

He grinned. "I'll admit it's stimulating, even as shallow and meaningless as it is. It's starting to make me tumescent, as a matter of fact. Look for yourself."

"No, that's okay."

"Take off your coat," he said. He nodded at the mattress. "And your dress. Your shoes."

"You need to answer my question before I do any of that."

"No. Use your hand on me, woman."

"I will do more, Brother Arno, if you simply tell me if you've seen her."

"More?"

"That's what I said."

"Who is she again?"

"She's my friend's little sister. I'm worried about her, and I simply can't relax, until I know she's safe. Once I know that, I'm fine."

"And then . . . are you prepared to . . ." He didn't finish the question.

"Yes," she said.

The pink tip of his tongue licked his lower lip. He was trembling, clearly becoming more aroused.

"I *have* seen her."

It wasn't much but it was enough to keep her pushing this facade. "When?"

"Just once. Over a month ago? She was a neophyte."

Colleen lowered the photo. "Was she okay?"

"Yes."

"How did she look?"

He shrugged. "Like anyone else."

"Where is she now?"

He shrugged.

"Is it possible she's gone on this pilgrimage with Brother Adem?"

"I am not sure. They don't tell me everything."

"Have you spoken to her? Ever?"

"No." He nodded at her coat. "Take off your shoes."

"I will—soon. But I need to know."

"I've not spoken to her."

"Who would know?"

"One of the elders."

"Where are they?"

Shook his head. "I've told you more than enough." He walked over to the mattress, began unbuttoning his shirt.

"Where's my application?" Colleen asked.

"They are not approved freely. You need me. I must go to the office."

"You said this was the office."

"Take off your shoes. I want to see your feet."

Colleen stifled a groan of frustration. "Where is the office?"

"I'll tell you when I've finished!" he snapped. "We could have been done by now."

She exhaled. "I need to clean up."

He shook his head. "No, you don't. That is one of the guiding principles: reël four."

"Well, *I* need to clean up."

"You're fine."

"I haven't been with a man since my husband. I need to clean myself."

He gasped in frustration. "Two doors to the left."

"Thank you." She turned.

"Stop!" he said, climbing up off the floor. "I'm coming with you."

"No," she said.

"I'm coming with you," he said firmly.

He didn't trust her. For good reason.

"Fine," she said. "Hurry up."

She went to the door, stood in front of his jacket while he pulled his pants on, buckled up. Surreptitiously she slipped her hand in a side pocket. Nothing. The other pocket. Same. While he was zipping up, she felt into the breast pocket. A wallet. *Come to mama.* It was in the pocket of her overcoat in no time.

Once dressed, his collar askew, they went next door to the restroom.

She opened the door. There were several stalls. He followed her in.

"I need privacy," she said.

"You will learn that that is another fallacy that has been hindering your growth."

"For the time being," she said, "I'll have my fallacy."

Their eyes met. He sighed. "Very well."

He left, waited outside the door. She could hear him breathing heavily, even with the disoriented music and crowd milling around in the church downstairs.

She went into a stall. Stood, went through his wallet. A frayed blue membership card, in Afrikaans, to Die Kerk. It recognized him as Bröer Arno. It had an address on the back—99 Pacheco Street. She pocketed it. The rest of the wallet did not contain much. A driver's license. Brother Arno was Leonard Gunther from St. Paul, Minnesota. There were a few dollars. She left them. She flushed the toilet. Went outside.

He was waiting.

"I'm ready," she said.

His tongue was working his lower lip vigorously.

They returned to the storage room. He quickly got undressed. While he stepped out of his shoes, she slipped the wallet back into the breast pocket of his jacket.

He turned, dropped his pants again. "Come on, woman!"

"I'm so sorry, Brother Arno," she said. "But I just can't."

His mouth fell open. "Wha—*what are you talking about?*"

"Since my husband . . . I just can't."

"It's part of letting go!" he snapped. "You will see that."

She shook her head. "Next time. When will I see you again?"

"There will be no next time. You will lie with me now, woman. Or I will summon the guards."

"What—in your tatty underwear, Brother Arno?"

He reddened with anger. "Don't you dare disrespect me, girl!"

"Rule number fourteen and a half: it's 1978, so we don't call women 'girls.' Not if you want to jump their bones, that is."

"How dare you!" He stormed over, grabbed her arm, hard, hurting her wrist. "Get on the mattress. Now. Do as I say and it will be over soon."

She jerked herself free, raised her knee into his groin, full force.

Brother Arno *oofed*, collapsed to the floor like a fallen tree. The floorboards shook.

"You brought that on yourself, brother," she said.

He curled up into a fetal position, clutching himself. "You will pay for this!"

She left the room quickly, pulled the door shut. She broke into a run down the hallway. She heard the door open as she stepped down the stairs.

"Guards!" he shouted.

Down in the main church, the Farsi organ was louder. The place was emptying out. She looked around, saw no Pamela, pushed her way out through the crowd.

Pam was on that damn pilgrimage; Colleen just knew it. Vintage Pam: pick the worst possible option and go for it with gusto.

Colleen found the front door, shoved herself past the two guards in robes.

CHAPTER TWENTY

Next morning, Colleen stood outside a spear-pointed wrought-iron fence on 99 Pacheco Street, hands in the pockets of her leather coat, collar up, hair in a tail under a black ball cap. Sunglasses hid her eyes.

Behind the fence, beyond a sizable lawn, lay a former mansion from another time painted a jarring matte black, trimmed in gold, with gold columns and balustrades.

Die Kerk van die Volmaakte. Church of the Perfect.

The main office was nestled in Forest Hills, where San Francisco's old money resided on rolling streets lined with established trees. Die Kerk took up the corner of a block, obscured by gnarled old cedars, making it look less incongruous with its conservative neighbors.

Constructed by a prominent stockbroker who lost it during the Crash of '29, the building had been a speakeasy during Prohibition, and later traded hands amongst wealthy San Franciscans as property values escalated. The current owner was a reclusive rock 'n' roller whose *Summer of Love* anthem became a worldwide hit in 1967 that continued to generate royalties that kept him in the jet set. He no longer lived here, having donated the five-thousand-square-foot building to his church. From Colleen's research at the public library on Van Ness, the place was as ominous as the two Dobermans that came bounding across the lawn at her now.

She jolted as the beasts rooted themselves on the other side of the fence, snarling with barred teeth.

She moved on to the front gate.

Die Kerk demanded complete "bevestiging"—attachment— from followers, which prohibited communication with the outside world. Much about the church was unknown, although charges had been filed for extortion and physical violence against those that spoke out against it.

All too similar to Moon Ranch, Pamela's last fixation. Pam obviously needed answers, answers that Colleen hadn't provided as a parent. Being in prison for most of Pam's young life hadn't helped.

She had to find Pamela, soon.

At the front gate she rang an intercom buzzer.

A man answered, his electronic voice crackling with static. He had an accent, somewhere from the eastern side of the world.

She introduced herself as Ms. Aird, interested in learning more about the church.

"Are you with the press, Ms. Aird?"

"No."

"The IRS? A law enforcement agency?"

"No. Why?"

"You do realize that if you attempt to infiltrate the church under false pretexts, Die Kerk will take the strongest legal action available?"

"I'm a file clerk—all quite mundane. I'm just at a point in life where I want some answers to things."

His tone shifted. "That's certainly a normal step in our short time on earth, Ms. Aird. God knows there will be hell to pay for what man has done. Repentance is the only way. And who is your guardian?"

She consulted Brother Arno's membership card, which she had pulled from her coat pocket. It had gotten her this far. But it might not be wise to reference him, even though she suspected he might not be in a hurry to advertise a lost card after his failed encounter, may not even know the card was gone yet. His groin was most likely still smarting from last night. She hoped so, anyway.

Even so. Tread warily. For Pamela's sake.

"None yet," she said. "How do I meet a guardian?"

"New members are sought out, not the other way around. If a guardian feels that someone is a suitable candidate, they will let it be known to them."

And, before she could answer, he clicked off.

She looked at the elegant black-and-gold structure.

A sheer curtain moved downstairs. The shadow of a figure moved.

She left, drove home, made a sandwich that she didn't really want but nibbled because she hadn't eaten since lunchtime yesterday. In her office with the Bay Bridge poking through fog, she made out an envelope to Moon Ranch, slipped the locker key to Fletcher's stash of acid in. He was scum but he had delivered. And she might need him again.

She lit a cigarette. Sat back. The fog was swirling away. The tip of the Transamerica Pyramid was visible downtown.

How to get into Die Kerk's office?

Another person came to mind.

CHAPTER TWENTY-ONE

Steve Cook lived in the Mission in a Victorian apartment building he owned and had nearly lost due to financial difficulties. His twelve-year-old daughter had recently been kidnapped but, thanks to Colleen, rescued, and was now living with her father in what could be termed a challenging relationship. But Steve was up to the task. From '60s British teen idol to international fugitive to down-and-out murder suspect, Steve Cook had done more in his three decades on earth than most men could dream of in three lifetimes. And he'd done it with panache, and a voice that sold a million albums, and a look that had once riveted masses of teenage girls—Colleen included. Now that he had his daughter back, he was raising her solo, singing with a local band, and dreaming of a comeback, while he recovered from the emotional and financial upheaval of her kidnapping.

SF's Mission District, the Latin part of town, rarely had parking so Colleen nosed the Torino up onto the sidewalk in front of Steve's building and into the narrow driveway, just kissing the carriage-style garage doors built long before cars.

Getting out, she saw that the once-deteriorating Victorian was now prepped and primed and ready for paint. Steve's Union Jack hung over the first-floor bay window. From the flat above, the boom of Patti Smith at volume competed with the street noise: "Because the Night."

She took a breath and stepped up onto the porch. She and Steve had spent a night together, and although it was not to be forgotten, she wasn't sure it should be repeated. Most days anyway. Steve had his hands full. And so did she. But still.

At the newly sanded glass-and-wood door to Steve's flat, Colleen heard the rhythmic pounding of a hammer inside. She knocked.

Steve answered in a damp T-shirt and faded blue jeans speckled with sawdust. Medium height, well built, his body tight with manual labor, his safety glasses were pulled up on his tousled dark hair, leaving raccoon eyes on a handsome rough-hewn face, also finely dusted. He needed a shave about two days ago, as per usual, but Steve was the kind of man who looked good with five o'clock shadow. Steve would look good climbing out of a dumpster.

He was also looking more settled after his daughter's recent ordeal. His dark brown eyes sparkled again.

"Look what the cat dragged in," he said in his British working-class accent. "Nice to see you, love."

She returned the smile. "Likewise."

"Come in, come in." He stood back, holding the door, brushing himself off with his free hand.

The last time Colleen had been here, the interior of the flat was down to the studs, a complete gut-and-remodel that had gone off the rails when Melanie had been abducted. But now walls were in place, sheetrocked, mudded and taped, waiting for paint. Period doors had been re-sanded and rehung. An elegant glass light fixture hung in the hallway. Victorian molding and trim had been reapplied. That wonderful smell of new lumber and fresh plaster filled the air. The front small parlor, sitting room, and formal dining room had been opened up into one long living area, with French doors separating the old rooms to preserve the separation if need be. Cast-iron fireplaces had been stripped down to the metal and oiled. Wood trim had been sanded and cut glass and mirrors added light that hadn't been there before.

"My, my," Colleen said. "When you're done here, can you do my place?"

"Just say the word."

In the back, where the dining area would be, sat a drum kit under a plastic sheet. Colleen noticed Deena's paint-spattered Pittsburgh Steelers sweatshirt on top of the plastic-covered sofa. Steve's drummer was also a onetime fling. Colleen wondered if there had been a rekindling and experienced a pang of jealousy. That sofa was the same one Steve and she had consummated their whatever-it-was on.

"Fancy a beer, love?" Steve said.

"I hate to see you drink alone."

She followed him to the back of the flat to the kitchen, one room not completely torn out during the remodel. Stylish black-and-white tile and cabinetry to die for. One wall was a collage of Steve's rock 'n' roll heyday: Steve sitting at a piano with Aretha Franklin, Steve with Mick and Keith backstage, passing a bottle of Jim Beam back and forth while Marianne Faithfull gave a wry smirk. Steve with Otis Redding in a recording studio, Steve's ears cuffed in headphones. Steve and his old band The Lost Chords, British teenagers with their '60s mod cuts, hip hugger pants, ruffled shirts, Victorian military tunics. It was like a museum.

Steve opened the fridge, got out two oil cans of Foster's lager.

"Whoa," she said. "Half of one of those for me."

"Lightweight." Steve put one back in the fridge, got a glass out, popped the beer, poured half into the glass, leaving a perfect head, handed it to Colleen. He held the big can in his hand.

"Cheers, love."

Their eyes met for a moment. Was he thinking of that night, too?

"Cheers," she said, clinking glass and can, then sipping ice cold beer while he downed half of what he had in his can. She watched his Adam's apple bounce.

"How's Melanie?" she asked when Steve came back for air.

"In school today," he said. "Or she better be." A slight grimace crossed his face. "I've caught her playing hooky more than once."

That sounded like Melanie.

"And you two?" she asked. "Getting along?"

Steve shrugged, set the giant steel can on the counter. "Give and take, as the social worker says."

Steve realized he was still wearing goggles on top of his head, pulled them off with a laugh, tossed them on the counter as well. She fought the urge to straighten his ruffled hair, although it looked fine. The same way that his workaday sweat smelled just fine. It was all in the packaging.

"What about you, Coll?" he said. "Seeing anybody?"

"I really need to get you a book on the fine art of conversation."

"Right. So?"

She shook her head *no*, took a sip of beer.

"Well, I'm not seeing anyone right now, either, if you were wondering. I saw you checking out Deena's gear."

Colleen blushed. "There'll be a legion of eligible candidates next time *the band with no name* plays The Pitt."

"Life's too short to fuck around, Coll. Almost losing Mel taught me that. And you're the one who got her back for me." He came up close, so close she could inhale his wonderful natural scent. He didn't touch her, but she knew he wanted to. She wouldn't have minded. "That puts you at the front of any queue."

She looked into his eyes, took a breath, steadying heartbeats. "You're making my day, dude, but I want to see you and Melanie gel first—without some crazy ex-con in the mix." Melanie wasn't over her mother yet, didn't need complications.

"Long as you know where you stand."

"I really didn't come over here just to nose around, Steve, although it's been fairly productive on that front. I do have a favor to ask. A big one."

He dug a pack of Lucky Strikes out of his shirt pocket, shook one loose, pulled it from the pack with his lips. "Shoot."

She told him about the possible link to Pamela.

"That's bloody great, Coll." He leaned back against the counter, lighting his cigarette. "Boom said something about giving you a hand with something the other night." Boom was also the part-time roadie for Steve's band, how Colleen had met him in the first place. "I thought he was being deliberately vague, yeah?"

"The less you know, the better."

"Got it." He smoked.

She told him that she thought Pamela's last stop had most likely been Die Kerk. How she couldn't get her foot in the door. "You used to know the guy that bought the mansion they use for their headquarters. I remember you telling me about him. He was a big star, back in the day."

"Who's that, then?"

"Arnold Saint James," she said.

"Arnold Saint James," Steve said, nodding in recollection. "The Chords were the warm-up act for him, '65, when he came to the UK. Before my big fuckup. He'd just written that tune that'll keep him in silk knickers for the rest of his life."

Steve's "big fuckup" was waking up in a London hotel room in 1966 to find a dead girl lying next to him. It was the end of a career that had just begun.

"Arnold Saint James is Barend now," she said. "That's his *perfect* name."

"All sounds a bit new-agey," Steve said.

"If it was only just that," she said. "Arnold is my big favor."

Steve tapped ash into the empty beer can. "Go on."

"You could use your charm, of which you have an overabundance, and call your old buddy Arnold Saint James—Barend—and say you'd like a visit to Die Kerk. Tell him how you've seen the success of some of their members and wouldn't mind a piece for yourself. That you've come into some money now that your royalties are finally settled after all these years. When Die Kerk is done falling over themselves to invite you over for a tour of the facilities, you can bring me along as your date. And while you and Barend are regaling each other with sordid tales of rock 'n' roll excess, I can slip off and nose around. And find out where Pamela might be."

"All good—in theory. But it sounds like it could be potentially dangerous."

"I know you've got Mel to worry about. Your part will be minimal."

"I mean dangerous for *you*, Coll. If Boom was helping you out, this little venture ain't benign, yeah?"

She shrugged. "What Mel is to you, Pamela is to me. Only I hope Melanie never puts you through a tenth of the grief."

He took a drag on his cigarette, exhaled smoke away from her. It bounced off the glass cabinets. "It was worth a try."

"You were sweet to do so. But it's too late for that."

He dropped his cigarette in the beer can. It sizzled. "Then I, madam, can't find a good reason to turn you down."

CHAPTER TWENTY-TWO

After another fruitless visit to Mr. Philanderer's love nest, Colleen went home, cranked up the gas heater, took a shower, wrapped herself in her kimono, put on The Lost Chord's album from 1966, dimmed the lights, tried to relax. Tried not to think about Pamela. And wondering who invented motherhood.

The phone rang.

"Fancy going to a party tomorrow night, love?" Steve Cook said.

"Die Kerk?"

"They're going to make time for us."

"Can I bring a friend?" More people meant she'd have more of a chance to get away and sneak around.

"*The more the merrier*, as the bishop said to the actress."

"Guess I better pick you up," she said. "Since you don't have a *motor car*." She said the last two words in a poor attempt at a British accent.

"And since I don't know how to bloody drive one to begin with. We're supposed to be there at eight."

"See you at seven thirty. What about Mel?"

"Aunt Deena's babysitting."

Steve's drummer and ex-flame had a soft spot for Steve. "Ciao."

She called her friend Alex, in Half Moon Bay.

"Hey!" Alex said when the butler put Colleen through. "I was just about to call you."

"I wanted to catch you before you went out with your thrill-seeker friends."

"I was actually going to stay in for once. I hear they have these things called books."

Colleen was relieved Alex was giving her liver a rest. "Want to go to a party tomorrow?"

"Is that a trick question? I'll even shave my legs. What time should I pick you up?"

"I'll drive. Be here sevenish. But I need to warn you—it's not the kind of party you're used to. To be perfectly honest, it's not really a party at all."

"No?"

She explained about Die Kerk. Pamela.

"That sounds heavy, Coll. But I feel like I know Pam. I want to help any way I can."

"I'll make it up to you."

"Damn right you will." Alex laughed.

"Since you're in such a receptive mood, I guess this is a good time to tell you that Steve is going to join us."

There was a pause. "Okay." Alex had always been a little bit jealous of Steve.

"He got me in to Die Kerk," Colleen said. "And we're just friends."

"Uh-huh."

CHAPTER TWENTY-THREE

"What time do the vampires come out?" Alex said.

She was sitting in the back of the Torino, Colleen and Steve in front, the three of them looking at Die Kerk's black and gold mansion on Pacheco Street in between swipes of the windshield wipers. The car rumbled in front of the wrought-iron gates in the light rain. There was no obvious party noise, no music, laughter, which didn't surprise Colleen. All three of them were suitably decked out in their best gear, smelling good. Colleen sported a rust-orange patterned minidress with sheer flounce sleeves, white pantyhose, tan boots, and raincoat. She had her trusty leather shoulder bag ready for any potential information gathering. On the car radio, The Jackson 5 were blaming it on the boogie.

"I'll get them to open the gate," Steve said. His double-breasted light gray suit was unbuttoned, revealing a black T-shirt and the top of a hairy chest. "We'll park inside. It's raining."

"Hold off," Colleen said. "Let's park out here—in case we have to beat a hasty retreat."

"Good point," he said, sitting back. "I guess we get wet, then."

"That's why God invented umbrellas," Colleen said, holding up her collapsible.

"One umbrella for three people," Alex said. She wore a deep red sequined cat suit, platform shoes to match, and a black bolero jacket to take it down a notch. Elvis, Las Vegas era, one of her favorite themes.

"Sharing is caring," Colleen said, backing out of the Die Kerk's driveway with a squeal.

She parked down the street.

Moments later, they were clipping across Pacheco, shoulder to shoulder under the small umbrella, headed for the former mansion.

Steve announced them at the intercom, and they were quickly buzzed in.

As they hurried up the long driveway, a wood-and-glass door opened on the spacious portico supported by gold columns. White light spilled out as a plump man in a white kaftan appeared. He had a bowl haircut and a mild waddle.

"Steve!" he shouted jovially. "Long time, no see! You should have parked up here. You're getting wet."

"Now you tell me, Arnold!"

The three of them got under the overhang.

"It's Barend now, Steve," he said, coming out to greet them. He wore sandals. A strange cross with wings on it hung around his neck.

"Right," Steve said, taking his hand. "*Barend*." He turned to introduce Alex and Colleen as Alex and Carol Anne. "I brought a couple of friends, yeah?"

Barend, or whatever his name was, eyed Colleen, then Alex, with beady eyes at first, then a shrewd grin. Colleen could tell that, despite whatever suspicions he might have, he didn't mind extra women.

"Well, *hello*, ladies."

Colleen reached out to shake a hand, but Barend came in for a bear hug instead. He stunk of stale sweat.

He did the same to Alex, and Colleen caught her look of disgust over his shoulder.

He led them inside.

"Jeez, Louise," Alex whispered, fanning her nose as she gave Colleen a wrinkled grimace.

"One of the rules to perfection is bathing weekly," Colleen whispered back. "Whether one needs it or not."

Steve followed.

A large man in a black tunic that stretched across his broad shoulders shut the door behind them. He wore sunglasses that didn't hide the fact that he was seriously checking out Alex. He radiated a sharp pong of sweat as well, and had *bodyguard* written all over him.

Inside a red-carpeted foyer with harsh overhead lighting from a high chandelier stood an older Indian man in black shirt, baggy white slacks, and pointy shoes. His hands were folded in front of him like a salesman about to close in. He had white-gray hair swept back in a pompadour and piercing eyes. Behind him stood another man, tall and wiry, also in a black tunic.

On one wall Brother Adem Lea looked down from a large painting, stringy hair parted on either side of the slightly lopsided crucifix tattoo in the center of his forehead. His long nose pointed off into the distance with what was no doubt meant to be a sense of purpose. He was shirtless and the painting did not reveal anything below the waist but the feeling was that he was again naked. Underneath, a plaque read *Die Kerk van die Volmaakte Dood*. Colleen reminded herself to look up *dood* next time she was at SF Public Library.

At the bottom of the elegant stairwell, corridors led off on either side downstairs. Colleen wondered where the office was, where the member records might be. The foyer was large but still smelled like a gym on a hot day, despite the fact that a joss stick burned on a side table over an incense tray.

"Steve," Barend said. "I'd like you to meet Gust—our director of operations."

Gust was the Indian man Colleen had spoken to on the intercom yesterday.

"Brother Adem is on a pilgrimage," Gust said in a Pacific accent. "Otherwise he would have been here himself to greet you."

Colleen prayed Pamela wasn't part of that pilgrimage but her instinct told her otherwise.

"That sounds so interesting," she said to Gust. "Pilgrimage where?"

Gust ignored Colleen's question. "Before we proceed, we'll need to see some identification."

Colleen started. Alex gave a look.

"Get away," Steve said, not one to mince words. "Don't you bloody remember me, Arn—Barend?" He laughed.

"It's just a formality," Gust said. "Our house of worship has been the subject of more than one spurious attack."

Colleen had her bogus ID, but Alex and Steve didn't; although Die Kerk certainly knew who Steve was. But Alex, with her well-known last name and fortune, would be a prime target for a shady organization.

"Fine," Steve said in a tone that implied it wasn't as he got his wallet out of his jacket.

Colleen leaned over to Alex and dropped her voice. "You know what, Alex? You don't need to be part of this. Tell them your handbag is in the car, go get it, and don't come back. Wait for us in the car." She held out her car keys.

"Sorry, Charlie," Alex said. "You're not getting rid of me that easily."

Colleen shook her head and put her keys away as Alex fished her driver's license out of a minute beaded purse.

Gust collected licenses, turned in the direction of the far corridor by the stairwell.

"Wait," Colleen said. "Where are you going with those?"

Gust turned back, blinking impatiently. "To make copies."

Colleen stood forward, reaching out. "Just hand them back and we'll be on our way."

Gust looked at her with what only could be called aggravation.

"Very well." As she suspected, he handed everyone's license back, but without a word. The tension in the air thickened.

Colleen, Alex, and Steve were shown into a large hall by the big guard with the sunglasses. The room had the atmosphere of a sterile temple. More red carpet and white walls. Several rows of chairs faced a podium. The smell of incense emanated from a clump of joss sticks on an altar below yet another painting of Adem Lea. He had one of those sickly mustaches in this one, the kind that don't fill out. There was a list of eleven reëls—rules—in Afrikaans. Airy music played over the loudspeakers, flute and guitar with a man reciting in Afrikaans as well. For all they knew, he was reading the railway time-table. But it was still unnerving.

"Catchy," Alex whispered to Colleen.

"And so relaxing," Colleen added.

A very young woman, barely out of girlhood, in a thin white embroidered muumuu and dark braids, was running a handheld sweeper across the carpet, barefoot. She stood to attention, holding her sweeper in one hand, head down submissively. She had dark skin and eyes and would have been stunning if she weren't also trembling. Colleen shivered herself at the incongruity and what might be going on here. She hoped this girl hadn't been subject to a nude shaming like the two women at the service she'd attended.

"Tea?" the girl asked, almost inaudible, avoiding eye contact.

No one wanted tea. She excused herself with a whisper, silently left the room with her sweeper.

The three of them were left with Sunglasses the bodyguard, who stood at the back of the room, hands behind his back, watching impassively, Alex mostly. Colleen and Alex took a seat in the front row, while Steve stood before them, hands in his pockets.

"What the bloody hell is going on?" he whispered to Colleen, rattling change in his pocket to cover his words.

"I don't think they know what to do with us," Colleen whispered back.

"No shit," Alex said brightly, looking around.

Barend entered the room, red-faced. He'd probably gotten his ear chewed off for inviting guests who had the temerity to question Die Kerk's security procedures.

He called out to Steve, "Gust can show you around now, Steve. And then you and I can catch up."

"Just me?" Steve said.

"Right," Barend said tightly.

"What about my friends here?"

"They'll have to wait here."

They were being punished for questioning the ID system.

Colleen said, "Go ahead, Steve. We're good."

"Great," Steve said to Barend with a hint of sarcasm, giving Colleen an uncertain look.

Then it was just her and Alex, under the watchful eye of Sunglasses.

"We don't rate a tour," Alex said.

"I need to snoop around," Colleen said quietly. "How good are you at intriguing big burly guards?"

Alex lowered her voice too. "You mean the kind that don't bathe?"

"Bingo."

"I'm not just a pretty face." Alex winked, stood up, sashayed over to the guard in her slinky red pantsuit. He had been pretty much glued to her the whole time anyway. She started making small talk, beginning with how long he'd been with the church. Colleen noticed Alex made a point to get in close. Within no time, Alex was touching his arm.

"Say, you must work out."

"A little," he stammered.

"More than a little, I'd say."

Colleen left her bag on the chair, got up, headed to the door, stopped at Sunglasses and Alex on the way.

"I'm sorry," she said to the guard. "Where is the Ladies' room?"

"To the left of the staircase," he said. "But wait—I'll get someone to take you."

Alex patted his arm playfully. "She knows how to go to the restroom all by herself, you know. She's not three years old."

He laughed, awkwardly. "Yes, I know. But . . ."

"Are you married?" Alex asked him. "I don't see a ring."

"Die Kerk does not recognize marriage."

"How interesting. Neither am I."

Colleen slipped out the door.

No one in the lobby. She headed under the stairwell where dimly lit hallways led off to either side. She took the right because she heard a murmur of voices in that direction. Passing several closed doors, she overheard Barend speaking. "All I can tell you, Steve, is that Die Kerk changed my life." Colleen had no doubt about that. "My ability to focus now is incredible. I've reached another level. My new album is proof."

"I do like the sound of that," she heard Steve say.

"All you've got to do is let go and let Adem be your guide."

"I'm not so sure about that, though, mate."

"Trust me. It'll revive your career. I just know it. Hell, I'd be willing to take a personal interest in you, Steve."

"You don't say," Steve said.

"I *do* say. There is a wealth of experience here to draw on and support you."

It sounded to Colleen as if they would be chatting for a while. Good.

She traveled the rest of the hallway, trying doors. Many were locked. The ones that weren't were a small kitchen and storage room.

She turned around, crossed over, did the other side of the building. At the far end was a door leading outside, to the back grounds, marked "Exit." It was latched and locked. She unlatched it, twisted the lock open. She might have an opportunity to come back later, root around.

On the way back to the lobby, she peered down a dark stairwell leading to a basement.

"Excuse me," a timid voice said.

Startled, Colleen spun.

The young girl who had been sweeping up in the main room.

"Just looking for the Ladies' room," Colleen said.

"It's back this way." Face down, the girl pointed to a door near the entry to the foyer.

"Ah," Colleen said. "Thank you."

"You're not supposed to be here unescorted."

"I'm so sorry. I had no idea."

The girl actually made eye contact for a split second.

"What's your name?" Colleen asked. Their eyes met again, before the girl looked away.

"I don't have one yet."

"Well, what did it used to be?"

"I'm not permitted to say. I'm in 'bevestiging' and my past must be washed away."

"Do you have any idea what your new name will be?"

"Roos," she whispered, looking away.

"That's a pretty name," Colleen said. Pretty *weird*.

"It will be my *perfect* name."

An Afrikaans name of some sort. Colleen introduced herself as Carol Anne. She wanted to ask about Pamela but it felt risky to implicate Pam until she knew Roos better. Instead she asked her how long she had been there, how old she was.

"Adem says we are all ageless."

Great. Colleen wanted to shake some sense into her. "So you speak Afrikaans?"

"I am learning it. We all must."

"And how long have you been with Die Kerk?"

Roos looked around, nervous. "I mustn't be caught chatting. And you must go back to the hall. I could get into trouble."

"I certainly don't want to get you into any trouble, Roos."

"Yes, thank you. But that is not my name yet."

"Got it. By the way, what does *dood* mean?"

Roos blinked at her as if she might be simple. "Why, *death*, of course."

Colleen fought an involuntary shudder.

Die Kerk van die Volmaakte Dood.

Church of the Perfect Death.

"What is this pilgrimage that Adem is making?" she said, recovering her composure.

Roos was looking profoundly nervous. "I must not discuss church business." It sounded as if she was reciting a rule. She closed her eyes and hummed. Then her eyes opened. "I'll take you back to the others now. *Please.* Before someone sees us?"

"Of course," Colleen said.

In the hall Alex was still chatting up the big guy. She gave Colleen a look of relief when she saw her come back in.

It was a good hour before Steve returned.

*   *   *

"When I die and go to hell," Steve said, smoking a cigarette as Colleen drove back to her place, "Die Kerk will be where I end up." He blew smoke out of the open car window into the rainy night air. Alex was in the back seat, looking out the window absentmindedly.

"Anything interesting?" Colleen asked Steve.

"Apart from the fact that they want my money? Which I don't have?" Steve smoked, blew another stream out the window. "There are about two hundred and forty-odd members on some retreat. That's why Brother Adem—aka Angel 22—isn't around."

"Where the hell are they?" she asked.

"Don't know." Steve shook his head. "But there's some bloody village they're building near some volcano they seem to think is important."

Jesus, Colleen thought. Moon Ranch was looking better by the day.

"Come on," she said. "I'm a big girl, Steve. Let me have it."

"They said I would learn more when I became a member. I can't put my finger on it, but it's not good, Coll. You saw that bloody bunch."

"*Die Kerk van die Volmaakte Dood*," she said. "Church of the Perfect Death. Did Barend mention that part?"

"Fuck me." Steve looked at her, grimaced. "No, he bloody well didn't."

"Funny they forgot that," Alex said from the backseat.

"Die Kerk is sounding like a suicide cult," Colleen said, her heart palpitating. "Did you see any files, Steve? File cabinets?"

Steve flicked ash out the window. "Along the wall of the office. Four or five of 'em."

"I've got to find out what kind of involvement Pam has."

"Let's hope *none*," Steve said.

Colleen bet Pam was on that pilgrimage. She turned on Vermont, up to Alex's Jag parked in front of her building. Steve got out, held the door for Alex. Alex gave Colleen a peck on the cheek on the way out. "Next time, I pick the party."

"Deal," Colleen said. "Thanks for diverting the big guy while I snooped around."

"You bet." Alex winked. "Hope Pam is okay."

"You going straight home?"

"Yes, yes. I'm giving my liver a few days off—per your instructions."

"Good girl. We'll get together soon."

Alex climbed out of the Torino, gave Steve's arm a squeeze. "'Nite, Steve. I better be on the guest list next time your band plays."

"Done and done," he said.

Alex got into her Jag, started it up with a rumble, sped off. Steve climbed back into the Torino, heaved the door shut.

For a moment, Colleen thought about asking him up to her place for a drink. But that sounded like a bad idea. Or a good idea. Whatever it was, Steve had Mel to look after now. And she had plenty on her mind.

"I'll run you home, Steve."

"Right."

She headed down 19th.

"Tell me you're not going to do anything rash, Coll," Steve said.

"Okay," she said, dodging the pothole she always did. "I'm not going to do anything rash."

"Lovely. Now say it like you mean it, yeah?"

She mustered up her inner Elizabeth Taylor, laid on the acting skills. "I do this kind of thing for a living, Steve. No need to worry."

"So what *are* you going to do?"

"I'm going to think on it," Colleen said.

"So you're not planning on breaking into Die Kerk or anything daft like that? Nose around in the file cabinets?"

She forced a laugh. "That would be crazy, Steve."

"Yeah, I know," he said. "That's why I asked."

"I'm going to run it by my buddy Owens at SFPD."

"Good idea." Steve nodded. "Bring in the police."

Not really, but she needed to allay Steve's fears. "I thought so."

"And it's also something I know you're adverse to."

She shrugged. "People change, Steve."

"All I'm trying to say is that if you're going to take those fuckers on, don't do it alone, yeah? I mean, I can help you."

"You with the eleven-year-old daughter who needs looking after."

"Twelve."

"Twelve. Is Melanie going to help too? Now that I think about it, maybe that's not a bad idea." Steve's daughter was a handful.

"You might actually have something there," Steve said.

Colleen turned, looked at Steve. "I'm not going to do anything dumb, Steve."

He looked at her with pursed lips. "Scout's honor?"

"Dib dib dob."

They pulled up in front of Steve's apartment building.

"I guess I'll just have to take your word for it," Steve said.

"Yes, you will."

They sat there for a moment. The engine growled in idle.

"Fancy coming in for a drink?" Steve said quietly, giving her a candid look.

Did she? How many times had she thought of that night? "It's a school night," she said. "Isn't it?"

"Dunno. I flunked school years ago."

"But Mel will be in bed—won't she?"

"She better be," Steve said.

"That's what I thought."

"At Auntie Deena's," Steve added.

"Oh." Colleen turned. Steve was looking directly at her with a sly smile. "I did not know that."

Steve feigned surprise. "What? You thought Auntie Deena was staying at *my* place?"

"I guess I did at that."

"No, Mel's over there. For the night. The *entire* night. Auntie Deena's taking her to school in the morning."

"Is that a fact?" Colleen said, thinking of the possibilities.

"It is," Steve said. "Got the place all to myself tonight."

"Well, thanks for clearing that up." Colleen turned all the way in her seat.

Steve returned bedroom eyes.

She reached over, tousled his hair.

"Good looking guy," she said.

"You're no old boiler yourself, love."

"I think that might be the nicest thing anyone ever said to me," she said.

"I always mean what I say."

"I like that."

"Especially about not doing anything rash."

"Actually, I *was* kind of thinking of something rash," she said.

Steve raised his eyebrows. "Care to elaborate?"

"God, but you're simple sometimes."

"I thought you liked them dumb."

"I do. Dumb as a box of rocks. And hot."

"Well, that would be me, then—wouldn't it?"

"Not really." She tousled his hair some more. "You were pretty slick over there at Die Kerk." She brushed her fingers along his cheek. "But you've definitely got the *hot* part down."

"Can't help it, love."

"I'll need to verify that, though. I am, after all, a trained investigative professional."

"A lot of big words in a row. But I think I got the gist of it."

"I need a shower after that locker room church. Jeez."

"Me too," Steve said.

"Want to save water?"

"Are you proposing what I think you're proposing?" he said.

"It's the environmentally correct thing to do, isn't it?" she said.

CHAPTER TWENTY-FOUR

The Dobermans came trotting out of the shadows, emitting low growls in unison, making Colleen's spine prickle.

She stood outside Die Kerk's wrought-iron fence with the spears on the posts in her gray rain jacket, hood pulled up against the steady drizzle that had been falling all evening. The front of the building was lit up, the gold trim and columns shiny with rain.

She followed the fence around to the far side of the building. The dogs tracked her, throats rumbling. She stopped under a tree, pulled the tinfoil bundle from her pocket. It crinkled as she unwrapped it. She caught a whiff of liverwurst.

The dogs watched intently.

She extracted one cue-ball-sized piece of doctored lunchmeat and held it up for the animals to see.

Their eyes connected. They were bonding.

"Good boys," she said. "Nice boys."

She tossed one ball over the fence. Dog One caught it on the fly. She quickly tossed the other. Dog Two followed suit.

They barely chewed as the food went down.

Then the snarling resumed.

"Sweet dreams, guys." Colleen headed back to the Torino parked down the street in the shadows. Got in.

Boom was sitting in the passenger seat, reading *Probability and Statistics* with a small flashlight.

"I hate to keep messing with your finals," she said, rolling down the window.

"No big," Boom said. "The hours are perfect for my busy class schedule."

Colleen lit up a cigarette, blew smoke out the window. "Not too many college students specialize in Breaking and Entering as a sideline."

Boom looked up, ambient streetlight flashing off his glasses. "Or ripping off drug dealers."

"A man of many talents." She smoked, tapped ash out the window.

"After Nam and working for you, Chief, an office job is gonna be kind of boring—if anybody will give a brother a job."

"They'll give a smart guy like you one. And, if you ever need a reference, let me know. I can vouch how good you are with a shotgun."

"I appreciate that," Boom said. "How much time do we have?"

"About fifteen minutes."

"What did you give Flopsy and Mopsy?"

"Valium." Alex had most of a bottle left over from when her father was dying and she'd been a nervous wreck. Three five-milligram pills would sedate a ninety-pound dog for a good few hours, if not the rest of the night.

"As long as you didn't give them any Moon Ranch LSD," Boom said.

"Good point. We don't need nasty guard dogs tripping on acid."

Boom flipped a page, went back to his chapter.

Her goal was the office downstairs where Steve had met with Barend, where he'd seen filing cabinets.

* * *

"It's starting to come down," Boom said.

Colleen and Boom stood on the far side of Die Kerk, rain pelting off Colleen's hood cinched around her chin, and Boom's camouflage Boonie hat. His broad shoulders stretched his USMC jacket to capacity. A military surplus shoulder bag looked like a kiddie pack on his big frame.

"It is that," Colleen said. "But no snarling pups so we're good to go." Hopefully there wasn't any other threat on the immediate horizon.

Boom crouched down by the six-foot wrought-iron fence and clasped his hands together with his fingers, making an impromptu step for Colleen.

"Ready when you are, Madam."

Colleen placed one wet Pony Topstar in Boom's big hands and tested the fit. Her trusty hiking daypack was secured on her back. "I want you to know I can still get into the dress I wore to my court sentencing ten years ago, Boom."

"You're light as a feather, Chief. I can tell."

She grabbed two fence spears for stability. "Let's do it."

Boom counted her off—*one-two-three*—and heaved Colleen up as she simultaneously sprang, and threw her over the fence. She cleared the spears and landed on the wet grass without falling. Slipping, yes, but catching her balance. She stood up, hefted her daypack up her shoulders. Keeping one ear cocked in case either one of the dogs were somehow still awake.

Boom gave her a thumbs-up. Then he scaled the fence as if it were a stepladder, landing smartly, springing on both feet.

"Show-off," Colleen said.

They jogged across the wet grass into the shadows back behind the building, taking it easy, the grass wet and slick.

The doghouse behind Die Kerk buzzed with snoring Dobermans.

"Sleeping on the job," Boom whispered as they headed up to the back door Colleen had unlocked the night before. Colleen was just happy the dogs were out of the rain.

The back door she had unlocked last night was once again locked.

"I knew it was too good to be true," she said.

"Can you pick the lock?"

Shook her head. "There's a latch on the other side. Whoever locked the door probably took care of that too."

"We could bust it," Boom said. "But it would make one hell of a racket."

"Let's look for a window."

They scoured the ground floor, staying close to the building. Every first-floor window, front and rear, was shut. They headed back around to the rear of the building.

"There." Colleen pointed at a narrow upstairs window, revealing a gap of a couple of inches. It also had the advantage of being above a small ornamental balcony for access.

"I'd never get through," Boom said. "But someone who can still get into her sentencing dress should have no problem."

"How do I get up there?" There was a drainpipe, but contemplating it made her armpits ticklish. Plus, who knew how much weight it would bear?

Boom unhooked his bag as he squatted, came out with a coil of 3/8-inch braided white nylon rope. He tied a one-pound cannonball fishing weight to the end. Colleen slipped on her beat-up leather gloves.

Boom stood up, holding the rope, the weight dangling from his hand. He stepped back, flung the weight up into the air toward the mini balcony, letting the rope spool out of his hand. The weight went over the stone banister but didn't catch.

"Dang." Boom gave the rope a yank and the weight clunked over the banister and came back down. He caught the weight but there had been enough noise to make the two of them nervous. Colleen put a finger up to her lips, cocked an ear.

Just the wind through the trees, and a distant car shifting up.

"Try again," she whispered.

Boom did and this time the weight flipped around the banister in between the carved wood columns and made a complete loop.

"You just won a Kewpie doll," Colleen said.

Boom tugged on the rope. Secure. "You sure you're up for this, Chief?"

"No," she said. "But let's do it anyway."

He handed her the rope. She yanked on it. Solid.

When climbing a wall on a rope, the trick was to walk in a crouch, use your feet over your arms. Hand over hand, sure, but walk up the wall. And don't wrap the rope around your hand. The faster you go, the easier it is. Easier being a relative term.

Colleen nodded, on edge at the prospect.

Boom squatted down near the wall, facing it, patted a shoulder, signifying for Colleen to climb up. She did. Slowly, Boom stood up, raising her five feet off the ground. She gathered up the rope and, limbs quivering with apprehension, put the sole of one sneaker on the stucco wall, which, although wet, had some rough surface to grip.

She pulled herself up, hand over hand, got purchase with the other foot, took another cautious step. It was unsteady and took more strength than she expected, but the small balcony was only a couple of feet above her head now.

"You got it!" she heard Boom hiss below.

She negotiated another step and her sneaker slipped on the rain-wet stucco. Her knee banged the cement-hard surface. It hurt but not enough to cry out. What bothered her more was the noise. Heart thumping, she saw the base of the balcony was eye level.

"Keep going!" Boom whispered.

Colleen sucked in a breath, braced her right foot against the edge of a drainpipe, kept at it. She was rocking side to side but covered the last few feet easily enough.

"That's it!"

At the top of the balcony, she pushed her right foot hard against the drainpipe, grabbed the banister. Almost there.

She got both arms over the banister, about to pull herself up, when she heard an ominous crack. The banister shifted towards her a fraction.

She hung on, ignoring the image of free-falling to earth and life as a paraplegic.

The banister stayed in place.

"You're cool," Boom whispered, standing below her.

Colleen sucked in a breath and heaved herself up over the wet banister. It creaked again as she climbed onto the tiny balcony. She got into a squat, ears pricked. All she could hear was the wind, the rain blowing, hitting windows, roof, gutters, downspout. Her face was soaking wet. As unpleasant as it was, it provided good sound cover. She unhooked the one-pound weight from the rope, unwrapped the rope from the banister, tossed everything down to Boom.

She pointed to the exit door below that had been locked, indicating she would attempt to use it on her way out. Boom gave her another thumbs-up, went off to hide in the shadows.

The open window was about a foot and a half wide. Quietly, she slipped her gloved hands onto the bottom of the lower sash and slowly—*slowly*—slid the window up. It screeched ever so slightly. She stopped, listened. Okay. She slowed down more. Eventually she got the window open enough to stick her head in.

She was looking into an upstairs toilet.

She unhooked her daypack, reached in, set the pack on the floor next to the toilet.

Climbed in after it. A tight fit. The secret was being quiet. She clambered onto the commode. Once inside, she pulled the window shut back to its original position. It was dark and she didn't want to switch on the light so she waited till her eyes adjusted. She got her day bag.

Ready.

She opened the bathroom door, peered out into the upstairs hall. There was faint ambient light, coming from the entrance hall most likely. Her heartbeats were pumping steadily. But she'd made it this far.

She ventured out.

The office where Steve had met with Barend was downstairs.

She tiptoed to the top of the stairs, looked down into the tall foyer. There was one lamp on a side table, throwing light on the ridiculous painting of Adem Lea. In the current setting, it looked even more surreal. The air was stale with the smell of burnt incense and old sweat.

She stepped down the semi-circular stairwell, generating a creak. She stopped, listened, picked up speed to the bottom of the stairs. She headed into the hallway downstairs, not far from where she'd had the conversation with Roos when she'd been snooping around last night.

She stopped, stood, listened. There were the sounds of a big house at night, the rain and wind outside pattering against the windows and roof. Somewhere a boiler clicked off.

Her first stop was down the hall towards the exit door she had unlocked last night. She found the door, which had indeed been relocked. She didn't see an alarm. She unlocked it. Her exit set, she turned around, headed back to the other side of the building where the office was.

She passed the door that led downstairs to the darkened basement. It was ajar. She stopped, thought she heard snoring. Some kind of dorm? Night watchman? She wasn't about to investigate. But she did pull the door shut, twisting the knob quietly to reduce any sound that might travel from upstairs.

Over to the office.

The office was locked, as expected. A Yale cylinder pin-tumbler lock. Soon she had a tension wrench in the lower part of the lock, fishing with a pick from her toolkit with her other hand. Yales needed a light touch.

The lock gave that satisfying click.

Tools back in the bag over one shoulder, she stepped inside the office, gently pulled the door behind her. Got her flashlight out. She wasn't going to turn on the overhead light or a desk lamp.

Using the flashlight, she headed to the file cabinets on the right side of the room. Four of them. All locked. But any snoop who couldn't unlock a file cabinet deserved to have her license revoked. Which reminded her, she needed to check the status of her investigator's license. Sacramento was dragging its feet.

She had the Chicago locks popped open with a simple lock pick in no time. She'd seen it done with a paper clip. Flashlight in one hand, she started digging through files. It was a little clumsy with gloves but so be it.

The first cabinet was bookkeeping. Bills and such. She flipped through the files in the drawers quickly. Moved on.

The second cabinet contained various operational and strategic documents. They were thick files, with drawings, documents, notes, photographs. She dug through those, several referencing Verligting.

The name rang a bell.

Brother Adem had mentioned Verligting in the film at the service on 555 Fillmore, the one she'd attended with Brother Arno. A sanctuary of some sort. She remembered a jungle setting and sounds.

Leafing through she saw several files containing information on what were called "Verligting pelgrimstogte." *Pilgrimages* or *pilgrims* would be her guess. They were ordered by year, three in total, from 1976–1978. 1976 was thick, with plans for a compound and pavilion. A list of approximately two hundred names, all single-word Dutch-style names. "Perfect names," she assumed, remembering Roos. There were photos of people toiling in a jungle, clearing land, building cabins, a pavilion.

Was that why so many people were on a pilgrimage, to finish building a utopia? Or make use of a utopia already built? *Verligting?*

She recalled Steve mentioning a volcano during his discussion with Barend. She remembered Adem Lea speaking on film at the service as well.

A newer folder caught her eye: *Tungurahua Pelgrimstog, 1978.* Current.

She pulled it, opened it.

Tungurahua was the volcano in Ecuador. There was a photo of a smoldering peak. The photo had an English caption. Translated from Quechua it meant *throat of fire.*

Leafing through the file folder, she found a list of names at the back. Eight pages; 245 names. Brother Adem had said something about 242 in his film. Steve had also mentioned 242. Close enough.

On the top of the first page was a note in pencil, circled: *Tennant Shipping, October 29th.* The date itself was also circled.

Each individual name was a perfect name, followed by a single word, in Dutch, or Afrikaans, or whatever it was: *timmerman, loodgieter, rekenmeester, vroulike offer.* Some sort of designation.

Colleen sighed. The "perfect" names gave her no idea if Pamela was on the pilgrimage.

She set that file back, shut the drawer.

Keep going.

The third and fourth cabinets contained personnel records. Hundreds. Many hundreds. The good news was that they were filed by "old" pre-perfect name: first name and last name, in alphabetical order. Her heart beat faster as she leafed through them. Maybe she wouldn't find a thing on Pamela. Maybe this was all a wild goose chase. She could live with that. Quite easily.

But, in the top drawer of the fourth cabinet, her fingers stopped at a tab with a very familiar name: Hayes, Pamela.

She sucked in a deep breath.

Proof. Actual proof that her daughter *was* involved with these madmen.

But was she on that trip?

Nerves thrumming, she plucked the folder. Flashlight in one hand, she opened it.

She hadn't seen Pamela for months and even then, only from a distance, the day Colleen had gone up to Point Arenas up the coast a couple of months back and spied on her from the ridge. Above the communal house by the sea. Through binoculars she recalled the feeling when she saw her daughter laughing at something one of the Moon Ranchers had said.

Paper-clipped to Pamela's file was a black-and-white headshot. Pam's hair had grown out and her face was gaunt. Her cheekbones looked sharp. Her eyes had rings around them and stared at the camera with a cool virulence. Her mouth was a flat line. But something about her had matured. More confident, perhaps. Colleen took some comfort in that, hoping it meant Pamela might ultimately take better care of herself, hopefully see danger coming before it was too late.

Then she chided herself for seeing what she wanted to see in the middle of the night, her heart full of fear for her only child.

As a child, Pamela had always been the one that other children took advantage of. Shy, unable to make friends easily, too eager to please the wrong kids, too easy to make a bad trade when it came to toys or comics, too willing to let the other child have their way. Too ready to try whatever the other kids were doing, regardless of the consequences.

She'd found proof of Pamela's existence.

But how did she find Pamela?

This was the most recent photo of her. She unclipped it, flipped it over before she slipped it in her pocket. Writing on the back. A date. *Fenna.*

Pamela's name was now Fenna. Her perfect name. She had joined the church in early October.

Colleen set the folder on the floor, planning to go through it and photograph it, went back to the other file cabinet, pulled *Tungurahua Pelgrimstogte, 1978.*

With shaking fingers, she leafed through the list of names at the back.

Found the "F"s.

There she was. Fenna.

Fenna: vroulike offer.

And knew that her worst fear was just confirmed: Pamela was on that damn pilgrimage.

Pulse racing, Colleen checked at random some of the other members whose skill was listed as "vroulike offer."

All feminine-sounding names.

Colleen's nerves rattled. She placed the Verligting 1978 file on the carpet next to Pam's personnel record. She unhooked her bag, getting her Polaroid camera out, attaching a flash.

That's when she heard a sound.

Footsteps.

Footsteps coming upstairs. From the basement on the other side of the building.

Her heartbeats rushed.

CHAPTER TWENTY-FIVE

Colleen heard the muffled sound of a door opening on the other side of the building: the door at the top of the stairs she had shut on her way here. Her nerves ratcheted up.

No time to photograph the documents that lay on the rug before her. For a moment, she thought about swiping the files but that might only implicate Pamela when they were found missing. She grabbed the two file folders, jammed them back into their respective slots in the file cabinets, shut the drawers quietly, pushed the four Chicago locks in.

Threw her Polaroid camera in her bag, bag over her shoulder.

Footsteps came steadily down the hall.

She tiptoed over to the door, locked it. But whoever was coming probably had a key. She spun, eyed two straight-backed chairs at a small worktable. Rushing over, she grabbed one, took it to the door, jammed the back up against the door handle, wedged it in, back legs off the floor. She tested it. Good and lodged.

Another escape route was needed.

The window. She dashed over, heaved it open with a judder. Wind and rain blew in.

Then she noticed the desk drawer. That gave her an idea. She went back, pulled on it. Locked. She pulled the deeper side drawer. Also locked.

Footsteps approached the door.

"Who's there?" It was Gust. The doorknob rattled.

She had her mini crowbar out of her bag and jammed it in the deeper drawer, made a particularly messy job of ripping the drawer open, shredding wood. Once open, she found what she was looking for: a metal petty cash box. She pulled it, threw the cash box into her bag. This would look like a burglary, divert attention away from the files.

"I've called the police!" Gust shouted outside. "I've got a gun."

Not what she wanted to hear. A key went into the lock.

The door opened but banged against the chair. Gust pushed. Jammed.

Bag over her shoulder, Colleen headed back to the window. Wind and rain blew as she climbed out, Gust shouting at her. The sill was slippery.

Fortunately, it was a short drop to the ground.

Landing in a sloppy crouch, she raised herself up. Hefting her bag, she charged around the back of the building on the wet grass. Slipped on a corner, went down with a thump, got back up. Past the doghouse with the still silent Dobermans, back to where she had climbed up the wall.

Boom was waiting in the shadows.

"Someone coming," she said before he could speak. "Head for the fence."

"Roger that." Boom grabbed his bag.

Lights came on. The slam of the door inside.

They pounded across the sodden lawn. Reached the fence as the back door flung open and smacked the wall. A shaft of light spilled out and a man came out in a striped robe, holding a flashlight and, much to the detriment of Colleen's nerves, what looked to be a pistol.

"Who's there?" Gust shouted.

At the fence, Boom squatted down to cup his hands together again for Colleen's sneaker. She stepped in quickly, still shaky from her climb up the wall and her tumble out the office window. Boom heaved her over the fence. This time one of the iron spears caught her shin and it hurt like hell. Stifling a yelp, she made it over, onto the grass at first, then rolling onto the sidewalk.

Somehow Boom got over the fence with little effort.

Landed beside her in a crouch.

"You okay, Chief?"

"Fine," she lied. "Let's go."

"Stop!" Gust shouted, running towards them. The flashlight beam bounced as it caught them.

Boom helped her up.

"Don't let him get a look at your face," Colleen said. Boom's build was not as distinctive as his race was.

They ran down Pacheco to where she had parked. The flashlight beam followed but faded in the misty rain.

"I've called the police!" Gust shouted again. All the while the flashlight beam flickered through the railings. But Colleen wasn't convinced Die Kerk would want the police anywhere near their business anytime soon.

As they got to her car, an uneasy mix of feelings rushed though Colleen. She finally had something to go on. She just didn't like where it was leading her.

CHAPTER TWENTY-SIX

It was past one in the morning when Colleen's Torino rumbled up in front of the Pink Palace, the public housing projects on Turk in the heart of the Western Addition. Even so, a few people were hanging around out front. That meant young black men. One swigged from a bottle. The twin ten-story buildings were an eyesore, as well as a precarious place to be this time of night. Colleen and Boom were drying out, the car heater on high, windows steaming up.

Boom opened the passenger door to the Torino, got out. He looked into the car.

"Let me know when you want to proceed, Chief."

"Better lay low for a while," she said. "Besides, you've got a final tomorrow." She had asked a lot of Boom. "Say 'hi' to Grandma for me." Boom's grandmother had raised him.

"Ten-four," Boom said, tapping the roof. "Semper Fi."

She watched Boom head over to the floodlit, weed-strewn front of the building. A couple of the ne'er-do-wells nodded to him as he went in.

Colleen put the car into gear, headed back home.

A couple of days ago she'd had no idea where Pamela was. Now, she knew her daughter was connected to a shadowy cult church with an obsession for death, and a volcano named the Throat of Fire. Where Pam was most likely headed. If not already there.

And the clock was ticking.

* * *

Back up Potrero Hill, the rain had stopped and night fog crawled along Vermont Street. Colleen circled the block. No suspicious vehicles. She parked in the dirt lot behind her building.

Upstairs she flipped on the gas wall heater and headed to the bathroom where she peeled off her jeans, took a look at her shin. She'd had worse but it smarted. She cleaned up the wound, winced as she applied Mercurochrome, slipped on her kimono. In the kitchen she made herself a cup of strong black coffee with a healthy splash of brandy and downed a couple of aspirin. She took her spiked coffee into her office with her day bag. Swirling fog billowed over Potrero Hill. She turned on the desk lamp, got out the cash box, opened it with her lock picking tools at leisure.

Two hundred and thirteen dollars in an envelope and a load of receipts. She put the money aside for The Salvation Army. St. Peter would surely let her slide on the thievery if she did that. The receipts were nothing special. She put the cash box to one side.

She got out a pad of paper and a pencil, and the English-Afrikaans dictionary she had purchased at Stacey's bookstore earlier that day. And started writing while her memory of the break-in was still fresh. She had to hunt around to get the spellings right.

Timmerman—carpenter.

Loodgieter—plumber.

Rekenmeester—bookkeeper.

These were the attributes listed by the volunteers on the Tungurahua pilgrimage. All were skills needed to build a utopian hideaway in the jungle. Verligting. Which translated to "enlightenment."

But Pamela couldn't hit a nail with a hammer without hitting her own thumb. Couldn't measure once, even twice, before she cut, and, more to the point, didn't want to. Not at least when Colleen knew her. So what was her skill for the venture?

There was *vroulike offer*—the attribute listed by Pamela's—and other female names.

Colleen leafed through her pocket dictionary.

Vroulike: *Female.*

Offer: *Offering.*

Colleen felt the blood drain from her head. Light and dizzy now.

Some of the members were destined to work.

Others were intended to offer themselves.

Sex servants? From what Colleen had seen, Die Kerk's treatment of women left a lot to be desired. But in the light of the fact that the church was named after the *Perfect Death*, "offering" had a much more sinister connotation.

She took a sip of fortified coffee, realized her hand was shaking. Her sense of foreboding had transcended standard parental dread. If her theory was correct, some or all of the 242 or so people were on their way to their deaths, perfect or otherwise.

Including her daughter.

If they were not already dead.

Colleen sat back, taking a deep breath.

She needed advice. Late as it was, she picked up the phone. Called her lawyer, Gus Pedersen, expecting to get his fancy answering machine. But, to her surprise, Gus picked up. Pink Floyd was playing in the background, the thundering, windswept expanse of "One of These Days." Old hippies never died. They just became radical lawyers. And they seemed to work all hours—at least not the regular ones.

"Ms. Hayes," he said in a smoky voice. "Moon Ranch giving you a hard time again?"

"They're the least of my worries right now," she said. "You could almost say we're friends."

"So you gave them their ball back?" Meaning the bag of acid.

"As good as." She had mailed the locker key. She told him of Pamela's connection to Die Kerk. When she was done, she heard Gus take a breath.

"I guess Moon Ranch wasn't bad enough for Pamela," Gus said.

"I need help."

"Yes you do, if Die Kerk is involved."

"Can we go to the police?"

Pink Floyd played in the background. "With what?"

"The possible deaths of hundreds of people."

"Hundreds of *willing* people. Adults who joined the church of their own volition. Going to some far-flung place. Out of judicial reach."

"This is madness."

"I know. You know. But the law has precedents."

"They're on their way. If not already there."

"Based on a grainy film at a cult church service, which could have been taken last year. You don't have a timeline. And that's what you need before we go any further. You need some proof that these people were taken against their will."

He was right.

"So I need to keep digging," she said.

"And you need to do it without breaking and entering."

"You know what's weird?" she said. "I didn't even know my daughter had a passport."

"There's probably a lot you don't know about her."

"How would I find that out?"

"I can resolve the passport issue more quickly—and legally—than you can."

She thought about the note on the file folder she'd seen at Die Kerk—Tennant Shipping. She wished she'd had time to have gone through Die Kerk's accounting records and dig deeper. She mentioned it to Gus. "Sounds like they might be using Tennant to transport church members down to Ecuador," she said.

"I'll make some calls first thing, reach out to the Feds, see what we can jump-start. But don't hold your breath. In the meantime, whatever you do, keep it *legal*. Not like last night, please. You don't want to land back in prison. You don't need that kind of trip down memory lane."

No she didn't.

And neither did Pam.

CHAPTER TWENTY-SEVEN

"And what do you need a copy of the shipping manifest for again?" the receptionist with 1960s big hair asked. It was sprayed to a sheen you could bounce a ball off.

"Proof of shipment," Colleen said, standing before the grand teak desk on the eighth floor of the Tennant building at 215 Market Street, home to San Francisco's venerable shipping company. Behind the bouffant a credenza loaded with model ships displayed a visual account of Tennant's history over the last century. The tall picture window showed the silver Bay Bridge across an uncharacteristically sunny San Francisco morning. But one wall of the reception area was lined with moving boxes and men in white overalls were busy carting them away on hand trucks. "For insurance purposes. I did call about it earlier this morning. Chris Hood in Accounts Payable is who I spoke to."

The receptionist spun in her chair, dialed a number, asked for Chris Hood. Explained the situation.

She turned back around, smiling wonderfully, exuding a whiff of flowery perfume.

"Please take a seat, Ms. Aird. Chris is a little busy this morning but will be out as soon as possible."

"There does seem to be a lot of activity," Colleen said, nodding at the moving men heading back down the hall with their hand trucks loaded.

The receptionist dropped her voice. "We're moving offices." Then she added, almost inaudibly, "Downsizing."

"Ah," Colleen said, noting for the first time that the newspaper on the woman's desk was open to the want ads. Looking for a job. "I hadn't heard."

The receptionist flashed her perfectly arched eyebrows. "Yes," she said. "Not good." She mouthed the last two words.

"I'm sorry to hear that." It looked like Colleen might be here for a while. She went over to the waiting area, sat down, smoothing her sensible Glen plaid skirt. Picked up the *Wall Street Journal* from the coffee table. The Dow Jones was down to 800. It was a good thing she was too poor to own stock. But people were hurting everywhere.

Eventually a young man appeared, the sleeves of his white shirt rolled up to his elbows. His curly brown hair was cut short. He looked tired. To Colleen's disappointment, he wasn't carrying any papers.

She stood up, gave him one of her *Carol Aird, Pacific All Risk Insurance* cards.

"I'm so sorry, Ms. Aird," he said in a high-pitched voice, holding the card with both hands apologetically. "But we're swamped. I'll get your shipping manifest into the mail tonight, I *promise*. Sorry for the wasted trip."

Colleen suppressed a sigh. "Isn't there any way you could run off a quick copy? My client needs it to qualify for next year's coverage. We're almost out of time."

Chris Hood frowned. "Don't they have a copy?"

"Not a signed one showing trip completion." She frowned herself, as if in sympathy, then dropped her voice. "Just between you and me and the lamppost, with the recent downturn, we're being extra careful."

"Tell me about it." He blinked, obviously thinking it over. "I'll be right back."

Five minutes later, Colleen was descending in the elevator, reading the copy of the shipping manifest.

Die Kerk's 245 cases of "misc. consumer goods" were delivered to the port of Guayaquil, Ecuador, on November 5th. Actual delivery was 243. Two weeks ago, to the day. Signed off for by customs. The ship was the *Fortuna*. It had set off from San Francisco, Pier 48. The captain's name was Spring.

The elevator stopped on the ground floor with a ding and the guard held the door for Colleen. She thanked him, went out to the lobby, the heels of her mild platform loafers echoing on the marble floor. Stacks of moving boxes were lined up here and there now.

Two hundred forty-five cases of miscellaneous consumer goods. Two hundred forty-five Die Kerk members destined for Ecuador. Two hundred forty-three had arrived. A company in financial straits. An insane church.

Outside at a payphone near the Embarcadero, the Ferry Building standing guard, she called Gus Pedersen, her lawyer.

"Your daughter has no record of applying for a passport," he said.

"So if Pam's in South America, it's not legal. And whoever took her there is breaking the law."

There was a pause. "Yes, but as I said before, I caution you to hold off doing anything that might affect your parole. I understand there's a congressman involved in a case against Die Kerk. I've got a call in to him."

She looked at her watch, wondering how long it would take her to get to Pier 48. It wasn't far, just down the waterfront.

"Duly noted, Gus. Thanks so much."

CHAPTER TWENTY-EIGHT

The sun was shining on the bay as Colleen crossed the Third Street drawbridge over Mission Creek into the southern waterfront, the gridded steel surface rippling her tires. Pier 48 was the first dock this side of Mission Bay. Unlike Pier 50 just past it, which bustled with activity and vehicles, 48 was pretty much a desolate lot, a victim of San Francisco's declining waterfront. Colleen parked the Torino in the near empty lot, saw a single ship moored bayside. It was pleasantly warm as she walked from the weed-strewn parking lot to the dock, the midday sun overhead, a definite change of late. It felt good to stretch out her limbs, her brown leather bag over her shoulder with some of the tools of the trade, including Little Bersalina of twenty-two caliber fame. She left her jacket in the car. Her green sweater, matching the rest of her Jane Office outfit, was more than sufficient.

The *Fortuna* was a dark blue cargo vessel generously stained with rust. About two-thirds the length of a football field, it took up half the dock. A yellow crane was mounted on its deck, pre-container. Colleen didn't know anything about boats, but this one looked old and worse for wear.

And, as she got closer, she could smell it. Like a giant urinal.

It was also quiet. No one around. Perhaps it was lunchtime. Perhaps the *Fortuna* was out of service. But a gangplank was out. She dug in her bag, found her trusty bogus badge in its authentic beat-up NYPD belt clip holder that she used in situations like this. She clipped it to the strap of the bag hanging over her shoulder. Looked plenty official if one wasn't looking too closely. She strode up the springy gangplank, squinting at the sunlight reflecting off the water. She'd left the bag unzipped, the heel of the Bersa just visible.

The *Fortuna* smelled even worse once on board, stinging her nostrils.

"Hello?" she called out.

No answer.

"Anybody home?" Maybe it should be anybody *aboard*. But still no answer. Just the water sloshing, the sounds of trucks and machinery on Pier 50 in the distance. Seagulls.

She walked the deck, found no one. But the cargo hold was open. She entered the bridge, which was the opposite of clean. Charts, cups, papers everywhere. A sweatshirt hanging over the back of the captain's chair.

A dining room at the front of the boat looked like it might have been abandoned. Plates and cups on tables. Sacks full of used paper plates against a wall. A lot of paper plates. Bottles, cans. A small galley had not been cleaned in some time. Pots and pans, one tipped over on the stove, dried sauce hardened.

A lot of people had been here at one time.

She checked seven of the eight small cabins, four bunks each, all well used, smelling of people. Sleeping bags, blankets, a sock, a broken toy doll. Magazines, newspapers. More dirty paper plates. The captain's cabin was locked. She knocked on the door. No answer.

She skipped going into the heads and bathrooms proper, cracking the doors and calling out *hello*. The stench told the story.

Down below she found a metal door. *Crew Only.*

She opened it, peered into a sizable cargo hold devoid of cargo. The giant hatch was open and the midday sun beat down overhead, thankfully dispersing much of the odor.

But dozens of ratty old mattresses covered the floor. More sleeping bags. Blankets. Papers. Discarded clothes.

And there, by a paper plate of unfinished brown glop: a book.

By Adem Lea.

Die Perfekte Dood.

The Perfect Death. She picked it up, flipped through it. Written in Afrikaans, it wasn't of much use to her. She already knew what Die Kerk was all about. But it told her one thing.

They had been on this boat.

Which had just returned from Guayaquil, Ecuador.

Two hundred forty-five or so members would be her guess.

"Who the hell are you?" a man's raspy voice said, slurry.

Startled, she spun.

At the door to the engine room stood an emaciated middle-aged man in dungarees, his shirttails hanging out. He had a dark comb-over that had fallen out of place and a pale complexion.

And, in his right hand, a pistol, like the rest of him, swaying. He was good and drunk. She was more worried he might fire by accident.

"Whoa," she said, putting her hands up partway. "I called out several times before I boarded."

"And that makes it okay?"

"Special Agent Aird." She nodded at the badge on her strap. "State Attorney's Office. I'm looking for Captain Spring."

"You're talking to him."

"Please put that damn thing down first before you shoot someone—like yourself."

He lowered the gun halfway.

"Be thankful you're not under arrest for pulling a gun on a law enforcement officer."

"Arrested for what? You walked onto my damn boat without permission." He grimaced, waved the gun sloppily. "Let me see that badge. Then you can get the hell off my boat."

She unclipped the badge, held it up. "I take it you don't want this investigation to go smoothly."

"Investigation into *what*?"

"Human trafficking." She raised her eyebrows.

"Bring that damn thing over here." He gestured with the gun, some sort of revolver. "I've got a good mind to report you."

She walked over slowly, holding up the badge.

Up close, he reeked of booze. Not a huge surprise.

"Intoxicated in command of a seagoing vessel," she asked. "How bad do you want to lose your license, Captain Spring?"

"What the hell are you talking about? We're docked." He grabbed the ID. "What is this?" He squinted at the badge. "Registered Chauffeur, State of Arizona?"

"Looks pretty authentic, doesn't it?" Colleen had her Bersa out now, pointed at his gut. "Picked it up in an antique shop. I put it in an official holder. Not bad, huh?"

Now it was his turn to jump. His gun was off target by now, pointed at nothing.

"Give me that thing," she said. "Butt first."

He handed over the gun sideways. She took it, tucked it in her bag.

"Let's start again." She took the ID badge, tossed it in her bag, stood back. "How many made it to Guayaquil?"

He flinched. "How do you know that?"

"Because I'm a private investigator," she said. "And my daughter's one of them."

He went round-eyed. "Your daughter?"

She reached into her bag, found the Die Kerk black-and-white mugshot-like photo of Pamela. Held it up.

He frowned. "Yeah, she looks familiar."

"How many, total?"

"Two forty-three," he said. "Two got off in Panama. Dysentery."

"I'm surprised there weren't more than two," she said, looking around at the squalor. "But not *her*, right?" She held the photo up again.

"No," he said. "She made it."

Colleen gave a heavy sigh. "Where were they headed to after Guayaquil?"

"Why should I tell you? With your goddamn chauffeur's badge?"

"Because you are likely to spend some time in prison," she said. "My daughter doesn't have a passport. Those people were taken illegally. The more you cooperate, the better."

"They went of their own accord."

"Doesn't make a damn bit of difference," she said. "And those people are most likely on their way to commit suicide."

"What?"

"Oh, yeah," she said. "And you transported them."

He shook his head sadly, let it hang. "I didn't spend much time with them," he said. "They're bat shit crazy. Their leader had a freaking cross tattooed on his forehead. They talked about some volcano. In between chanting and praying." He wiped his forehead, pushed his comb-over back up. "Sweet Jesus."

"The Throat of Fire."

"Yeah, something like that. They were going to walk there."

About 125 miles from Guayaquil. A week of hiking. Maybe more. And they arrived in Ecuador two weeks ago.

Colleen had her work cut out for her.

"One last question," she said. "*Why?* Why did you do it?"

His face broke into a brutal frown. "Tennant is downsizing."

"And you're one of the lucky ones."

He nodded. "Twenty-eight years."

"So Tennant doesn't know the whole story? About Die Kerk's 245 cases of 'consumer goods'? 243 which made it."

"Put it like this: they didn't go out of their way to look into things. Not when Die Kerk paid a premium for shipping. They were happy to take their money."

"I bet Die Kerk paid you a premium, too."

"What difference does it make? Those nutjobs would have found another way to get there. And Papa needs to eat."

"Papa needs to drink, by the looks of things."

"Who are you to judge me? With your insane fucking daughter." She shook her head. "You need help."

Colleen took one last look around, left, heading for the door to the hold. She went up on deck, her mind full of turmoil. She couldn't deny the truth any longer. Pam was headed to that damn death volcano, if she was still alive.

She stepped down the gangplank, the afternoon sun blinding.

"What about my gun?"

She looked up. Captain Spring was on deck, teetering.

She stopped, got his .38 out of her bag.

Tossed the gun into the water. The gun splashed, gurgled down, while Captain Spring looked on, speechless.

"I just did you a favor," she said.

CHAPTER TWENTY-NINE

"My advice, Colleen, is to seriously rethink this," Gus Pedersen said, taking a sip of jasmine tea, setting his cup down neatly on its saucer.

Four fifteen in the a.m., they were sitting at a Formica table in Hot and Juicy, a 24-hour burger joint just off Castro. Colleen's lawyer bulged in his chair like a man playing tea party with a child. Gus was linebacker material, with a long thick brown ponytail over his fringed suede jacket. He wore a bushy mustache and sideburns. Colleen had never seen his wide-set eyes without his tinted aviator glasses.

The small diner was packed with the kind of people that came out after dark and stayed out until daylight turned them into ash. At the counter sat a man at least six feet tall, wearing a blue dress, dangling a man's size-12 pump while he checked his makeup in a compact. A bodybuilder type in minimal clothing was engaged in quiet conversation with a handsome elderly Asian woman in a striking fur coat. On closer inspection, the handsome elderly Asian woman was a handsome elderly Asian man. To round things out, a trio of thrill seekers in full disco gear, two coeds and a slight young man, were drunkenly stabbing at a plate of French fries. Like the clientele, the decor was over the top, along with the music. "I Will Survive" drifted from a loudspeaker at a decent volume.

"I take it you don't have children, Gus," Colleen said, tapping ash from a Virginia Slim into the ashtray. She sipped coffee she didn't really want but needed to stay awake. Too late to sleep; too early to rise. She wore her red tracksuit and white Pony Topstars. Her traveling outfit.

"But what you're proposing is just plain dangerous," Gus said. "Breaking into Die Kerk and uncovering a plan to transport hundreds of people to Ecuador for a possible suicide pact might have been beautiful detective work but it's illegal—not to mention physically risky to go down there yourself. Die Kerk can get nasty."

She knew about Die Kerk's penchant for revenge. But it angered her more than it frightened her. Pam was the reason.

"I've spoken to a Congressman Waters," Gus said. "He's heading up an investigation into Die Kerk's activities in South America. A number of his constituents are down there."

"Do you know where exactly?"

"Somewhere near Baños."

That's what she knew.

"Their Social Security checks are being sent to Die Kerk and they're pretty much being held, as far as their relatives are concerned. Most have no passports. There's no way they can leave easily. Adem Lea is also facing labor law violations here. People are pushing for action. I spoke to Representative Waters about your situation. He wants to meet. With what you've uncovered about Tennant Shipping, the Fed's case against Die Kerk is strengthened. Waters is planning on going down there soon, along with several family members and legal counsel. We can get you to join him. Safety in numbers."

"All of which takes time," Colleen said. "Time I don't have. That Pamela doesn't have."

Gus put his big hands up in appeasement. "A little patience. All I'm asking."

"How much patience?"

Gus picked up his tea, swirled, took a sip. "Within the month."

She shook her head. "A month is an eternity where a suicide cult is concerned."

She told him about the term *vroulike offer*.

He set his cup down. "I admit, it's not good." Gus rubbed his face, blinked behind his tinted lenses.

"I can't wait." She reached down, got her bag, set it on her lap, pulled out two bulky manila envelopes. One was marked *Sergeant Matt Dwight*, the other, *Inspector Owens*. "Here's everything I've got on the two cases SFPD are handling. One concerns the rumor about the mayor being shot, the other is my friend Lucky, beaten to death by the bikers connected to the rumor. If you don't hear from me within a week, these go to the respective parties."

Gus reached across the table, took the envelopes. "And where are you going to be exactly? As if I didn't know."

"Ecuador," she said, smashing her cigarette out. "Baños. Near the volcano. It shouldn't be impossible to find Verligting." She checked her watch. "I booked a flight to Quito. Leaves SFO in a few hours."

"You're not going alone, I hope."

She nodded.

Gus sighed, adjusted his sunglasses. "What about your friend Boom? Can't he go with you?"

"It's too much to ask. He's in the middle of finals. He's taken a couple of chances helping me already." Illegal ones. "And I'll move faster alone. I'll keep you posted. If anything should happen . . . well, you know who to contact: Dwight, Owens, the Feds, Congressman Waters."

"I really wish you'd give this some more thought."

"I have."

"I know." Gus nodded, looked at his watch, gathered up the enve-lopes. "I know you have."

She gave a single nod. "Pamela's my daughter."

CHAPTER THIRTY

The bus groaned to a halt on the dark mountain road a mile above sea level. A grouping of huts and buildings clung to the edges of the narrow highway, all shut save for an empty cantina. The rain forest loomed on one side, the volcano on the other. A hint of pink glowed from its crest.

The bus door hissed as it popped open.

"Last stop," the driver said in Spanish. He was a heavy-faced mestizo, bent over a steering wheel that seemed a yard in diameter. It vibrated along with the diesel engine, in chorus with the fringe balls hanging from the windshield. On the radio, Latin pop music played, a tune laden with syrupy strings.

"We're stopping here?" Colleen asked. She was the only remaining passenger. "We're still at least five kilometers from Baños."

She'd learned Spanish growing up in West Denver.

"Tungurahua," he said, nodding up the mountain. *The throat of fire.*

With the door open they could smell a hint of sulfur, the volcano more active of late. What did that mean for Die Kerk's schedule?

Colleen stood, gathered her light pack from the overhead rack. She hoped she wasn't too late.

"The militaires are evacuating the town," the driver said. "They won't let you in."

Evacuating over five thousand people was no small feat. "I'm actually looking for a place called Verligting. A settlement. Know where it might be?"

He squinted at her. "You're not one of *them*, are you?" Meaning a Die Kerker.

"My daughter is," she said. "I came down here to find her."

His scowl turned to a grimace of concern. "Near the town of Mera, I'm told. Beyond Baños. Twenty-five kilometers? Who knows exactly. Get too close and you're likely to be shot at."

She nodded at the cantina. "Let me buy you a meal. Or a beer. And you can tell me what else you've heard."

"*No gracias.* I've got to get back to Ambato. And if you've got any sense, you'll stay away from volcanos and the people who worship them."

She thanked him, got off the bus, in jeans, hiking boots, layers of outdoor wear, with her small pack, and watched the bus make a laborious U-turn, then lumber off down the mountain road.

She was left with the sounds of the Andes, the wind, an owl hooting.

Was Pamela listening to this? Smelling the same sulfur? How far away was she?

Minutes later, Colleen had a warm sandwich wrapped in greaseproof paper to go. The aroma of pork and onions made her stomach growl.

"The basilica in Baños is a meeting point," the woman in the cantina said. "If you can get past the soldiers."

"Thank you," Colleen said, and headed up the mountain road in the dark.

CHAPTER THIRTY-ONE

It was past midnight by the time Colleen reached Baños. The faint glow of the volcano pulsed on the peak of Tungurahua. The narrow road into town was dusted with a fine layer of ash, tire track imprints here and there. Despite the altitude and cold night air, five kilometers of dark mountain road had filmed her with perspiration. Worrying over Pamela kept her awake.

The radiant mountaintop was contrasted by the darkened mountain town, buildings shut, without power.

Shouts echoed off in the distance.

At the modest bus station on the edge of town, a dirt lot with a smattering of single-story structures, military vehicles and soldiers were posted.

An adolescent soldier stopped Colleen. He had sharp features. A rifle was slung over his shoulder.

"Turn around, Señora. The town is under evacuation orders."

"I'm looking for my daughter," she said.

He called over a sergeant with a peaked cap and tunic neatly tucked in. He had a perfectly trimmed mustache.

"Your daughter is in Baños?"

Lying to South American soldiers didn't seem like a good idea.

"I believe she's in Verligting," Colleen said.

"You're not a *volcanario*, are you?"

"My daughter is. I'm hoping to go to the church, see if she might have checked in." In Colleen's wishful mind, Pamela might have come to her senses, decided to leave Die Kerk. "Before I head to the settlement. It's near Mera, I'm told."

"Sorry. No can do."

"Can't I just pass through?"

He shook his head. "Orders. If she's at that settlement, then you're too late anyway."

That's what she was worried about. She headed back the way she came. On the outskirts of town, she ventured off road, headed back toward Baños, wading through grass on an overgrown trail. She'd skirt the town. But the undergrowth was quickly becoming formidable and the incline up to Tungurahua started almost immediately. From her pack, she drew the hunting knife she had purchased in Quito in its canvas sheath, strapped it to her belt.

It promised to be a long night.

After less than a mile what little trail there was became non-navigable in the dark. She was a sweaty mess. Baños lay to her left, dark and unnerving. Tungurahua loomed to the right. She'd sneak back into town here, connect up with the main road, head east, towards Verligting.

As she got onto a dirt road into Baños, passing through rough sections of vacant cinderblock housing, she reached a once-grand colonial building, dark and empty. A door was open and the clatter of breaking glass from within quickened her pace. Men's voices. Her nerves tightened at a small group of men who appeared on a side street.

"Hey, Chica!" one shouted. "Where are you going on such a beautiful night?" Another laughed.

"Need some company?"

If there was once thing Colleen could do, it was run. And she did.

Further into town, the twin white steeples of the Church of the Virgin of the Holy Water rose up out of the dark volcanic stone bell towers, lit up where other buildings were not. A large circular stained-glass rosette window above the entrance blushed in the dark. A generator chugged away.

Colleen moved her sheathed knife to the side pocket of her backpack.

Several soldiers were posted outside. An armored car sat in front of the park. A soldier in his thirties, with a pockmarked face, asked Colleen her business.

"I think my daughter may have checked in here."

Thankfully, this soldier let her through.

Inside the church, where paintings of the local history of eruptions and the ensuing miracles performed by the virgin lined the walls, cots were lined up in the aisles alongside the pews. People slept, idled, milled about. Waiting to be evacuated, looking for loved ones. Nervous chatter echoed off the high church ceiling.

A middle-aged nun in a white wimple checked a longhand-written list of names when Colleen asked if she had heard from or registered a Pamela Hayes.

The nun looked up with a frown, shook her head.

"Fenna, by any chance?" Pamela's perfect name.

The nun checked the list again, shook her head no.

"I guess my next stop is the settlement," Colleen said.

"Please be careful," the nun said, excusing herself to tend to a woman with a child that needed a diaper.

Outside, Colleen filled her canteen from one of the huge plastic water barrels that had been set up by the park. Then she headed east, out of town, toward the edge of the Amazon rain forest. She was soon back on darkened road, flanked by looming greenery. Everything grew with vigor near the equator.

She still had a good fifteen to twenty kilometers to go and it was the middle of the night. It was a good thing she wasn't tired. Fear for Pamela's life was good for something.

Behind her, she heard a truck grinding up as it approached. Without even looking, she stuck her thumb out. Any ride would be welcome.

The truck swung around her, a beat-up green thing from another time, with a fenced open back full of bleating goats.

It slowed down, engine grumbling.

She shifted her backpack up on her shoulders, picked up her feet before the driver could change his mind. She had her knife, just in case.

CHAPTER THIRTY-TWO

"Where to, Chica?" the grizzled driver said, staring at Colleen from the steering wheel of the truck cab. He was barrel chested with a gut, a good twenty years her senior, in a faded red-and-white FPF futbol shirt. He had a round face to go with his belly. Both shook with the vibrating of the truck.

Colleen stood on the running board, sizing him up. She was a woman alone, traveling late at night in a country where *norteamericanas* were sometimes considered easy. The seats were torn and duct-taped, the cab littered with trash. On the radio, a mountain song played in Quechua, a language foreign to Colleen. An empty beer bottle rolled on the floor.

But beggars couldn't be choosers. There wouldn't be many rides available. And she had to get to Verligting sooner rather than later.

"Mera," she said.

"Hop in."

She scrambled up, pulled the creaky door shut. The cab smelled of farm animals.

And booze. She noticed the bottle wedged between the driver's thighs. He put the truck into gear and it groaned out onto the narrow road.

She could feel him looking her over. She stared straight ahead at the green branches moving by, lit up by headlights.

"Leaving town?" he said. "Good idea."

"You think she's going to blow?"

"Any day. She's quiet now but not for long." Then, "Your Spanish is good."

"You speak it a little different down here."

"So, what's a pretty gringa doing out all alone this late at night? All on her own, eh?"

Uh-oh.

"Looking for my daughter," she said.

"Your daughter lives in Mera?"

"Verligting."

"Oh, man. You're not one of them, are you?"

"Not in the slightest."

He took a swig from his bottle as the truck swerved, rested it between his legs. "You sure you know what you're doing, Chica? Those nutters have shot at more than one trespasser."

"I'm sure. Any idea how many there are?"

"Hundreds, I'm told."

That sounded right. They drove for a minute or two.

He took his hand off the wheel and pulled the bottle again, a noisy swig.

"Want a drink, Chica?"

"No thanks."

He shook the bottle at her. It sloshed. "Go on. *Aguardiente.* It's good."

Cheap firewater. "I'm not much of a drinker."

She heard him swig his aguardiente. The truck veered when he did that. "So what do you like to do for fun, eh?"

"I'm not much in the way of fun these days." She switched her bag to her left shoulder, placing a barrier between the two of them, the side pocket with her knife handle poking out within easy reach.

"I can take you to Verligting, if you like," he said casually. "Well, the property line, that is."

"How far is it?" Verligting wasn't on her map. It wasn't on any map.

"Oh, fifteen kilometers."

Ten miles. "But where?"

"Not far." He wasn't going to tell her.

"Off the highway?" There was only one road as far as she knew, and they were on it.

He didn't answer.

They began a steep decline, the mountain behind them, headed down into a long, dark valley, the twisting road following the river. Getting closer to Pam, after so long, and so far from home, felt surreal. Unsettling.

"So, what do you do when you get lonely, eh?" he said, slurring slightly.

He wasn't going to let up. "I don't."

"Come on. Everybody gets lonely."

She ignored him.

"All I'm saying is that it's a shame, a good-looking woman like you."

She didn't respond.

"Go on," he said, brandishing the bottle again. "Have a drink already."

She shook her head.

He muttered something to himself, swigged.

Not long after she heard the river, growing louder as it tumbled out of the mountains to her right. She knew a considerable waterfall lay ahead. It was a point of interest. A painting in the basilica depicted the virgin saving a man whose car had gone over in the 1920s.

Down another bumpy incline, they pulled off to the right.

"Where are we going?" Colleen asked, her nerves on high alert.

"The Devil's Cauldron." A grin crossed his face. "It's worth seeing. You'll like it."

The waterfall. He was planning on parking, spending a little time with her. It would be a good place to ditch this guy.

He pulled into a small lot up to the waterfall, shut the engine off with a residual clatter. The crash of the water was thunderous. In the darkness, spray soaked the windshield, and beyond that, a sense of openness. Frightened goats bleated from the back of the truck.

"Well?" he shouted over the tumbling water.

"Since I can't see a thing, I'll have to take your word for it," she said.

"And this?" His meaty hand rested on her thigh.

"Hands to yourself, amigo." She gently moved his hand away.

"Do you need money, Chica?"

"No."

A moment later he came in at her, like a football player for a tackle. She shoved him back.

Before he could come in for a second try, she had her knife out.

His mouth dropped. He froze.

She reached over, pulled his keys from the ignition. "Where's the turnoff for Verligting?"

"There's a dirt road," he stammered, "just before Mera. On the left. After a ranch—Estancia Guadalupe."

"See?" she said. "That wasn't so hard."

"What are you going to do with my keys?" he said, voice quavering.

"See that wall over there?" There was a blur of a stone wall through the windshield, overlooking the waterfall. "That's where I'll leave them. But get out of the truck before I'm gone and over they go—into the river." She shook the keys for effect. "And, try to come after me, I've always got this." She showed him the knife.

"*Puta!*" He spat the word at her.

"Thanks for the ride," she said, opening the door latch behind her. Knife in hand, she hooked her bag over her shoulder and got out, climbing down the running board in reverse to keep him in her line of sight. She left the door open. It would slow him down.

The waterfall was thunderous as she headed for the road. Water soaked her as she marched over to the wall, but cooled and refreshed her, too. She placed the keys squarely in the center of the stone post of the wall. No need to put his livelihood in jeopardy. He probably had a family somewhere that depended on him.

Soon she was pacing down the winding mountain road. She pressed the button on her Pulsar watch. Red digits indicated one thirty in the a.m. Pam was still the better part of a day away. Colleen hefted her bag on her shoulders, picked up the pace.

The roar of the waterfall behind her helped pound her thoughts into oblivion. Sometimes thinking only got in the way.

CHAPTER THIRTY-THREE

The first rays of daylight filtered through the tree canopy as Colleen climbed the steep dirt road. Early-morning fog tumbled down through the trees like wet smoke.

The night of hiking had drained her. Her quads burned. But hopefully Pamela was close by. If nothing else, the trek had taken the edge off Colleen's anxiety.

Up ahead, a farm tube gate blocked the road. Padlocked shut. About four feet tall and topped with barbed wire. A sign was posted, in both Afrikaans and Spanish.

Trespassers beware! Stay out!

Die Kerk van die Volmaakte.

Verligting. Finally. Colleen stopped, inhaling deep breaths. The rich damp smell of vegetation was contrasted by what most likely lay beyond.

Hostile territory. Her only hope was that Pamela was alive and would listen to her.

Rusty barbwire fence ran along either side of the gate, much of it obscured with undergrowth. Off road, Colleen followed the uneven fence. Slogging through brush, taking her time; she didn't need to twist an ankle.

A hundred yards in, the fence broke around the sharp spine of a huge rock jutting out of the mountainside. Using all four limbs, she climbed up and over the rock. Birds chirped a shrill morning song that carried on the wind.

She surmounted the rock, stood in more underbrush, looking up, catching her breath.

A gap of light up the hill. She recalled the photos and sketches of the clearing in the Die Kerk file. She waded through scrub, layered with sticky sweat. Even this early in the day, mosquitos and gnats buzzed around her.

And then she saw something move in the brightness of daylight up top, amidst the wisps of fog. She froze.

A critter? No. A *person*.

The head of a person. In a broad-brimmed hat. Looking downhill. At her? Slowly, *slowly*, she hunkered down, keeping motion to a minimum. Squinting up into the light through the bush.

A patrol?

Shrouded by foliage, she waited until the figure disappeared, insects droning, then moved sideways to the cover of a tree. She pulled the brim down on her dark green fabric bucket hat, anonymous, obscuring her head and face.

The next half an hour was painstakingly slow as she negotiated rough, sloped ground, rocks, dense brush, branches. The head never reappeared, but she couldn't be sure when it might. As she drew closer to the ridge, wind blew down through the trees, carrying the sounds of people. Shouting. Hammering. Sawing. Some kind of work effort. A motor chugged.

A loudspeaker barked, echoing through the compound: a voice in Afrikaans, some sort of instruction. The work sounds diminished. The high-pitched tone of a Farsi organ followed, reminiscent of the service at 555 Fillmore Street, made more strident by the echoing loudspeaker.

She checked her watch. Six a.m. The loudspeaker repeated its command. Calling people to service?

The sounds of people stopped. She could possibly move a little more quickly.

As she got to the top, the heat of the day seeped through the opening of light.

Standing on the slope just below the rim, she peered through tall grass.

There was indeed a clearing. She recognized it from the photo she had seen in Die Kerk's file. She saw a number of wooden structures, tin roofs, some half-finished, some open. Tents were erected here and there. There were even vehicles, construction equipment. Across the clearing was the large pavilion she recognized, open on the sides, where a mass of people was now gathering under a huge roof. Her plan was to join them, blend in. She could see another peak beyond, gleaming green in the morning sunshine.

A man's voice reverberated through loudspeakers in Afrikaans. She recognized the portent tenor.

Adem Lea.

The beginning of a sermon.

She ditched her small pack behind a tree, leaving the knife with it, not wanting to be caught armed. She scrabbled over the ridge, brushing off leaves, straightening her clothes, pulling her hair under her bucket hat, tugging the brim down on all sides, shielding her eyes. Fatigue lingered. She pushed it back, taking more deep breaths.

She snaked around the dirt clearing, staying low in a crouch, toward the pavilion.

Adem Lea switched to English. His accent had that fruity South African lilt.

"I speak to you today in your old language, people, as I know many of you are still learning the tongue of our creator. So many new members. But, after our journey here, we are ancient. And as one."

Colleen hid behind a bulldozer, assessing the landscape. The thought of Pamela nearby made her heart beat with anticipation.

A voice barked at her in Afrikaans. Startled, she turned.

A heavyset middle-aged man wearing a black beret and a hunter's vest with a rifle over his shoulder stood twenty yards away. He snapped at her again, pointing at the pavilion. She was obviously late for the meeting.

"*Ja,*" she said, giving him a thumbs-up, exhausting her Afrikaans. She nodded at a porta potty in lieu of an explanation. She hurried to the pavilion, joining one or two other stragglers.

Under the huge aluminum roof, she saw Brother Adem at a podium onstage, dark sunglasses, long hair under a floppy hat. The crucifix tattoo on his forehead was just visible.

"*The Throat of Fire is Mother Earth's portal to the subconscious mind of all mankind. But not all can enter. We can, though, children— the chosen ones. Some pretend to learn from books, but they are the books of man, books of ignorance, books of pride and sin. Some try to bathe away their sins, put on airs and watch clocks and punch timecards and try to order their lives to the hopeless little things they make, living in little boxes with artificial light to hide from the darkness of what awaits them . . .*"

As one, the congregation agreed: "*Ja Adem.*"

Colleen took a seat towards the back. In the rising warmth of the day, the smell of unwashed bodies wafted. One or two faces eyed her, but she kept her eyes to herself. There were several hundred people, if not more. More. So far, so good. She could hide in the crowd. But tension crawled over her clammy skin, as she wondered where Pamela might be. If she was here. If she was alive.

"*It is only when we shun all of these man-made distractions that have destroyed the creator's world, and give over to the unending power of our mother and realize how we have violated her and how we must become one with her again, that we can reach perfection.*"

Ja, Adem.

More adjusted with her surroundings, Colleen looked around. So many faces.

"*Because we are flawed,*" Brother Adem continued. "*Too imperfect to live in this world, the world that was perfect until we appeared on it, like sores. We must end our imperfection before we destroy the world. Only then will we ourselves be perfect.*"

His words chilled her. But the crowd was acquiescent.

And then, Colleen saw her, sitting onstage next to the podium, wearing a long beige hippie dress, her red hair asunder. *Right in front of her.* Her heart pounded.

Pamela.

CHAPTER THIRTY-FOUR

Colleen couldn't quite believe her eyes. Pamela was sitting with several other attractive young women onstage, like a harem, beside the man whose church had brought her all the way to South America to venerate a volcano. And most likely sacrifice her life.

But here she was, after all this time and all these miles, her daughter—finally.

She hadn't seen Pamela for months—and then only from a distance. Had not spoken to her in almost a year, thanks to Moon Ranch's restraining order.

It was pure Pamela to throw herself into the deep end of things.

Now, the hard part began.

Pamela's normally fair face was darkened by the sun, heavily freckled. So were her neck and arms. Her eyes were narrowed, squinting perhaps, or a sign of dissatisfaction. Colleen had seen that look on her as a child, when something disappointed her. Pamela's mouth was a rigid line, another hint that she had grown—or somehow changed. Was this trip into self-discovery not satisfying her either? That could be a good thing—a wonderful thing—if Colleen could get to her in time.

Colleen wondered about making eye contact. In a room of hundreds of hard-core supporters of Brother Adem, things could turn against her. Pamela could turn against her. Colleen needed to meet her in private. Somehow.

Colleen listened to Brother Adem talk about geographic studies that showed locations on earth which were purer, out of range of mankind's evil. Cities were evil. They were also within range of nuclear attack by the corrupt and evil government. Mother Earth established her own points of energy, eight altogether, dotted around the world, to counter the evil that man created.

Tungurahua was the first epicenter, the gateway to Mother Earth.

God had come to Adem in a vision and told Adem the sobering truth about man.

"Men oppose Mother Earth's wishes. Pollution. War. Industrialization. We are a cancer on her beautiful skin."

Ja, Adem.

"Perfection requires that we grasp the ultimate flaw—ourselves. We are what is wrong."

Ja, Adem.

"A vision from God called me to the United States."

Colleen knew that Adem Lea fled South Africa after charges of tax evasion and human trafficking.

"The United States was a place to start but presented one huge problem."

Ja, Adem.

"The Russians were targeting our cities with their nuclear missiles. Just as the United States does. To kill its own people."

Ja, Adem.

"But there exists a direct path from north to south, where evil is weakest, focusing on the Throat of Fire. And it is here where we can surrender ourselves to the earth, atone for man's sin."

Colleen refrained from shaking her head as she saw her daughter's face light up, as she chanted "Ja, Adem" along with the others.

"In two days, we begin our journey, as Tungurahua calls us with its coming eruption. In two days, to perfection in select numbers, in multiples of eleven, sacred numbers. So that we can continue to host this astonishing settlement we have built—Verligting—so that others may join us and make the same journey of perfect death. The first wave of members has been selected for the first offering. Twenty-two special members, signifying my own designation from God himself—Angel 22. I ask you to stand as I read your perfect name, that name you have earned, so that your brothers and sisters may share your glory on your path to perfection."

Ja, Adem.

Adem Lea read names from a list. Dutch names. As he did, members stood, and the others chanted their name back, along with the phrase *perfekte dood.*

All who stood were women. Young women.

In all, seventeen stood.

Colleen counted her blessings as Brother Adem flipped the page on his list. For Pamela had thus far remained seated. As had the other four women sitting with her onstage.

"Finally," he said, "those close to me, signifying my own personal sacrifice—my own *vroulike offer*—as I relinquish them back to the earth they have violated."

And then he called five more names.

All the women onstage stood up as he did.

Last of all was *Fenna.* Pam's perfect name.

And up stood Pamela, tears of joy in her eyes.

CHAPTER THIRTY-FIVE

Colleen sat stunned as the meeting came to an end with a hymn sung in Afrikaans. Members rose, their voices echoing off the metal roof of the pavilion. They began to clap in unison as the Farsi organ pierced the air.

Her daughter was going to die. There was no longer any way to deny it.

"*Kom, suster, kom saam!*" the man next to Colleen said.

She looked up.

"Come, sister, join us!" he said, pulling her to her feet. "Perfection comes soon."

She allowed herself to rise, to clap, to sing of perfect death. And the tears in her eyes matched those of her daughter, who sang and swayed on the stage, a look of serenity on her face. Pamela's face was wet with tears of happiness; Colleen's, tears of sorrow.

Colleen filed out of the pavilion as the sermon finished, crushed. She must act. She must act now.

She walked over behind the bulldozer parked on the edge of the settlement. Watched the others come out.

Eventually she saw Pamela emerge. Walking with Brother Adem and another girl. A look of purpose on her face.

But, under that look, another one, one that was core Pamela. Tightness around the eyes gave it away. Uncertainty. Unsure of herself. Emotions that allowed others to take control.

Other members arrived at the construction area, picking up shovels and picks, returning to work on a rough patch of ground with a foundation outlined in orange string.

"*Kom werk, vrou!*" a man shouted at her, pointing at a shovel.

She picked up the shovel, scraped around as she watched Brother Adem head off to a white prefab hut on the edge of the camp shielded by trees. One arm around Pamela, the other around another girl about the same age. A couple of bodyguards followed at a respectable distance, both wearing black berets, one man with a length of board lazily over his shoulder, a pistol slung low on his belt. He swaggered like a cowboy. The other man had a rifle over his shoulder, the barrel level with the ground, patrol style.

Colleen watched Brother Adem and his two women go up to the hut. One of the guards fired up a generator. An air conditioner on the window jumped to life, chugging away, doing double time. Other huts did not appear to have the same luxury. Brother Adem's hand fell to Pam's waist as he opened the door, lingering for a moment on her hip before he went in. Pamela looked up at him, submissively, a weak, needy smile. Always wanting to please those who would take advantage of her. Just like with her father.

They went inside.

The door shut and the two bodyguards took up position on either side. One gave the other a wry smirk and looked at his watch.

Colleen leaned her shovel against the metal tread of the bulldozer, slipped off behind a porta potty into the trees. Down the hill into the shadows where her pack was hidden behind a tree.

She had two days to save Pamela. Two days.

CHAPTER THIRTY-SIX

It wasn't until early evening that Colleen was able to steal another glimpse of her daughter. She had positioned herself up the hill in the trees outside Verligting, where she had a clear view of the camp. One concern was the guards who patrolled the perimeter.

Sticky from the day's heat and plagued by mosquitos despite the repellant she had slathered on, she was good and hungry. She was rationing the fruit she had packed in Quito and was down to one bruised banana and a soft candy bar. Her canteen was empty.

The door to Brother Adem's quarters finally opened, after a day of being shut. Colleen picked up her field glasses and zeroed in. Pamela stepped out in a pair of denim cutoffs, flip-flops, and a Led Zeppelin T-shirt. What had most likely taken place in Brother Adem's lair filled Colleen with both anger and sorrow. Pam was little more than an instrument of pleasure for a man who would soon let her die.

She watched Pamela head off to an open dining area by the pavilion, along with a section of the camp. They ate in shifts. Through the binos, Colleen saw Pamela pick at a plate of something, sitting at the end of a table with others but not talking, keeping to herself. When Pamela was a child, it would dishearten Colleen to no end when her daughter didn't make friends. Few things saddened her more, and she recalled a Sunday school meeting where she picked

Pam up. She had been waiting out front of the church early, by herself, while other children played inside. Pam's eyes were moist and she was embarrassed and hurt. She either tried too hard or didn't try enough.

But now, to see that same glumness as she played with her food only made Colleen hopeful even as her heart went out to her. Yes, her daughter was despondent in this godforsaken place, had never found happiness, and Colleen knew, as a mother, she shouldered much of the blame. But perhaps it meant Pamela could be swayed— if Colleen could somehow get to her. Talk some sense to her. But she dared not risk venturing down there with everyone around. She had gotten away with morning service, where there had been a crowd to hide in. She'd have to wait until Pam headed out on her own some- where. There were communal showers, not that this group was much into bathing. There were toilets near the edge of the camp, not far from where Colleen had positioned herself. Eventually, she theorized, Pamela would have to face the call of nature. If Brother Adem didn't have his own private toilet.

Colleen perked up when she saw Pamela get up from her table, take her paper plate over to the side of the camp, toss it onto a huge pile of garbage, as many had done.

Maybe Pam was going somewhere Colleen could intervene.

But Pam went back to her table, sat by herself. Colleen ate her chocolate bar, her mouth dry with no water. She had seen Lucuma trees and knew the green fruit was a source of nutrition and fluids.

Then Pam got up from the table again, headed over by the pile of garbage, said something to a guard in a black beret, rifle by his side.

And she walked off into the woods.

Yes!

Colleen lowered her field glasses, hopped up from where she was hidden, made her way through undergrowth to where Pamela had wandered off. It took longer to travel around the football-field-sized camp than she had expected, and when she got close to where she thought Pam had gone—a rough path into the trees leading away from the camp—she heard water splashing and birds calling. She peered over a clump of rocks at the path. And saw Pam returning back through the trees, returning to camp. She wouldn't be able to catch her in time.

She thought of calling out to Pamela but held off. Who might overhear her? Guards were everywhere. And what kind of reaction would she get from Pam? Colleen's history of intervention had not been well received.

When Pam was gone, she made her way down and snaked around to the path Pam had taken.

She found a small waterfall cascading down a wall of rocks, secluded in the cool of the trees. Pam had a sanctuary.

Colleen went over to the waterfall, cupped her hands, drank her fill, splashed water on her face.

And knew where to be next time Pam ventured off. She just hoped there was time.

CHAPTER THIRTY-SEVEN

Another jungle dawn crept over the compound as Colleen readied her binoculars.

It had rained heavily that night. She had hunkered down in the trees in her plastic poncho, but still gotten good and wet. She had managed to sleep, however, in between fighting off bugs and waking to bats flapping about in the branches, and sustained herself with Lucuma fruit, so she could almost say she was refreshed. The approaching heat of the day was already making her skin sticky.

The loudspeakers barked with instructions. She focused. Die Kerk were gathered under the pavilion. Another six a.m. sermon.

Colleen saw Pam enter, trailing Brother Adem and the other woman, wearing her hippie dress. Colleen decided to skip this service; no need to push her luck. She knew the timeline. Tomorrow they were headed to the Throat of Fire.

When the sermon ended, members filed out, went back to work.

Through her binos, Colleen followed Brother Adem to his prefab with the brunette from yesterday and another girl this time, a shapely young blond with a sly grin.

No Pam. Maybe they took turns. Maybe Pam was on the outs. Colleen wasn't heartbroken over that. Perhaps it would provide her an opportunity to catch her.

With her knife in its sheath on her belt, she headed to the waterfall where Pam had gone yesterday. Waited in the shadow of a large spreading fern, hoping Pam might appear.

Then, with a rush of excitement, she saw Pam approach, alone. Her face was drawn, eyes down. This might be her chance.

Pamela picked a passion flower and sat on a log by the waterfall, turning the flower in her thin fingers, staring at it, the purple-and-white petals blurring. She looked so sad. Colleen felt for her, more than she thought possible, but it also gave her hope. Hope that this time—*this time*—Colleen would not be shunned. She was prepared to take Pamela by force, if need be, but that was the last resort.

She was close, as if across a room. Colleen's heart pounded.

Finally, she mustered up the courage to speak.

"Pamela," she whispered.

Her daughter looked up, startled, stared at the fern.

Colleen stepped out from behind the fern, took a breath of moist rain-forest air that shook her body with nervousness.

"Pamela," she said again. "It's me."

"What?" Pamela shook her head, as if in disbelief. "No!"

Her daughter's voice was deep, as she remembered it. She hadn't heard it in so long. But it was still her. "It can't be," Pamela said, rubbing her eyes. She jumped up.

Colleen put her hands up in conciliation. "I know this is a surprise, Pam."

"That's the understatement of the year." Pam shook her head again. "How on earth did you get here? *Here?*"

"Long story, Pam. Bottom line, I found you. And I can't tell you how good it is to see you again." *Alive.*

Pam stood erect, rearing back. "I'm sorry but I can't say the same about you."

The same old story, Pam's residual anger.

Colleen took a step closer. "That doesn't matter right now. What does matter is what's about to happen to . . . with this church. And especially to you."

Pam placed her hands on her hips. Her voice trembled with anger as she spoke in measured tones. "You have no right. No right whatsoever. This is my life. *My* life. I'm not a child anymore. You can't tell me what to do."

Colleen laughed bitterly. "Could I ever?"

"No—because you were in prison the whole time I was growing up."

One of Colleen's biggest regrets. "Not the whole time, Pam."

Pam flat-mouthed a smile. "Oh, right, there was that time when you killed my father. I almost forgot. I guess you were around for that, weren't you?"

"I did what I did for a reason . . ."

"Yah, because you were fucking angry! It was all about *you*! What about *me*?"

"Why do you think I was so damn angry, Pam? I came home, saw what that bastard had done. To you. *You!*"

Pam shook her head. "He was still my father. You had no right to kill him."

"Pam, he used you. *Raped you!* Betrayed your trust, and mine. Betrayed everything a father is supposed to be. I wasn't about to let him do it again."

"It wasn't your decision!"

During her years in prison, Colleen had read about Stockholm Syndrome. In her eyes, Pam might have been her father's special girl even if she was nothing but a victim. It might take Pam a lifetime to see that, though, if ever. "You know what, Pam? You're absolutely right. That's why a jury found me guilty and sent me to prison for the better part of a decade."

Pam's voice rose and Colleen feared they might be overheard. "And now you think you've got some God-given right to keep following me? Hounding me? You followed me out to California. Then Moon Ranch. Now here. When will you leave me alone?"

"Pam, I followed you to California because you fell in with a bunch of bikers who committed murder."

"No one asked you to."

"No one had to. I'm your mother! I saved your damn life! Then you joined up with those . . ." She stopped before she said something negative about Moon Ranch.

"Great. So we're even. For killing my father. Now leave me the hell alone."

Colleen ran her fingers through her damp hair. "Is it just possible that you're angry at your father, too? And might be misdirecting that anger at me? Because I'm the only one left to blame?"

"You sound like those damn therapists."

"Pam, if there was any way I could take back what I did, don't you think I would? I spent ten years thinking that very thought every single day, but, most of all, how I wasn't there for you."

"Well, water under the bridge, as they say. Now you've got to let me live my own life."

"I'm all for letting you live your own life, Pam. But that's not what's about to happen. Just the opposite."

"How would you even know what happens at Die Kerk?"

"Oh, I know. I know they plan on letting a number of you go to your deaths tomorrow. Twenty-two *vroulike offers* to start."

Pamela flinched. "Stay out of my life!"

"I will, if you promise to have one."

"Everybody dies! Everybody! No one gets out of this alive!"

Colleen's head shook with a flurry of desperate thoughts. It was like holding back a flood. "In their own good time, Pam. Not through suicide. Not when they're just out of their teens. You've got your whole life ahead of you. I've made plenty of mistakes, but don't you think you might have just made one or two yourself?"

"Do you know what your generation has done? Destroyed this planet."

"So rebuild it."

Pamela shook her head violently. Gritted her teeth. "The government is planning to kill us all anyway! You have no idea."

"Is that what Brother Adem tells you?"

Pamela shot a finger at Colleen. "Don't you *dare* talk about something you know nothing about."

"Pam, all I'm asking is for you to give yourself a breather, take a break from this, think it over. *Please.*"

Pamela crossed her arms over her chest. "I've thought it over. I'm at peace with my decision. Humans have failed."

Colleen gave a deep sigh. "*I* might have failed you, Pam, but there are still a lot of good people out there you haven't met yet. And these people you're with now—let's just say they're misguided."

"Ever think you might have too many opinions?"

"Most days." Colleen laughed a sardonic laugh. "But I can't stand by and watch my daughter kill herself."

"No one is killing anyone! We're making amends. Offerings. To appease Mother for our sins."

Colleen wondered if Pamela saw the irony of her words.

There was no preparation for arguing with a child who wanted to commit suicide. The best Colleen could do was try to remain sensible, although she was beginning to doubt even her own sanity. "I'm sorry, Pam, but I can't see how you've done anything that warrants your dying. You have nothing to apologize for. The state of the world is not your fault."

Pam took a deep breath, as if thinking over Colleen's words, and Colleen prayed some of what she said might be sinking in.

But when Pam spoke, all she said was, "I have given it thought. A lot of thought. And I've made up my mind."

"Is that so? That's not the look I saw on your face yesterday at that sermon or whatever it's called. I'd say you looked pretty unsure about the whole thing. And I can't say I blame you."

"Were you spying on me? *Again?*"

"What of it, Pam? I'm your mother. When you're a mother, you'll understand exactly why I did what I did. Ten years ago—and now."

"You are not my mother!" Pam spat. "You never were."

If there were words that could slice her like a razor, her daughter had just said them. And they made her shake inside, like the tree branches blowing in the breeze. But she stood, legs trembling, because that's what you did when you didn't know what else to do.

"Pam, I'm sorry. You don't know how sorry. But, right now, you've got to listen to me."

"I'm done listening to you, Mom. Done."

At least she called her "Mom." Talk about a small win.

She could take Pam by force.

But that didn't seem to be the way to play this if Colleen ever wanted Pam to truly trust her again. Colleen still had a little time. A day.

"So, tomorrow is the day?" Colleen asked.

"The first day of offering," Pam said piously. "*Die eerste kudde*— the first flock of angels."

The day twenty-two members would give themselves. Young women. Sacrificial virgins came to mind, but Brother Adem and Die Kerk had, no doubt, made sure none of these poor girls were still virgins.

"The day you jump into a damn volcano," Colleen said. "My daughter."

"I wouldn't expect you to understand. You never understood me."

Another slice. Colleen fortified herself with whatever inner strength she had left.

"I'll come with you," she said.

Pam actually laughed, the first real laugh she could recall since she was a girl.

"Nice try." She shook her head. "No, you won't. This isn't your life. Moon Ranch wasn't your life either. Get it into your thick head—you're not part of my life."

"I'm more than happy to butt out if you promise me to do that—have a life. Come back with me to San Francisco and simply think about it. I promise I won't bother you again."

Pam frowned as she blinked in thought, and Colleen thought for one hopeful, ecstatic moment that she might just acquiesce. But when Pam spoke, her words were eerily calm.

"I appreciate your concern. And that's why I'm not going to call the guards on you now. Do you have any idea what they'd do to you?"

"I don't care, Pam."

"They'd kill you. They've done it before."

A shudder ran down Colleen's spine.

"Pam," she said. "Come home with me."

"*What* home?"

A third slice.

Pamela spoke: "You need to leave now, Mom, before they find you. Leave now, and let me live my life. Please."

As ridiculous as it sounded, Pam's words were words of encouragement to Colleen's twisted heart. Because Pam cared enough to spare her.

"Can I have a hug before I go, Pam? I did come four thousand miles."

Pamela's face softened a millimeter. "I have to get back. We have to make our preparations for tomorrow."

To hike up Tungurahua. Become an offering.

Colleen came over, wrapped her arms around her daughter's stiff shoulders.

"I love you, Pam," she whispered. "Ever since I first saw you. I always will."

Pam's shoulders eased as she hopefully took in Colleen's words. "You better leave now. They're going to wonder where I am."

Colleen let go, stood back at arm's length, her vision smearing with tears. There was nothing else to say. She wiped her eyes, watched her only child turn, walk through the trees, disappear into the rain forest as tanager birds sang.

CHAPTER THIRTY-EIGHT

Colleen headed into the trees with a broken heart, leaving Verligting behind her. She simply couldn't change Pamela's mind.

Not today at least.

But she still had one more day before Die Kerk were to begin their "offerings." And she was damned if she was going to let her only child literally throw her life away.

She'd head back to Baños, notify the military about Die Kerk's planned activity tomorrow. Surely, they would intervene. And, if not, she would—somehow.

She picked up her backpack she had hidden behind a tree and made her way down the mountain, tracking the dirt road but staying off of it, flanking one side. The sun was breaking through the tree canopy, cutting the darkness of the woods with slices of daylight.

That's when she saw something. Someone.

She ducked below a clump of foliage. Peered back over the top.

Two men wearing black berets. Carrying rifles. One was at the gate. The other was patrolling along the fence. Both were looking her way. She was obscured by underbrush and trees, but she had no doubt they had spotted her. Her pulse raced.

"*Wie gaan daarheen?*" one shouted. It sounded like the Afrikaans equivalent of *who goes there?*

She drew her knife, for all it was worth. A knife against two guns. "*Wie gaan daarheen? Wys jouself!*"

She stayed low, the wind picking up, rushing up through the trees.

The two men spoke in low tones to each other.

She stayed put.

A rifle shot rang out, echoing up the hillside toward her. Then another. A bullet zinged a rock nearby. Her back tightened.

The shots grew closer. Bushes rustled. The two men were coming her way.

Another shot tore leaves off a bush next to her.

Colleen got down on her stomach, knife in hand, crawled for a tree farther away from the road. Shots popped.

How she wished she had a gun.

She could hear them talking quietly in Afrikaans. Getting closer. Her heart pounded.

She needed to create a diversion.

She reached the tree, got up into a crouch. She was at the top of a steep incline, the one she had scaled on her way up a couple of days ago. About twenty yards down was the ridge of stone she had clambered over. Beyond that more steep hill. She slipped the backpack off her shoulders, went through it, pulling her emergency cash and her binoculars. Her passport and most of her money was already in the pockets of her jeans. She fastened the bag back up, stood behind the tree, peered out, eyed the hill below as another shot rang out.

Lifted her backpack over her head. She hated to lose it but it would only slow her down, especially when she got to the barbwire fence down the hill.

With all her might, she hurled the bag high toward the huge rock.

It bounced and picked up speed, crashing down the hill through the foliage. Just what she wanted, the sound of a person rushing down the hill.

"*Sy het so gegaan!*" one of the men shouted.

She heard them thrash through the bushes toward the fallen backpack, shouting in Afrikaans. They came into view down the ridge, heading for the rock. One stopped to fire his weapon at an imaginary suspect.

Heart pulsing, knife in hand, Colleen kept low, crouch-ran in the opposite direction, headed for the dirt road. She would be more visible but she'd make better time and the men were well out of the way now.

At the road she cut a sharp left, downhill, picking up speed on the flatter surface. Headed for the gate. Heard them shouting at her, off in the thick of foliage, fifty yards away.

She reached the tube gate, down the hill a ways from the compound. Barbwire on top. She wouldn't be climbing over.

She got down flat, shimmied through the bottom bars, squeezing herself through as two more shots echoed. One dinged the metal gate. Shaking, her legs seemed to take forever to pull through, especially with her still tender shin.

But, finally, she cleared the gate. Scrambled up, in a squat, off road again, raising up, running downhill, watching where she put her feet. But making good time now.

Another shot cracked out. But further in the distance. Their voices were indistinct. She'd shaken them. She gave a massive exhalation of relief as she slowed down to a trot.

She swung back onto the dirt road where she could make better time, kept jogging until she reached the two-lane highway along the river. Gasping for air, sweating, she sheathed the knife, turned uphill, back towards Baños. A good twenty-five kilometers. She needed to flag a ride before the Kerkers sent out a search party. But she was off their property.

By the time she reached the waterfall where she had rebuffed the truck driver, she found a couple of vehicles parked. Sightseers. She stopped for a moment, removed the knife in its scabbard from her belt, tucked the scabbard in her right hiking boot. Awkward but no one was likely to give her a ride with a knife showing.

She asked the sightseers in Spanish whether anyone was headed to Baños. No luck. She ran back to the road. Couldn't run quite as fast with the damn knife in her boot. If it got to be a problem, she'd have to toss it.

Not long after, she heard a large vehicle groaning up the mountain. She spun.

A beer truck crawled around the corner.

She stuck her thumb out. If he didn't stop, she'd jump on the back of the thing anyway. He was going slowly enough.

She cupped her hands around her mouth and shouted in Spanish that she was headed to Baños. That he didn't have to stop, lose his momentum, she could jump on board.

He gave a thumbs-up, shifted down, slowing the truck. She dashed over, climbed up on the running board, got into the truck as he shifted back up.

She needed to get hold of the military before Die Kerk headed up to Tungurahua tomorrow.

CHAPTER THIRTY-NINE

It was early evening by the time Colleen finally reached the Church of the Virgin of the Holy Water in Baños. With the sun down, the north side of Tungurahua's crest glowed pink above town. If it hadn't been so threatening, it would have been beautiful.

It was cold, and she did up her jacket. She was hungry. But that was the least of her worries.

A big soldier standing guard in front of the church had his rifle slung over his shoulder like a toy, barrel pointed to the ground. She asked where she could find the officer in charge of the evacuation.

He told her she would have to come back in the morning.

"Too late," she said. "Die Kerk is planning to come en masse to the volcano tomorrow. Hundreds of people. Many will die."

He called his superior on a radio. A crackled conversation ensued. When he was done, he told her she would need an escort to see Lieutenant Colonel Martinez. And that would take time.

"How much time?" she asked.

"I wish I could tell you. Everyone is tied up at the moment."

"Please just tell me where I can find Lieutenant Colonel Martinez."

He stood, blinking, eyeing her.

"I'm not going to mention how I found out," she said.

He directed her to a hotel near the police station, about six blocks into town.

She thanked him, dashed through the twilight streets. Few people were out, the odd soldier. Everything was dark, shut down.

The hotel was a stately old colonial building across from a park. A generator chugged. It had power. She pleaded her case with a soldier at the door who got hold of Lieutenant Colonel Martinez's adjutant. She waited in a narrow old tile lobby, cool and musty, visited the restroom, drank deeply from the faucet, rinsed her grubby face and hands, tucked in her shirt, pulled her hair into some semblance of normalcy with her fingers.

She met the lieutenant colonel's aide, a slender man with dark eyebrows. He told her to wait while he went and spoke with Lieutenant Colonel Martinez.

In the hall, the hotel staff eyed her warily. She was a sweaty mess and disheveled to boot. Plus, she wasn't local.

The secretary returned.

"This way."

She was shown into the hotel restaurant where the only patron was the lieutenant colonel finishing dinner at a table facing the entrance. The waiter was taking away an empty dessert plate. The officer, a man in his fifties with a fresh haircut, wore a smart uniform jacket and tie. He was lighting a cigar. A snifter of brandy and a cup of espresso sat on the white tablecloth before him. When he saw Colleen, he stood and asked her to sit down, despite her bedraggled appearance.

She sat. Her stomach rumbled as she eyed the bread rolls in the basket.

"I am told you have new information regarding Die Kerk," he said, sipping coffee. She would have loved a cup of coffee. And a meal. Or two. But she pushed ahead, told him about the imminent suicides.

He set his cigar in an ashtray. "You attended one of Die Kerk's sermons?" he said, incredulity creeping into his voice.

"Yes. I heard all this firsthand—from Brother Adem himself. Two days ago. At Verligting."

"Are you a member of the church?" he asked cautiously.

"Not at all. My daughter is."

"And you came all the way from the United States to find her?"

"To rescue her before it's too late. She's going to die, along with many others if something isn't done." She described how the volcano was an opportunity for the church to sacrifice members—*vroulike offers*—to an angry god.

He relit his cigar, took a puff. "It's not that I don't sympathize with your situation. But my men are busy clearing out Baños."

"We're talking about a minimum of twenty-two deaths tomorrow," she reminded him. "There will most likely be more. And, if Die Kerk aren't stopped, many more down the road."

"*Possibly,*" Martinez said, tapping ash. "We're also talking about a bizarre sect living in the jungle. Foreigners who have fired shots at our people—citizens who need my immediate help. I have my orders. And less than half a battalion to carry them out. It's a matter of priorities. I can't divert precious resources to save some crazed suicide cult bent on their own destruction." He frowned, took a puff on his cigar. "And who knows—these Kerkers may not even go through with it. Meanwhile, the volcano is a real threat to the city. It continues to get worse up there."

"How is it going to look when people jump to their deaths on your watch? Most of them *norteamericanas*?"

He blinked in sympathy. "I'm afraid that is a risk we will have to take."

"When the worst happens, the international media will put you—and your superiors—under the magnifying glass. There will be inquiries by the American government."

"Are you threatening me?"

"With a few men, you can stop this from happening."

He sighed. He was a decent man, just one under pressure.

"Isn't there any way you can send a small contingent up there with me?" she asked. "A few men? Think of what you'll be preventing."

Lieutenant Colonel Martinez set his cigar down.

"Let me see what I can do," he said. "No promises."

A wave of relief washed over her.

"Thank you," she said. "*Thank you.*"

CHAPTER FORTY

Several hundred yards from the summit, Tungurahua glowed, lighting up the night sky for a moment before disappearing into a cloud of ashy fog. Colleen and half a dozen Ecuadorian soldiers negotiated the rocky path above the tree line, this side of the mountain, safe from the worst of the eruption. At fifteen thousand feet they puffed thin air, having hiked for much of the afternoon. Muscles were sore. The reek of sulfur was persistent. Near the top the wind grew bitter, whipping up the mountain. The ground was muddy as they plodded, much of the snow cover having melted due to the heat of the volcano.

"I didn't expect it to be cold," she said to Marcos, one of the soldiers, puffing along behind her. He had grown up in the area, a Mestizo boy with smooth Indian features. "The air is sucked into the crater, like a fireplace," he said.

They saw no lava yet. Marcos said most of it ran on the western side. They were on the east.

"What about in there?" Colleen asked, nodding at the crater.

"A different story," Marcos said. "Hot. Hotter than a sauna."

Colleen stopped, caught her breath. Up above, toward the rim of the Throat of Fire, they saw no one. Where was Die Kerk?

"I don't get it," Colleen said, lapsing into English for a moment. She repeated it in Spanish. "Die Kerk said *today*."

"Maybe the *volcanarios* are waiting for a complete eruption," Marcos said, bracing his leg on the mountainside, leaning into it.

"A wasted trip," the lieutenant said, catching up. He was a slender man in a flat top military cap with the country's coat of arms on the front. His face shone from the climb from Baños. Behind him the rest of the men grunted their way up the winding path. Moods were mixed, between those cautious of a potential clash with armed sect members, to those concerned about heading into the mouth of a volcano due to erupt. As they drew closer, with no Kerkers in sight, they seemed more worried about the latter.

"I heard Brother Adem with my own ears," Colleen said to the lieutenant. "Tonight's the night."

"You heard an insane man make a wild statement at a sermon in order to motivate his flock."

"Today is the twenty-second of November," she said. "It's a significant date. There are twenty-two females for the first offering. Adem Lea is Angel 22. Numerology plays an important role in what they do. They'll be here."

The lieutenant shook his head. "We have work to do." He turned to the men. "Five minutes!" he shouted. "Then we head back to Baños."

The men stood at ease, one even breaking out cigarettes at this altitude.

Colleen lifted the binoculars from her neck. Turned, fixed them beyond the twin towers of the Church of the Virgin of the Holy Water two miles away. Past town. In the direction of Verligting. She scanned the black horizon. Back and forth for the next several minutes.

Nothing.

How could she have been so wrong?

"We need to head back," the lieutenant said.

Colleen scoured the darkness down the mountain. Nothing. East now. Toward the river that ran to Mera, where the waterfall was, the dark terrain bouncing through the lenses.

Dots of light swam through her binoculars as she searched. She stopped, shifted back.

Sparkles. She tightened the focus.

"I think we have company, Lieutenant," Colleen said, handing the lieutenant her field glasses. She pointed down the mountain.

With a frown he took the binos. Put them up to his face.

"Those are torches," she said.

"You're right," he said, adjusting the focus. "You are right."

*   *   *

"They're getting closer," the lieutenant said, looking through his own field glasses now. "Quite a number judging by the number of torches."

"About half of Verligting, I would say," Colleen said. It would have taken all day to hike here. They were still a couple of miles away.

"And only six of us." The lieutenant turned to one of the men, his hand out. "Give me the radio. We're going to need reinforcements."

*   *   *

It took well over an hour for the Kerkers to arrive, taking the same path the soldiers had to the summit, on the undisturbed side of the mountain. Torches led the way. The time felt like an eternity, Colleen wondering if Pamela was in the procession—she most likely was—and what was going through her mind right now. Hoping she could read her mother's thoughts, her distant plea.

Through the binoculars, Colleen spotted Brother Adem at the front of the line, several hundred yards away, sitting on the shoulders of a big man with a beard in black leather, who carried him like a child. Adem wore a rain poncho and a white surgical face mask. Several men in black berets walked on either side, some with face masks, all armed with rifles. Here and there along the line of people, rifle barrels poked out as well. Some members wore hooded ponchos in the cold.

"Quite a few guns," Colleen said to the lieutenant, who was watching as well through his field glasses. "There were about thirty guards at the camp. Not all of the camp is here but much of it is."

The lieutenant nodded silently as he scanned the approaching line. The soldiers were obscured in shadows. The Kerkers would not be expecting anyone waiting for them. But the numbers were not good for a potential conflict.

The group drew closer and they could hear them chanting in Afrikaans, low and guttural. Colleen shuddered at their tone, primitive and forbidding. Death held a power that overcame anything else.

"*Dios mío*," one of the soldiers said. Another mumbled in agreement.

And then, to her dismay, Colleen saw Pamela, walking behind Brother Adem with the twenty-two women, all in white robes. In the light of the torches, Colleen saw Pam's red hair tied up with a garland. Her face was as pale as her gown, as if anticipating the death that awaited her. Colleen's temple pulsed with worry. Her only child. How could she have let this happen? Her eyelid flickered. She needed to keep her wits about her. *Control, stay in control.*

Other members trailed behind, dressed in this and that, more ponchos, more face masks against the sting of sulfur.

Colleen lowered her field glasses, turned to the lieutenant. "Can't we do anything?"

He lowered his binoculars, frowned. "We need reinforcements."

"But that might take hours."

"If it even happens." He motioned to the men. "Fall back!" They shifted to one side, with only a small rise to protect them. They waited while the group approached. Behind them, the wind shifted for a moment and they heard the volcano pop and hiss.

The procession stopped when they saw Colleen and the soldiers over the rise. No one moved.

The lieutenant strode out partway, shouted to Brother Adem in Spanish. "You are not permitted up the mountain. Turn around and go back the way you came." He switched to passable English and repeated his command.

No one moved.

"Pamela!" Colleen yelled. "Just leave! Go! *Please!*"

Pamela, clearly surprised, looked her way. Then she turned away, a troubled look on her face.

A murmur of discussion between Brother Adem and his immediate men followed. The nerves along Colleen's spine tingled.

They pressed forward.

"They're not leaving," the lieutenant said.

She hadn't really expected them to. "Can't anything be done, Lieutenant?"

The lieutenant took a deep breath.

"Ready arms, men," he said tightly.

The soldiers spread out, unslinging their rifles.

"There are hundreds of them," one soldier said.

"Not all of them are armed," Colleen said. "Just the guards."

"Go back!" the lieutenant shouted again at Brother Adem. "Or you will be placed under arrest."

Brother Adem barked an order to his people. His "mount" fell back, presumably for Adem's protection. He was swallowed up in the crowd.

A number of Kerkers in black berets emerged from the group, rifles raised. They opened fire. The pop of gunshots broke the air amid the rush of wind. Colleen dropped to the muddy ground, as did the soldiers, getting into prone position, rifles ready.

"Return fire!" the lieutenant shouted.

Shots cracked the air, carrying on the wind. Although they were horizontal, the squad was partially exposed on the rise. Colleen prayed Pam was not in range.

Die Kerk returned a barrage of gunfire.

One of the soldiers shouted in pain, grabbed his side, slumped into a heap.

"Fall back!" the lieutenant shouted to his men, waving his pistol.

Unarmed, there was nothing Colleen could do apart from help another soldier drag the fallen man back to safety. Once out of the way, his head slumped lifelessly. The soldier who had helped her crossed himself. Colleen said a silent prayer, the soldier's death drenching her with guilt. She noticed that the dead man carried a sidearm in a holster. She unholstered his pistol, a Walther PP, stuck it in the waistband of her Levi's. The other soldier eyed her.

Brother Adem's men kept firing, pinning them down as the procession filed past up the mountain. The best the soldiers could do was to hold off in a fallback position. Covered by the gunmen, the Kerkers proceeded up to the crater. Finally, the gunmen retreated up the rear of the line as well, falling in with the group. They shouted in Afrikaans and it was clear they were not in the least concerned with the consequences of their actions. People embracing death had advantages others did not.

Colleen's thoughts were riveted on Pamela as she watched the Kerkers wind up to the crest into the red glare through ashy fog.

"Now what?" she asked the lieutenant after he radioed in his status. One man dead, another possibly wounded.

"Still waiting for reinforcements. And a medic. The good news is that they are on their way. I requested four squads, but we'll take whatever we get."

"Hours?"

"Possibly." He chewed his lip. "But I did request air support."

Colleen felt a jolt of encouragement. "I didn't know you had any."

"We have two helicopters available for emergency evacuations. Who knows? Perhaps we'll get one."

In the meantime, Brother Adem and his flock were determined to continue their death ritual.

Colleen couldn't wait.

"I want to thank you and your men for your support, Lieutenant. Can one of them please lend me a poncho?" She wanted to blend in with the Kerkers.

"No," the lieutenant said, shaking his head. "Out of the question. You are *not* going up there alone."

"I'm afraid so. My daughter's up there."

"I simply can't allow it."

"I'm not holding you responsible for my safety," she said. "But I have to do whatever I can before something happens to her."

"Wait for reinforcements," he said.

"I don't have that kind of time."

He gave a sigh that became a nod. "Very well. I'll radio in again. Stress that the situation is dire."

"I appreciate it," she said.

Marcos stood forward, holding out a green poncho. She thanked him, took it, slipped it on.

"I can go with her, Lieutenant," Marcos offered.

"You will do nothing of the kind," the lieutenant said. "We've already lost one man. We'll wait for reinforcements. That's an order."

"Yes, sir," Marcos said reluctantly.

Colleen thanked Marcos, headed off, poncho flapping. Hoping that Pamela might come to her senses.

CHAPTER FORTY-ONE

The stench of sulfur and smoking earth stung Colleen's nostrils as she approached the summit. Smoke smarted her eyes. Close to the rim, she heard the groaning of the volcano over the chanting of voices.

Finally, she reached the top, peered over the lip of the crater. Hundreds of Kerkers stood on a huge shelf of earth facing a chasm on the other side churning orange. Her face warmed, even from where Colleen stood, like standing too close to a campfire.

Torches blazed.

The Kerkers sang in Afrikaans, low and dissonant.

She pulled the poncho's hood over her head, drew the pistol from her waistband, racked it, which cocked the hammer back. The gun hidden in her poncho, she made her way down the short incline into the crater to join the group.

Brother Adem sat on the shoulders of the large bearded man adorned in black leather, their backs to the cauldron, facing the crowd. His surgical face mask was down below his neck.

The Kerkers were in a state of euphoria, standing in an arc around him. Twenty-two women in white stood off to the one side, closer to the pit. Colleen couldn't see their faces yet, tell which one was Pamela.

Colleen scrambled down the inside of the rim, joined the congregation along the edge. Chanted along. Gun at her side under her poncho, she wormed her way through the crowd. Jostled behind the front row. The hissing lava in the basin was mesmerizing, a sea of boiling rock. Waves of heat wafted from the pit, like a giant sauna.

The women in white robes stood in line along a length of rock jutting out. Their gowns clung to their bodies with sweat. Their faces were feverish and pink.

With a shock, Colleen spotted Pamela in the line. Pamela's eyes were closed in calm resignation.

In the face of her daughter just turned twenty, Colleen saw the face of an eight-year-old child broken by a father who had taken her innocence. Pamela had never recovered, no matter what she thought; she continued to follow men who lied and captivated and used her, each one progressively worse. Her father. The biker in Santa Cruz. Fletcher at Moon Ranch. And now Brother Adem, enticing women to their deaths to feed his sick ego.

Adem spoke to the crowd in solemn tones Colleen could not understand. The group responded with mumbled song. The other side of the crater responded, hissing, belching up a chunk of white rock that fell back into the pit, leaving a white arc of light.

Brother Adem gave a command and the women turned, formed a single line, pointing at the fire.

Lining up to jump. Pamela was third.

Colleen felt her stomach tighten.

From the front of the crowd, a drumbeat thumped, slow and steady.

Under her poncho, she had her pistol ready.

Brother Adem squeezed his knees together, commanding his human steed to bend down. Adem dismounted. The big man in leather stood to one side.

Brother Adem strode over to the line of women.

"*Vroue, berei jou voor vir die perfekte dood.*"

Colleen understood the last phrase well enough: *perfekte dood*—perfect death.

"*Ursula,*" he said.

The first woman in line closed her eyes, made a sign of prayer with her hands, pressed them together, released them, straightened them by her side.

She broke into a sprint.

Then, like a swimmer off a diving board, she leapt into the cistern of lava.

There was brief silence, followed by a high-pitched scream.

The crowd chanted.

Perfeksie!

Brother Adem nodded with satisfaction, spoke in Afrikaans.

Colleen had to act soon, or her daughter would follow.

She saw Pamela, second in line, her eyes clenched shut, her face a mask of fear and uncertainty. Thank God for her indecision. Colleen only prayed it wasn't too late.

Colleen realized that what she was about to do would probably end in her own death. But so be it. Over ten years ago, she had let her anger take priority. Now Pamela would.

Brother Adem was speaking. She could make out the words "vroulike offer."

Pistol under the poncho, Colleen pushed through the front line, marched quickly out toward Brother Adem.

"*Wat maak jy?*" someone said. It sounded like *where are you going*?

She dashed behind Brother Adem on the ledge. It was feverishly hot on her back. One or two more members raised questions in Afrikaans.

Brother Adem turned, looked at Colleen in surprise.

"*Wat dink jy doen jy?*"

She brought the gun up fast, amidst the gasp of the crowd, pointed it at his head.

His mouth dropped.

She clinched her free arm around his neck, tightened the gun on Brother Adem's temple.

"There's been a change of plans," she shouted.

CHAPTER FORTY-TWO

The Kerkers stood along the ledge inside the crater of the volcano, staring in disbelief at Colleen holding the pistol to their leader's head. For her part, Colleen stayed well behind Brother Adem, using him as a shield, one arm around his neck. He wasn't any taller than she was. Up close he reeked. The pit of lava behind bathed her back in heat. The molten rock whistled and popped.

"What do you think you're doing?" Brother Adem said to her in trembling English.

"Exactly what it looks like," Colleen said.

"You're insane," he gulped.

"*I'm* insane? Oh, that's good." She had been worried Brother Adem might take a nihilistic view of his own existence and actually welcome death in whatever form it took, and that this intervention would be worthless but, as it turned out, when push finally came to shove, survival was the first thing on his mind.

She saw Pamela, second in line to jump. Her mouth was agape as she looked at this woman in the hood, unaware that it was her mother holding Brother Adem hostage.

Brother Adem shouted out a command in Afrikaans to his people, reverberating in Colleen's ears. She gathered it was along the lines of "stop this person."

Several men in black berets stepped forward, rifles at the ready. A shot rang out.

Colleen held the pistol up alongside Brother Adem's head, fired into the ashy cloud. Her hand jolted with the shot, which cracked the air next to her and Brother Adem, making him flinch. Her own ear buzzed as well.

The guards stopped in their tracks. Noise and commotion broke out amongst the ranks.

"One step further and Brother Adem dies!" Colleen shouted, the tip of the gun barrel to his temple again. Brother Adem shook with fear and the disorientation of the shot. She realized that if he called her bluff and his men charged her, she'd have to shoot Brother Adem, whose head was inches from her own. She'd be covered in brains and blood, and then they'd kill her. Pamela's death would follow. She couldn't let that happen.

"Tell them to stop," she instructed Brother Adem between her teeth.

Brother Adem shouted for the gunmen to desist.

The crowd froze. A momentary feeling of relief washed over her.

"The military is on their way," Colleen yelled. "Reinforcements have been called. You have two options: stay here and take your chances with the soldiers, or leave now, and hope you get down the mountain before they arrive."

Members watched, uncertain, fearful.

Gun to Brother Adem's head, Colleen released her grip on him for a moment, pulled her hood back.

Pamela stood forward, mouth open, blinking in disbelief. Her white robe loosened from her sweat-steeped body, blew in the breeze.

"You have no right to do this!" she shouted. "*No right!*"

"I'm sorry, Pamela," Colleen said. "But all the same, I'm doing it. It's over. Please! Stop this madness."

Pamela shook, her teeth clenched with rage. Her eyes shut tight and Colleen sensed her frustration, her humiliation at her mother's interference. This kind of thing was not covered in Parenting 101.

"You can't stop us from jumping!" she yelled.

"You're absolutely right," Colleen said. "But the next person who does is responsible for Brother Adem's death." She pressed the gun tight to his temple, making him recoil.

"Stop!" Brother Adem yelled. "Don't jump, children!"

"There are hundreds of us," someone said. "And only one of you. We can easily overpower you."

"And Brother Adem can just as easily die," Colleen said.

Brother Adem was shaking in her clenched arm.

"And I don't think he wants that," she said. She spoke to Brother Adem. "Do you?"

"No," he said in an unsteady voice.

"Then tell them it's over, Brother Adem. Tell them to disperse. Now."

Brother Adem began to speak in Afrikaans. She cinched his neck. "In *English*!"

"Do as she says, my children," he said in a wavering voice. "Return to Verligting. We'll regroup there. Tonight is not the night for perfection."

The man in black leather, who had been Brother Adem's "horse," stood forward.

"But, Brother Adem, is this not the most perfect death? The one you have always spoken of?"

"No, Haven," Brother Adem said. "A perfect death is one of our choosing—not one thrust upon us."

"But, Brother, if you stay and die, rather than leave, is that not of your own choosing?"

"Get out of that one," Colleen whispered to Brother Adem, her arm tight around his neck.

"It is not my time!" Brother Adem shouted. "I still have much to do."

"Not your time, Adem?" Pamela shouted, squinting, taking another step forward. "What do you mean—*not your time*?"

"I must guide all the flocks to perfection before I go to mine," Adem said in a voice that shook. Colleen felt him tremble in her grasp. "In multiples of eleven, remember? You are only the first of many. There will be more. Many more."

Colleen watched her daughter's face as it shifted into a suspicious grimace.

"You're a coward," Pamela said to Brother Adem. "Nothing but a coward."

"No, Fenna, you misunderstand, child. There are still many to make the journey. My role is to guide you to Verligting, then here, to perfection. Only when that work is finally done will it be my turn."

Colleen spoke: "Wise up, people. The way Brother Adem is playing this, it will never be his turn. He'll die an old man in his sleep while you jump to yours now. That will be his perfect death."

She watched several faces turn to doubt.

Then, over the ridge, they heard the *wup-wup-wup* of helicopter blades.

"What's that?" someone said.

"You can stay and face the soldiers," Colleen shouted, the gun still to Brother Adem's head. "Or you can leave now."

The arrival of the soldiers changed many moods.

"The military," one man said, turning. "I'm leaving."

"Where are you going, Brother?" Brother Adem said.

"I'm leaving, too," said another.

More members left, climbing over the rim, disappearing into the darkness. Guards surrounded the group loosely, many of whom stood by, watching in doubt. Some wandered about, as if lost.

The helicopter came into view, blades spinning with the reflection of the lava, blowing hot air and dirt far and wide. Then the aircraft lowered out of sight, settling on the other side of the crest somewhere.

More members scrambled over the rim.

Pamela stood, looking askance at Colleen and Brother Adem.

"What are you going to do now?" Pamela asked her.

"Wait until you leave, Pamela," Colleen said.

"And what makes you so sure I *will*?"

"Because you figured it out, Pamela. You need something in your life but it's not Brother Adem." *Thank God.*

People were frantically pushing to get over the crest, back down the mountain. They could hear soldiers over the ridge yelling.

Brother Adem was shouting at the fleeing Kerkers desperately in an apparent bid for unity.

Soon, less than a few dozen of the former members remained, surrounded by guards. Some followers began chanting in Afrikaans. Others simply did not seem to know what to do next. But for many, unlike the volcano, their fire had been extinguished.

More soldiers appeared over the ridge, rifles poised. People fleeing were ignored. The lieutenant instructed his men to disarm the Die Kerk guards and break up the group that was chanting. One Kerker guard shouted and a shot rang out, but soldiers quickly circled him, separating him from the pack. Another man flung his rifle aside, turned, and ran for the pit, leapt in, screaming as he plunged to his death. Colleen shuddered.

It took several minutes for the soldiers to subdue the crowd and disarm them.

The lieutenant approached Colleen, along with two men, one of them Marcos.

"One other woman jumped to her death as well," Colleen said in Spanish.

"Not your daughter, I hope?"

"Thankfully, no," Colleen said, nodding at Pamela, standing by, then at Brother Adem, still in her clinch. "Here's your instigator. If he had had his way, many would be dead. With many more to follow."

Colleen released Brother Adem.

"Take this man into custody," the lieutenant said to Marcos. "He is responsible for the death of one of my men." More Die Kerkers were slipping away, including guards now, eager to avoid arrest.

"We will need you to make a statement," the lieutenant said to Colleen.

"Of course. Tomorrow?"

"Yes. Do you have somewhere to stay?"

Colleen shook her head.

"At the very worst, you can probably stay at the church."

"That works for me. I'm just so grateful to you and your men for helping save my daughter. I'm so sorry you lost a man."

The soldiers cuffed Brother Adem's hands behind his back.

"I demand a lawyer!" he shouted in English.

"All in good time," the lieutenant said in English. "This isn't the United States."

They left, taking Brother Adem with them. Less than a handful of Die Kerkers remained, singing softly. Soldiers herded them away from the edge of the volcano.

Thankfully, Pamela was still there. She seemed to be waiting for Colleen.

The relief Colleen felt was immeasurable. Whatever happened next, Pam had been spared from immediate danger.

Colleen flicked the safety on her pistol, shoved it down the back of her waistband, went over to Pam. She told herself she was done interfering.

"Where do you go from here, Pamela?"

Pamela gave a heavy sigh. "I don't know," she said. "I don't know."

"Sometimes not knowing what comes next is fine."

"I can't go back to Verligting."

Colleen felt another release of tension. "You don't know how happy I am to hear that."

Pamela shrugged.

"Do you have a passport?" She knew Pam didn't.

Pamela gave a weary shake of the head. "Brother Adem took care of those things."

That sounded about right.

"The embassy in Quito can straighten this out," Colleen said. "Do you have any money?"

Pam replied that she did not.

"I can help," Colleen said.

"No. I don't want a thing from you."

Colleen suppressed the hurt. "No strings, Pam. Just to help get you back . . ."—she almost used the word *home*, but caught herself . . . "to the United States."

Pam stared at the ground. "I don't know."

"You can't stay here, Pam. This isn't your country. They won't let you stay. You've got nowhere to go, no money."

"I'll figure something out."

"Come back with me, Pam," Colleen said. "To San Francisco. I've got a spare room made up for you."

Pamela looked up, eyed her suspiciously. "I'm not so sure."

Colleen put her hands up defensively. "No strings."

"You keep saying that. But how? How do you figure? With your spare room 'all made up'?"

"Just until you get on your feet, Pam. You've been through hell and back. And a lot of that is because of me."

Pam shook her head. "You don't mean that."

"I'll be honest, there was a time when I wouldn't have. But what happened to you when you were little . . . I should have seen it coming. And I didn't. And I should have reacted differently." Differently than killing Pam's father. "I was wrong. I paid my debt to society—but not to you. Now it's your turn. I want to make it up to you, Pam, if you'll let me. Give me a chance. That's all I'm asking."

"I just want to get away from you."

Those words stung.

Colleen blinked away the beginnings of tears. "Come with me to the church in Baños tonight at least, Pam. We can talk. At least give me that."

Pam sighed. Her face softened. She gave a fragile smile. "I'll come but just until I figure out what I'm going to do next. Don't think this means I'm coming home."

Colleen returned a smile herself. She would take whatever she could get.

"Whatever you want, Pam. Whatever you want."

"Alright, then."

Alright, then. That was all she was going to get for now. But at least her daughter was still part of this world. Not Die Kerk's. Colleen would count her blessings.

"Alright, then, Pamela," she said.

CHAPTER FORTY-THREE

"Pamela—we're back," Colleen said, gently shaking her daughter's shoulder as the jumbo jet skidded on slick runway, late evening, SFO. She caught herself almost adding the word "home."

This was going to be work.

After many hours in the air, they disembarked the 747, with their shared fabric carry bag from the overhead compartment, clothes and toiletries picked up in Quito. Colleen's backpack was on a hill somewhere outside Verligting; Pamela had left her things behind as well.

As they walked up the jetway, Colleen searched Pamela's face for a trace of a smile. Nothing. Too tired, she told herself.

But inside, Colleen was ecstatic. For all they had been through and all the work that lay ahead, her daughter was alive. And they were reunited, in a sense, although that might be pushing things.

And then Colleen saw the newspaper headline, at a stand by the main terminal:

MOSCONE, MILK SLAIN
DAN WHITE IS HELD

Colleen stopped, mouth agape. The mayor—assassinated. As Lucky had predicted.

One of the city supervisors had been shot, too.

But the man being held for the murders was not the supervisor Lucky had warned her about—Jordan Kray. But another one.

She squeezed her eyes shut, reopened them.

The headlines hadn't changed.

They'd been after the wrong man.

CHAPTER FORTY-FOUR

The news left a ringing in Colleen's ears as she stood at the newsstand in SFO. Overhead announcements echoed. Travelers click-clacked through the terminal.

"Is everything okay?" Pamela asked. She wore a simple loose light-blue floral dress, picked up in the market in Quito, and flip-flops. Her pretty red hair had been washed and brushed and, although she was exhausted, the puffiness around her eyes was hidden by large, round sunglasses. Color had returned to her face. She had been sleeping and, although not eating much, thanks to a stomach bug picked up in South America, Colleen was elated with the improvement she saw. The longer she could provide a normal environment for her daughter, the better.

All in good time.

"The news . . ." Colleen said, gesturing at the *Chronicle* headline. She had put the case behind her. It was SFPD's now.

Pamela read the headline.

"Wow," she said.

"*Wow*, is right," Colleen said, not too astonished at her daughter's lack of concern after everything she'd been through. "Come on, let's get you home."

She reached out to take Pamela's hand.

"It's not *home*," Pamela said quietly, and not offering her hand.

Colleen caught her daughter's look of admonishment. "It's just a figure of speech, Pamela," she said, suppressing a sigh. "What I meant was, let's go back to *my place*. Get you settled, get you some rest." She raised her eyebrows. "Sound okay?"

Pamela frowned, nodded. "Okay."

"Okay, then." Colleen let her hand drop. *Don't push. You're here to repair the damage done, not vindicate yourself as a mother.*

It was late evening by the time the Yellow cab dropped them off on Vermont Street. Once upstairs, Pamela immediately ran to the bathroom where she slammed the door and threw up in noisy gasps. What the hell had she picked up?

Pam didn't think she could stomach soup. Colleen found a bottle of Seven Up in the fridge. She fixed Pam a glass. Pam downed it, handed it back.

"I'll pick up some Pepto-Bismol later," Colleen said, "and whatever else might help settle your stomach."

"Ice cream."

"Rocky Road," Colleen said with a little smile, remembering Pam's childhood favorite.

"No. Just vanilla."

"Right," Colleen said. "Why don't you get some sleep?"

Pam didn't seem dissatisfied with the arrangements in the spare room until she saw her old photo in a silver frame on the bedside table. It was a picture of Pam in better days, younger days, before her Goth phase, a young teen with freckles and a rare smile.

"Really?" she said, eyeing Colleen harshly.

Colleen went over to the bedside table, picked the picture up, tucked it under her arm. "Sorry. I've just always loved that picture." It had brought her much comfort in Denver Women's Correctional Facility. If Pam didn't want it, she'd keep it by her bed.

"I just don't want to be crowded," Pamela said.

"Got it," Colleen said, chiding herself. "I'll let you get some rest. I'm in my office. Shout if you need anything. I'll run to the store later."

"Okay."

Okay. By now, Colleen wasn't expecting a *thank you*. She left Pam to sleep and went into her office. Whatever anguish she was experiencing over Pam, bottom line, her daughter was home—yes, *home*—and safe. For the moment. She would look into counseling, whatever it would take for Pam to come back from the nightmare of Die Kerk, but for the time being, baby steps.

And she had that damn Mayor Moscone shooting plaguing her again.

At her desk she lit up the first cigarette in over a week, savored the nicotine rush, sat back, wondering what to do next. Wet fog ran down the window. Out there was a city in disarray, with a dead mayor, and a supervisor being held for his murder.

Lucky's accusation that Shuggy and his biker cronies had discussed Supervisor Jordan Kray shooting the mayor had kicked all of this off. But Supervisor Dan White was the shooter.

What had happened there?

She told herself to let it go, focus on Pam. Sergeant Dwight was handling the case. She'd been instructed to back off.

But Lucky had died for this. And so had the mayor and another supervisor, Harvey Milk.

Lucky had been right to a point. So this whole thing seemed to circle back to Shuggy Johnston.

She tapped ash. Shuggy had some sort of connection with Pamela, back during her Moon Ranch days, when she apparently delivered acid for them, not that long ago. It only seemed like a lifetime ago.

Colleen couldn't exactly ask Pamela right now, sleeping off Montezuma's Revenge, serious jet lag, and a trip to South America with a suicide cult. The two of them were barely on speaking terms to begin with. Pam might be asleep in the next room, but she was a thousand miles away.

Colleen called her answering service.

Two messages from Alex, worried sick about her and Pamela. Alex knew the reason for Colleen's trip to Ecuador. Colleen would call her back at a decent hour.

And one from Sergeant Dwight. But nothing from Inspector Owens, who'd been AWOL for some time now.

Sergeant Dwight wanted to talk to her ASAP. He'd left two numbers.

Even though it was late, she called Matt Dwight at the first number, which she recognized as the home number he'd jotted down on the back of his business card when he first stopped by. No answer. He was most likely working the Mayor Moscone shooting. She called the second number.

But before anyone could answer, Colleen's doorbell rang. She hung up the phone, went over to the front window, looked down onto Vermont Street.

A boxy beige Ford sedan sat double-parked. An unmarked police car.

Maybe it was Matt Dwight. It would make sense he'd want to talk to her with the immediacy of the shooting.

She went to the front door, hit the intercom.

The voice did not belong to Sergeant Dwight.

"This is Inspector Ryan—SFPD Special Operations. We need to talk to you."

An inspector. From the same department Sergeant Dwight reported to. Were SFPD sending in a bigger gun? Since there had been a mistake in the tip? Under the circumstances, she could see it. She buzzed them in, went to quickly check on Pamela. Pam was out like a light, head under the covers. Sleep—the best medicine. Put that damned death church into the past, get over that bug. Colleen pulled the bedroom door gently shut.

Back at the front door, she waited while two pair of feet trudged up the stairs.

Two men appeared.

One was a big, weary-looking, middle-aged man with a five o'clock shadow and a shaggy head of hair, weeks past a haircut, wearing orthopedic shoes and a roomy shapeless tan sport coat with sleeves that were too long. Looking like Fred Flintstone with a mean streak. He was followed by a short wiry bald guy in rimless glasses.

The big man showed his badge. Inspector Ryan.

She stood back, invited them in. "I ask that you guys try to keep it down. My daughter's asleep. We just got back from a trip and she's picked up some kind of stomach bug."

Ryan unveiled a fleshy grimace. "That won't be a problem—because you're coming with us."

Colleen's heart started. She had been the one to bring the matter to SFPD's attention to begin with. Now they wanted her downtown. With Lucky's information only partially right, maybe they were suspicious.

"Why can't we talk here?" she said.

"Because this is a murder investigation," Ryan said. "Now, is that okay with you or should we come back at a more opportune time?" The sarcasm was thick.

So it was going to be like that.

"Why didn't you just say that instead of walking up two flights of stairs?" she said with an edge. The trip hadn't been easy on him.

"Because we had to make sure you wouldn't decide not to come with us." He raised his eyebrows.

"Am I under arrest?"

"Do you want to be?" Inspector Ryan didn't like being questioned.

"If you say I'm not, I'm going to hold you to it. So is my lawyer."

"To hell with your lawyer. The mayor's been shot."

"And where are we going exactly?"

Ryan didn't like that either.

"850," he said.

850 Bryant. Hall of Justice. "How long will I be?"

"That depends on how forthcoming you are. If this is any indication, it could be a while."

"I'm going to get my jacket and leave my daughter a note so she knows where I am."

"Hey, take your time," he said mockingly. "We'll wait."

Colleen scribbled a note for Pamela, while she grabbed the wall phone, shut the kitchen door, called her lawyer. She tucked the note under the sugar bowl and positioned it on the corner of the kitchen counter. Late at night, Gus Pedersen didn't answer. She left a quiet message for Gus on his answering machine, the latest of technical gadgets, and told him when and where she was going and why. She mentioned the inspector's name. Gus knew her situation calling the anonymous tip line and talking to Sergeant Dwight. "I don't like the way this is shaping up," she said softly into the machine. Being an ex-felon, the police tended to think of you in one way.

Inspector Ryan scowled at her on the way out the door.

If there was one thing Colleen disliked, it was riding in the back of a police car. She was taken back to that night in West Denver, 1967, when she called DPD after she buried a screwdriver in her husband's neck and watched him die on the kitchen floor. Afterwards she called her mother to come over and pick up Pam, who was eight at the time, and when that was done, she called the police and turned herself in. Served close to ten years of a fourteen-year sentence.

And here she was again, trying to take care of Pam, being carted off by the police.

They drove in silence for a couple of blocks, the little man at the wheel peering over the top of it.

"What's the latest in the mayor's assassination?" Colleen asked as they bounced over the pothole she always avoided. "And the supervisor—Harvey Milk?"

The two cops looked at each other but said nothing. The silence was deafening. She realized it was also part of the treatment.

Then, she noticed they turned right on Potrero, rather than left.

"I thought you said '850,'" she said, as they headed south.

No answer.

Her heart thrummed. But they were playing her. The trick was to stay cool.

They bounced down Potrero onto 101 South, picking up speed, getting off shortly at Alemany Boulevard. The farmers market was nothing but desolate concrete stalls, shut for the night, next to a grim section of public housing. All jammed by the freeway at the bottom of the hill. Not the San Francisco in the postcards.

They pulled into the farmers market. Not many vehicles, and most of them not anything anyone would care about. The little man drove them to the very back of the lot, into the shadows of a fishmonger's truck. He stopped, set the brake, shut off the ignition.

The door locks clicked shut.

Colleen wasn't going to rattle, but her heart was thumping nicely. They were a long way from people who would give a damn about the police roughing up a suspect.

"Anyone bring a deck of cards?" she said.

No answer.

Inspector Ryan turned in the front passenger seat to Colleen, his arm over the back. With his bulk it was an effort for him. Even so, he was intimidating in the semi-darkness, his heavy face jowled with antagonism.

"Why did you tell Sergeant Dwight that Jordan Kray was gonna be the shooter?" he said.

So that's what this was about. "Because that's what I heard."

"From who?"

"Herman Waddell."

"Where can we find this Herman Waddell?"

"The morgue—if he hasn't received a county burial."

"He's dead?"

"That's generally how you get to the morgue," she said.

Ryan smirked. "So why didn't you tell Dwight about Herman Waddell?"

She actually had. Maybe Matt didn't write it down. Respectful of her concern for Lucky's privacy perhaps. "My client was worried his real name might get him in trouble." As it turned out, for good reason.

"That wasn't your call."

"Client privilege," she said. "He was staying in a flop hotel in a room next door to the characters originally throwing Jordan Kray's name around." She told Ryan about Shuggy and his two biker friends. "You really need to talk to Dwight," she said. It was Dwight's investigation. She wasn't going to get Matt into trouble, Ryan being a superior. "The same people are the ones who beat Luck to death."

"*Luck?*" Ryan said.

"Herman Waddell."

Ryan nodded; his bottom lip pursed. "How did this Shuggy and his friends get Jordan Kray's name?"

"Good question. You should ask him. I was instructed to stay away from the case."

"How many times have you met with Sergeant Dwight?"

They could find that out. But again, Dwight might have had a reason to keep things confidential. Maybe he didn't trust them. She certainly didn't. And they didn't seem to trust him either. Dwight might be under the microscope for appearing to drop the ball on the mayor shooting.

"I met him twice," Colleen said. "Once when he came by my place, introduced himself. Again at a bar where we touched base."

"And how did you come by Dwight in the first place?"

She told him about calling the anonymous tip line, then calling Inspector Owens.

"Why Owens?"

"I know him. I wanted to make sure it got looked into. I wasn't convinced the anonymous tip would be acted upon."

"Why?"

She weighed her words. "Because SFPD doesn't always have the most stellar image of following through."

The little guy gave a quiet harrumph and shot her an accusing look in the rearview mirror. Ryan's eyes narrowed. "What else?"

She told him about the neo-Nazi Klan party, Dr. Lange and Doris Pender.

"So you went to this Klan thing, even after you were told to stay off the case?"

"Lucky died on my watch. I wanted to find his killer. At the event, one of Shuggy's buddies pretty much said they did it—the little troll who calls himself Ace. Plus, I'm not crazy about Nazis and Klansmen in general—especially when they want to shoot the mayor. Call me sentimental." She wasn't going to share her concern about Pam and Shuggy. Pam was her business.

With some effort, Ryan dug out a business card. "If Dwight contacts you again, you call me right away. Got that?"

She took the card. They *didn't* trust Dwight.

"Lucky's information was close," she said. "Maybe the shooter and whoever he's connected with are smarter than we thought. Used Jordan Kray's name as an alternative when they really meant the real shooter—Dan White."

"Maybe you think too much," Ryan said.

"Maybe you're not thinking enough," she said. "Focusing on one of your own instead of the shooter."

"Right now, we're focusing on you. And information you sat on."

"I was told to stay off the case. I've been out of the country."

"We don't have to go easy on you, you know."

"What are you going to do—beat me up, leave me in some godforsaken parking lot by the projects? You could barely get up the stairs to my flat."

"We know all about you," Ryan said quietly. "Murdered your ex. We know your type."

A shudder went through Colleen. They were making this personal. But it wouldn't do to appear intimidated. "An ex-cop shoots the mayor and you guys spend your time harassing the citizen who tried to warn you. Why don't you find the people who did this? You can start with Shuggy Johnston and his pals. I think you'll find they're the ones who killed Lucky, too. Maybe it will lead to Dr. Lange. If you need any more help, let me know." She reached for the car door handle.

The door was locked. More pressure. Her pulse tightened.

"Let me out," she said.

"You get out when we say you do."

"I called my lawyer right before we left the house. Told him where I was going, who I was with. You said 850 Bryant. But you drove me down here instead. If I'm not home soon, safe and sound, he's going to file a complaint with SFPD Internal Affairs."

"Bullshit."

She shrugged. "Go ahead—call my bluff. I can sure use the money."

Ryan's eyes became narrow slits. He gave an irritated sigh, nodded at his partner. The little guy hit a button.

With relief, she opened the door. Got out.

Ryan said, "Best watch your step, bitch."

She leaned down, looked into the car.

"You call me 'bitch' like it's a bad thing."

She slammed the door, walked off into the shadows. She had no idea where she was going to find a cab in this neighborhood, this time of night.

* * *

It took a good hour to walk home through some of the city's less desirable neighborhoods. One positive was that she'd walked off a good deal of her nerves and jet lag. Now it was literally the middle of the night.

But now she knew it hadn't been Matt Dwight following her that day when an unmarked car first trailed her through SF up by Sears. It had been Ryan and his accomplice, following. Why?

At home, Pam was still nestled under the covers, seemingly unmoved. Colleen tore up the note she'd left for her under the sugar bowl, made tea, poured a shot of brandy in it, took it into her office overlooking the fog lifting over Potrero, sat down, stretched her legs and back. Everything cracked. She called her answering service.

Mrs. Philanderer wanted a status update. Now. The woman was growing impatient. Colleen made a note to call her first thing. She needed paid work, especially now. She'd been plowing through her finances at a clip. Now she had Pam to look after.

Her lawyer, Gus, had called, too. She'd called him, but he was out. She left an update on his message machine. She was tempted to call Matt Dwight again, give him a heads-up on Inspector Ryan, who seemed to be gunning for him. But it wasn't her business anymore.

Technically.

She was sorely tempted to pay Shuggy a visit.

Lucky had died trying to do the right thing, and that's all it seemed to get him: dead. Just like the mayor. And Supervisor Harvey Milk.

And dying for nothing didn't do Lucky justice.

CHAPTER FORTY-FIVE

Later that morning, Colleen checked in on Pam again, still bundled in a fetal position under the covers. She prayed that her daughter would return whole from the nightmare of Die Kerk.

Back in her office she called Mr. Philanderer's wife, informing her that she'd been out of the country and would pick things up where she'd left off. She also mentioned an overdue bill.

"I want that photo of the two of them together first," Mrs. Philanderer said.

"If you read our contract," Colleen said coolly, "you'll find you're past due for services already rendered—including numerous photos. But I'll check today and give you an update."

"You do that."

Mrs. Philanderer wouldn't get any more photos until she paid her bill. Divorce work was the worst.

But her mind kept coming back to Lucky and the dead mayor—especially after last night's car ride with Inspector Ryan.

Fog drizzled down the window. Out there was a city in disarray, with a dead mayor, supervisor, and another ex-supervisor arrested for their murders. The Summer of Love was a long way away in the rearview mirror.

She called Owens at work. Still out. Where was he? She knew he'd moved out of the house but didn't know where. She felt for him, going through an ugly divorce of his own. But she could really use his help too.

She called Sergeant Matt Dwight, tried to catch him at home. No luck. Probably at work.

She pulled on a jacket, drove over to Polk Street on the off chance Mr. Philanderer might be treating himself to a morning quickie before work. No lights on in the love nest and no baby-blue Dodge Magnum parked in the neighborhood. She made a record of her visit in her notebook. It was all going on the bill.

Colleen headed back home and got caught up around City Hall where a throng of demonstrators with rainbow flags and signs were holding up traffic, protesting former Supervisor Dan White's supposed special treatment by SFPD. White was the shooter of Mayor Moscone and Supervisor Harvey Milk, an openly gay politician who represented the Castro. News reports claimed White, a former cop, was being regaled with goodie baskets and a cell to himself, complete with color TV. This did not bode well with the gay community. Chants of "When you're White, it ain't called murder" filled the air.

She stopped at the Safeway near Castro to pick up meds for Pam and a few groceries. She hit the payphone outside the supermarket on her way back to the car, called Matt Dwight at work one more time. Thankfully, he answered. She heard multiple conversations in the background, all at a high volume.

"I'm pretty busy right now," he said.

"I have no doubt," she said. "But I need to talk to you—in private."

"Give me your number," he said. "I'll call you right back."

While she waited, she fed a quarter into the newspaper vending machine, thinking about Lucky who not too long ago made his living selling papers on the street. No more.

The shooting of the mayor was front page, no surprise. Apparently, an anonymous tip had been filed prior to the shooting, but the police had failed to act upon it. Well, she knew who the tipster was.

The payphone rang.

"I can talk now," Matt Dwight said. No extraneous conversations. He had moved to a private phone.

"You haven't been around," he said. "I tried to stop by last week."

"I was out of the country."

"Ah."

"What the hell happened, Matt?"

"Dan White recently resigned from his position as supervisor but changed his mind. Went to City Hall to ask for his old job back but Mayor Moscone turned him down. Moscone had only been too happy to get rid of White in the first place. White shot him four times."

"How did White get a gun into City Hall? Through the metal detectors?"

"Someone let him in through a side entrance. Being an ex-cop and a recent employee, no one thought too much of it."

"And Supervisor Harvey Milk?"

"After he shot Mayor Moscone, White stopped by Milk's office, shot him, too. He'd never been wild about the guy or what he stood for."

Jesus. "Meanwhile the wives of SFPD are baking cookies for Dan White," Colleen said.

"White's a popular guy. Not everybody in this city is as tolerant as people like to think we are."

Wasn't that the truth?

Colleen took a breath, measuring her words. "Whatever happened with my anonymous tip, Matt?"

There was a pause. "It got as far as Jordan Kray."

"And when you saw he was clean, you thought I was barking up the wrong tree."

"Not you so much. Your buddy."

Lucky wasn't the most reliable source of information. And he had been wrong—well, half wrong. But still, she was disappointed. She'd gone out on a limb and the information had been discounted.

"I'm sorry, Colleen," Matt said. "Not that it makes much difference now."

"Not to Mayor Moscone and Harvey Milk, it doesn't. But it also got Lucky killed, and no one's giving him a second thought."

"I am."

"My big question is," she said, "how did Shuggy and his pals come by the name Jordan Kray? Not that far from the truth. Jordan Kray is a supervisor and an ex-cop, too."

"Who knows? By the time Lucky overheard Shuggy and his pals crowing about it, it might've been 'pass the story.'"

Pass the story. The party game where a number of people relate a story told to them to the next person in line. By the time the tale makes its way around the circle, it's invariably altered.

"Maybe," she said. "Or maybe it was deliberate misdirection."

"Do you really think Shuggy is that central to the shooting?"

"Possibly. He's a killer. Or maybe it's someone further up the chain. One of Shuggy's neo-Nazi or Klan pals. Dr. Lange influences a lot of people."

"I ran Shuggy's sheet, as well as his partners. Usual biker stuff. I stopped by the Thunderbird but Shuggy wasn't home. I looked into your neo-Nazi guy, Dr. Lange, too. Clean."

"And that was it?"

"I didn't see anything out of the ordinary."

She would have taken it further. But she wasn't a cop.

"Look, Colleen," he said, "rest assured that everyone on your list is getting their rat cage shaken now. If White isn't some lone gunman and there was a coordinated plot, we'll find it."

Locking the barn door after the horse had bolted.

Lucky deserved more.

"Shuggy, Stan, and Ace beat Lucky to death. Ace pretty much admitted to it at that Nazi-Klan shindig," she said. "What's the status of that?"

"Not my wheelhouse. And Owens is still out."

Dwight wasn't Homicide. Owens was.

"I know he's going through a divorce," she said.

"That's putting it mildly."

"Know where I can find him?"

There was another pause. "The Breakers Motel on Lombard. But you didn't hear it from me. She's putting him through hell."

Poor Owens was staying at a motel.

"My lips are sealed," she said. Then, "I didn't just call about the case. I need to tell you something—about your senior. Also, in confidence."

"Of course. What's it about?"

"Ryan and some little weasel stopped by late last night. Drove me down to the farmers market on Alemany to try and throw a scare into me. They weren't entirely unsuccessful. They wanted to know all about my anonymous tip. They also wanted to know about you. And not in a good way. That's why I wanted to mention it."

"You don't say. That's the way Ryan works."

"If I didn't know better, I'd say they might be trying to pin SFPD's dropping the ball on the Moscone shooting tip on you. It was your case to begin with."

"You took a risk telling me that, Colleen. I appreciate it."

"*De nada.*"

"As much as I hate to say it, we've got one or two who think Dan White isn't that bad."

"Goodie baskets," she said. "Color TV."

"You got it. Watch your back. Steer clear of Ryan. Shuggy and his buddies, too."

She agreed reluctantly.

Matt said, "When all of this settles down to a dull roar, do we still have a dinner date?"

"I'll bring a doggie bag."

"That's the best news I've had in a while. Keep your nose clean, parolee."

He signed off.

She wondered how Pamela was holding up back at home. After Die Kerk, Colleen had planned to devote her time reconnecting with her daughter. But the Moscone shooting changed that. And Lucky's murderer was still at large.

She drove home, getting tied up around Castro, where the rainbow flag flapped over Bank of America. Protesters were chanting along to a man with a bullhorn.

When you're White it ain't called murder.

CHAPTER FORTY-SIX

Back on Vermont Street, Colleen circled the block, checking for suspicious vehicles before she parked in the back lot. She took the back stairs up to her porch, shifted her bag of groceries, got her keys out, let herself in.

From the kitchen she could hear Pamela getting sick to her stomach in the bathroom again.

Colleen set the groceries on the counter, went to the bathroom. The door was open. Pamela was on her hands and knees in Colleen's kimono, praying to the porcelain goddess.

"I got some Pepto-Bismol, sweetheart."

"Kind of late for that," Pamela gasped.

Colleen let it slide. "How about some tea?"

"Ugh," Pam panted, her voice echoing from the toilet bowl.

Then another thought flashed through Colleen's mind. How slow could a woman be?

"Pam—are you having diarrhea?"

"No! Now will you just leave me alone—*please*?"

No problemo, Colleen thought. She left Pam hunched over the commode, went back out, down the wooden stairs, drove down to the drugstore, picked up an Early Pregnancy Test. They had just come out that year. She drove back up the hill, keeping an eye peeled for suspicious vehicles.

Pam was sitting on the couch in her robe, smoking a cigarette.

"I didn't know you smoked," Colleen said.

"Well, now you do."

"I'm going to make some tea," Colleen said. "Want some?"

"Okay," Pam said, puffing away.

Okay. Colleen made tea. Plenty of honey for Pam, whose blood sugar had to be nonexistent.

They sat across from each other in the living room. The atmosphere was decidedly chilly.

"Feeling any better?" Colleen asked, sipping tea.

Pam put her bare feet up on the glass coffee table. She shrugged as she sipped.

"Is that a 'yes'?" Colleen asked.

"Yes," Pam said tersely.

"Good." A little color was starting to return to Pam's face. There was no time like the present. Colleen set her cup down.

"Pam," she asked, "when did you last have your period?"

Pam smacked her cup down on the glass coffee table loud enough to make Colleen jump. Tea splashed. Thankfully nothing broke.

"For God's sake!" Pam stood up, cinched the kimono, marched off into the spare room, slammed the door.

Colleen nodded, stood up, went to the spare room, stood outside the door.

"Pam, I'm on your side. If you're pregnant, we need to deal with it—the two of us."

No answer. Good. At least she wasn't shouting.

"Do you think you *might* be pregnant?" Colleen said to the door.

She thought she heard Pam crying. She put her ear to the door. Crying. She was taken back to her little girl who cried too much. A wave of remorse filled her. What terrible decisions she had made, the biggest one killing Pam's father. Not that the bastard didn't deserve it. But for what it did to Pam, she'd never forgive herself.

She gently opened the door a few inches.

Pam was sitting on the edge of the bed, bare feet on the floor pigeon-toed, hunched over, elbows on her knees, head hung between them. Slowly, she looked up at Colleen. Her blue eyes were red and shiny. Tears streamed down her cheeks. Colleen's heart melted for her. She gave Pam a sad smile.

"I missed a month," Pam said quietly. "Maybe two."

Colleen fought a wave of dread at who the father might be. "I picked up an Early Pregnancy Test. We'll make sure."

A weary smirk from Pam. "It's only going to tell me what I already know."

"Probably. But then we can get you in to see the doc." Colleen never went to the doctor, but Alex had a gynecologist she liked.

"And then what?" Pam said.

Colleen shrugged. "There are options."

"An abortion."

"That's one. There are others. But it's your decision."

"You're telling me if I have *his* kid, you're gonna be there for me?"

So it *was* that psycho Adem Lea. Colleen let the shock subside. Told herself that beautiful flowers grew out of manure.

"It's not going to be easy telling people I'm a grandma," Colleen said, "and no one's going to believe me, anyway"—she flipped her hair back with a hand, *la-de-dah*—"not with my youthful looks and all, but I actually kind of dig the idea."

"Do you? I call 'bullshit.'"

Colleen took a breath, let her hand drop. "I'm getting used to the idea," she said. "How's that?"

Pam squinted. "Even knowing who the father is?"

"What matters to me is you, Pam."

Pam sighed. "You really mean that?"

"I got pregnant when I was sixteen. I was scared to death. Your grandfather was going to throw me out of the house if I didn't marry your father. Worst mistake I ever made. *Very worst mistake.* Well, maybe killing him was, but one bad decision led to the other. But, Pam—the day I gave birth to you and held you in my arms—that was the happiest day of my life. I was one happy, terrified teenager."

Pam cracked a frail smile. "Really?"

"Really." Colleen let that sink in. "I'm not even going to pretend I know what you've been through recently, but I do know what it's like to be young, alone, and pregnant and not have any good options. But you're not in that position. I'm here for you. This place is here for you. You can come and go as you please. No strings. You can have an abortion, have a baby, keep it, give it up for adoption—your decision. All fine with me."

Pam's face softened. She looked down at the floor, crossed one foot over the other. A tear dropped on the hardwood.

"Thanks," she said quietly.

All Colleen wanted to do was go to her daughter and hug her with ten years' worth of missed affection. But Pam wasn't ready. Colleen would bide her time. Being in prison for almost a decade taught her how to wait. She'd wait.

CHAPTER FORTY-SEVEN

After fiddling around with the vial of purified water, medicine dropper, and a test tube that contained sheep blood cells, and waiting two hours, a dark ring appeared at the bottom of the tube. Pam was indeed pregnant. The EPT was almost anticlimactic. Colleen called Alex, got the name of her gynecologist, made an appointment.

It was close to midday. Pam's morning sickness had passed.

Back in the living room, Pam was smoking another one of her Virginia Slims. Colleen was tempted to yank it out of her hand but struggled with her motherly instincts.

"Hungry?" she asked.

"Starving," Pam said.

"Let's go to the Cliff House for lunch," Colleen said. "We'll celebrate."

"*Celebrate?*" Pam said with a wry smile. "Talk about putting a spin on things."

Celebrate connecting with her daughter.

"I'll wait while you get cleaned up," Colleen said.

"Okay," Pam said, obviously liking the idea.

While Pam took a shower, Colleen threw her pack of cigarettes in the trash. The doorbell rang. She walked over to the front window, pulled the blind open, looked down on Vermont.

No car double-parked. But a familiar beige Ford sedan was parked across the street. An SFPD unmarked. If it was Inspector Ryan again, she was tempted to go get Little Bersalina.

In the hallway she hit the buzzer.

"It's Matt."

Sergeant Matt Dwight. She let him in. A moment later he was jogging up to her landing in nice-fitting slacks, along with his herringbone jacket, blue Oxford shirt, burgundy tie.

"Is this about the Moscone case?" she asked.

"Yes and no," he said, coming in. He stood, hands on his hips. He raised his eyebrows, obviously listening to the water running.

"My daughter's staying with me," Colleen said.

He looked surprised. Maybe relieved it wasn't a man. Matt knew the reason for Colleen's ten years in prison but hadn't connected that Colleen's daughter was a factor in her life. Then again, she kept Pamela to herself. Pam was hers and no one else's. "I haven't seen her for some time."

"Nice." He smiled and she liked him for being happy for her. But it was a brief smile. His face grew serious, tense. He dropped his voice. "We need to talk." His eyes shifted toward the bathroom where the water was still running. "Just you and me."

She showed him into her office in the corner of the flat, shut the door. She had a guest chair and a spider plant but not much else besides her desk and the new, used IBM Selectric. The sun was trying to break through the clouds wafting through the spans of the Bay Bridge.

Matt chose to stand. She leaned back against the desk. She gave him an inquisitive look.

"Ryan has been digging into my file on your anonymous call," he said.

"So, you did have a file."

"Of course. But it was confidential—until he pulled rank and had the case assigned to him. Given the outcome of the shooting, it's no surprise. But he's been following up the leads and interviewing people: your friend Shuggy Johnston, to be exact. And his two buddies."

"Better late than never," she said.

"I know you think I dropped the ball," he said, "and I did, in a way. Once I checked out Jordan Kray, the chief felt everything could be taken down a notch." Matt let an ironic smile slip. "One thing I didn't quite level with you on was that I wanted to look into Dr. Lange further, but I got pushback."

The surprise must have shown on her face because Matt said, "Dr. Lange is the focus of another investigation I cannot share with you. We're talking high profile." He raised his eyebrows. "It's Ryan's case." Matt continued: "So pulling Lange in for questioning earlier was considered too risky."

"And once Kray was given the green light, the mayor rumor was back-burnered. To protect Ryan's case with Lange."

Matt confirmed with a nod. "You were good enough to warn me about Ryan. Now it's my turn to return the favor."

She was wishing she had a cigarette. She crossed her arms. "About Ryan?"

"Ever since he took over the case, he's been a busy boy. He just had Shuggy Johnston pulled in for questioning."

It made more sense that Ryan had been following her that day now, up by Sears. It still didn't feel quite right, though.

"Better late than never," she said. "Maybe Shuggy and his two thugs will go down for Lucky at some point."

"One of the detectives in the interview said Ryan was throwing your name around when Shuggy denied having any knowledge of Aryan Alliance. Said he knew for a fact Shuggy had been to one of their recent meetings. Said he had a witness who said she went to one such event with him."

Colleen's heart seized. "Did he mention my real name?"

Matt Dwight gave a solemn nod.

"My *real* name." She had used an alias with Shuggy.

"Your real name."

"And Shuggy put two and two together."

"It's not that hard. Who else could have gone to that meeting with him?"

"Jesus H. Christ."

"Tell me about it." He grimaced. "Ryan has a rep for being a bull in a china shop. Especially when he's doing things his way. He's protecting his turf."

And not worrying too much about anybody else. Colleen wasn't high on his list of people to look out for to begin with. In fact, Ryan might just have been doing a little bit of the opposite when he dropped her name around Shuggy.

"Looks like I better keep my eyes peeled." She better watch out for Pam, especially, who knew Shuggy from her Moon Ranch days. The two of them could *not* meet again. Ever. There was no telling what Shuggy might do to get at Colleen.

Matt slipped his hands in his pockets. "It's not going to be hard for Shuggy to find you, if he puts his mind to it."

Colleen was aware of that. "I'm used to making enemies." The water shut off in the bathroom.

"Since this is all off the books, I can't assign a cop to watch your house. But I'll swing by whenever I can. And if you even *think* you need help, you call me."

"I appreciate that." And she did.

Matt cleared his throat. "Do you own a firearm, Colleen?"

An unregistered one. "Who's asking?"

"I'm not going to ask about legality." He divulged a tight smile. "But keep it handy."

"I take it Shuggy isn't in police custody."

"Not yet."

"He and his pals killed Lucky. I'll make a statement."

"All in good time. Homicide is short a man right now. Hopefully, Owens'll be back in action soon."

"Do you think Ryan and Dr. Lange might have some other kind of connection?"

Matt frowned while he thought about it, shook his head.

"Took you a minute to come to that conclusion," she said.

"Can't see it," he said. "No, I can't."

She wasn't so sure. But she didn't like Ryan. Cops who threatened her tended to have that effect.

Matt checked his watch. "I've got a dozen things I need to do."

She pushed herself up off her desk, thanked him for the warning, as much as it troubled her, and showed him out. Pam was in the kitchen, getting a glass of water. She had taken over Colleen's kimono. Her wet red hair was combed back. More pinkness had returned to her cheeks and Colleen felt a flush of optimism.

Colleen introduced Matt Dwight simply as Matt, keeping the cop connection to herself. She saw Pam give him the once-over. She wasn't sure how she felt about that.

"I still haven't forgotten about that other thing," Matt said quietly at the door, meaning dinner.

Their eyes met for a moment.

"Good," she said. She liked the whole idea better now that she saw how he'd been compromised by Ryan on his case.

Back in the apartment, Pam was in the spare room, getting ready, with the door open.

"Boyfriend?" Pam said, brushing her hair. Conversations seemed to work better if they were in different rooms.

"Work related," Colleen said.

"You sure about that?"

"I barely know him."

"But you'd like to."

"He's a nice guy."

"Nice *looking,* you mean."

After ten years in prison, she had missed Pamela's adolescence. Pam was still her little girl. Having a conversation like this was new territory.

"I guess," she said.

"You *guess?*" Pam stuck her head out of the bedroom, grinning.

Colleen smiled back. "Okay. He's easy on the eyes."

"Just a little." She went back to brushing her hair. "You been to bed with him yet?"

Colleen felt herself blushing. "If I had, I sure wouldn't tell you."

"Ah," Pam said. "We have a prude in our midst."

"Not really. But I am your mother, believe it or not. I'm also not a big fan of kiss and tell."

"Sex is no big deal, Mom. It might loosen you up to get your rocks off."

Talk about a conflicted message. Her one and only—fathering the child of an insane cult leader—giving her mother sex advice. But, on the plus side, Pam had called her *Mom.* But none of that was important right now. Getting Pam somewhere safe was.

"Matt's visit does mean a change of plans, though," Colleen said.

"What? Why?"

"I'll be right back." Colleen ducked into her office, shut the door, and called Alex in Half Moon Bay.

"Hey, Duchess," Alex croaked, sounding groggy, after Harold the butler put Colleen through. Colleen checked her watch. Late morning and Alex was just rising. Another night out on the tiles? Colleen wasn't going to pry, but she worried about Alex's consumption of late.

"I've got a huge favor to ask," Colleen said. "Huge."

"Oh-kay . . ." Colleen could hear Alex light a cigarette.

* * *

"Pack your bag," Colleen said to Pam.

"What for?"

"You're staying with a friend of mine for a few days."

Pam furrowed her brow. "Why?"

"Don't worry," Colleen said. "Alex has a mansion in Half Moon Bay. Not to mention a butler and a chef."

"Great," Pam said. "But, again, why?"

"I'll tell you on the way."

* * *

Colleen and Pam drove along the Great Highway, heading south, beach sand blowing across the road. The skies were churning gray and the waves uncertain.

"This Alex," Pam said, brushing her red hair back off her shoulder. "She's a friend?"

"A good friend," Colleen said. "She's been dying to meet you."

"But why? One minute you and I are going out to lunch, the next I'm being whisked off to some rich chick's castle."

"I made an appointment with Alex's gynecologist tomorrow," Colleen said. "Alex is going to take you."

"Cool." Colleen felt a surge of relief. "But you keep avoiding my question."

Colleen frowned as she drove. "I've got a lot on my plate right now."

"So? I thought I wasn't in the way—am I?"

Colleen wasn't going to go into Shuggy Johnston. "I'm in the middle of a delicate case."

"*Delicate* means *dangerous*?"

Colleen was actually heartened. Pam cared enough to worry about her safety. But she still didn't want her anywhere near Shuggy. "No."

"So why don't you want me around?"

"It's just some tedious divorce work I'm on and I need to wrap it up. I'm going to be in and out at all hours. I won't have time to look after you for a couple of days. And you need rest. Better for you and me if you stay with Alex. Just for a little while."

"You sure you're going to be okay?"

"I'm sure," Colleen lied.

"Okay," Pam said. "I guess."

There was so much they didn't know about each other. But it felt like they had made some progress.

Colleen breathed a sigh of relief. Now she could deal with Shuggy. And whatever that entailed. Without Pam.

CHAPTER FORTY-EIGHT

Back in San Francisco, Colleen spent the afternoon staking out Mr. Philanderer's love pad, with no sign of him or his paramour. With a sigh she headed home, stopping at a payphone near Sukkers Likkers.

She needed to be prepared in case Shuggy or one of his pals came visiting. Her Bersa Piccola was lightweight and fit the back pocket of her Levi's without ruining the curve of her jeans but didn't quite cut it for handling multiple attackers and certainly wouldn't scare off people of Shuggy's ilk. Boom had such a weapon, but she wasn't going to involve him. He'd done his bit, and then some.

She dropped a dime into the payphone and called Al Lennox, a bail bondsman down by 850 Bryant who had put her in touch with some disreputable people in the past. She needed somebody disreputable right about now.

Al answered in his raspy but cheerful voice.

"I was just closing up shop, cute thing," he said. She'd never really seen herself as cute.

"Glad I caught you," she said. "I have a rush order."

"Oh, yes? You are singing my song." Al Lennox loved rush orders, because they meant rush order money. "Who's the lucky guy who needs bail at this late hour?"

"A friend of mine named Rodney Strong."

There was a pause. *Strong* was a code name. There were several Al used. *Sweet* was anything that might get you high. *Green* was a loan, fast, at high interest. *Strong* was a weapon.

"Give me your number," he said. "I'll call you right back."

Colleen gave him the number of her payphone. She waited for Al to leave the office, use the payphone at the bar nearby, his unofficial line. It would've been the perfect time for a cigarette. But she'd given them up for her future grandchild, if it came to that.

A few minutes later, cold wind blowing up Polk, the phone rang.

"Poor Rodney," Al said, and she could hear the exuberance of the after-work bar patrons where he was calling from. "What's he up for?"

"10-32," she said. Police code for a firearm.

"What kind?"

"Sawed-off," she said. "Portable and easy to conceal."

"Bail for something like that isn't gonna be cheap, you know."

She figured as much. "Why am I not surprised?"

He told her how much.

"Ouch," she said.

"And don't forget my fee."

Double ouch.

"Okay," she said. "But he needs it tonight."

"Oh, you kidder."

"Yes, I love to joke about things like this."

Al's tone turned serious. "Let me make a phone call and get right back to you."

"I'll need some shells, too."

"She sells seashells by the seashore." Al hung up.

She shivered in the cold San Francisco evening that was approaching, wishing she'd worn more than a denim jacket.

But, not long after, the phone rang.

"Clooney's," Al said. "Nine o'clock. Bring cash."

She went back home, rummaged around in the back of the pantry, found the can of Brim decaffeinated coffee she never used, opened it, fished her roll of emergency money out from the grounds. Shook it off over the sink. Paying for Rodney Strong's 10-32 was pretty much going to clean her out. But so be it. Maybe she could sell the damn thing back to Al when Shuggy was out of her life.

At nine p.m., she walked out of Clooney's bar on Mission with a large double paper bag weighed down, feeling just a tad nervous, a woman on parole with an illegal firearm. Her second illegal firearm. She put it in the trunk, drove over to O'Farrell Street, motored by the Thunderbird. No ratty Harley-Davidson with a white eye swastika on the tank parked out front. On the third floor Shuggy's light was off. Shuggy was out. Shuggy might even be out looking for her.

She headed back home, circled the block, no suspicious vehicles. No maniacs wielding swords, no Symbionese Liberation Army members brandishing submachine guns. But if Shuggy made an appearance, she was ready.

She parked in the back lot, pulled her Bersa from the gym sock under the dash, checked around before she locked up the car, trudged up the back stairs with her paper bag to her porch. Let herself in. Set the bag on the kitchen counter. Bersa in hand, she checked the flat. Matt Dwight's warning had her on high alert.

No one.

It already felt empty without Pam. Colleen went back into the kitchen, set Little Bersalina on the kitchen counter, checked the contents of the bag.

Pulled out an ancient Century Arms 12-gauge shotgun that was just over a foot long. The wood was grimy black, the metal oxidized. The barrel had been sawn back as far as it could go. Much of the stock had been lobbed off, too. Two rabbit ear hammers poked up.

A hillbilly handgun. She broke the weapon, sniffed the empty barrels. Not recently fired but there was definitely the tang of gunshot residue.

She looked in the paper bag. Four 12-gauge shells. Six would have been nicer. But Al Lennox never over-delivered.

She loaded up the gun with two shells, put the other two aside. She went and got her military surplus parka with the white fur-lined hood, put it on, popped the under-the-bed gun in the deep inside pocket.

Trotted around the flat, practiced whipping the gun out. Efficient. Stylish, too.

She put everything to one side, got herself a glass of water. Leaned back against the counter, drank.

She wanted to call Alex, see how Pam was settling in. But no. She'd keep a lid on her feelings, the need to be Pam's mother, the urge to fix things that might not be easily fixable. She'd keep her distance, no matter how lonely it felt. It wasn't about her; it was about getting Pam some semblance of sanity back in her life. Let her recover. Deal with her pregnancy.

She thought about being the grandmother to Adem Lea's child. It wasn't easy to get her head around. But she'd deal with it.

She took her glass of water and personal arsenal into her office and called her answering service. No new messages.

She hung up, took her Bersa and Princess phone on its long cord into the bathroom, set both on the edge of the sink, took a long steamy shower.

She stood under the water and let it needle her face, run down her body. She was still fuzzy from her trip to South America. Along with the images of Kerkers leaping into the volcano, things still felt unreal. She needed the opposite.

While she was in the shower, the phone rang. She leaned out, flipped her wet hair to one side, answered the phone. It clicked off.

She'd been hoping for a surprise call from Pam. She told herself to quit hoping. Now she was thinking of Shuggy.

Out of the shower, she pulled on her kimono, which smelled like Pam, which made her miss her more, grabbed the shotgun, did the rounds. Back porch—nothing unusual in the yard below. Front window, peering out from behind the blinds. Nothing out of the ordinary.

She made a cup of coffee. As much as she wanted a glass of Chardonnay, she needed a clear head.

The phone rang again. She answered.

"Hey, Mom."

The nicest two words she could have heard.

"Hi, Pam," she said, sipping coffee. "How's Alex treating you?"

"She went to visit a friend. It's just me, the butler, and the chef."

"Life is rough."

"It's a little weird having a butler float around after you. I asked him if there was possibly any ice cream. He said: what kind? They have several flavors. Homemade, of course."

"Decisions, decisions."

"Thought I'd check in on you."

"You don't know how much I like that you did."

"Oh, I think I might. You sure things are okay up there?"

"Absolutely."

"Alex says I can use a car if I want. Just stay away from the Jag."

"That was nice." Colleen hadn't even thought about her daughter being able to drive, then recalled that she had driven the drug delivery van for Moon Ranch. Her little girl.

"I could come up," Pam said slyly.

Colleen's heart melted. "Nothing would make me happier, sweetie, but I need you to stay right where you are for the time being. You need your rest. Besides, Alex is taking you to the doctor tomorrow, right?"

"I figured you and I could go."

Another warm rush filled Colleen's chest.

"There will be other opportunities. I really want to go with you tomorrow, but I'm right in the middle of this case. A couple of days and I'll be in the clear." She hoped so.

"You sure you're not in some kind of trouble? You can tell me. I know all about trouble."

Colleen laughed. "I know you do." It felt good to be able to joke about such dark issues. "But I'm fine, really. I've just got a client whose husband has a girl on the side and I need to get some photos pronto. All very grubby but it means I'm going to be very busy the next few days. And you really need your rest." She didn't want to ask whether Pamela was thinking of keeping her child. Let her make her own decisions.

"You know, it really means a lot, you helping me out."

"I can't think of anything I'd rather do."

They said goodnight. It was the nicest phone call Colleen could remember. She'd remember it for the rest of her life.

She turned the lights down, set the sawed-off on the glass coffee table, put The Lost Chords on the stereo, Steve's album back when he was a teen idol, a record she treasured. She recalled being a young mom living at home with a husband who was still alive and a little girl who was now expecting a baby of her own. She listened to a sixteen-year-old Steve singing about that river that time couldn't stop and wondered when Shuggy might show, if he did show. Her instincts were usually good. They were prickly now. She sipped coffee, her bare feet on the glass coffee table next to the shotgun.

But she was getting sleepy. Everything was starting to catch up with her. Somewhere in the middle of "Shades of Summer" she drifted off, her head tilted back on the sofa.

She didn't know what time it was when she woke with a start. A car door had shut quietly, down on the street, amidst the white noise of the elevated freeway up the hill. For some reason it had woken her up. It was late and a lot didn't go on around here then. Plus her feelers were on high.

She pressed the button on her Pulsar watch, the red numbers cutting the near darkness. Early in the a.m.

She stood up, cinched her kimono. The lights were off so she wouldn't be visible looking out the window. She went over to the front of the flat, pulled the curtain aside an inch or two. Two stories down, parked down Vermont, she saw a dark mid-sixties Impala, a boat of a car with a primered fender. Someone sat behind the wheel, someone next to him. Or *her*. And maybe someone in the back. Her biker trio came to mind.

She went, got her binos. Focused on the driver.

Shuggy. Did he wear anything besides his denim and leathers? And, in the passenger seat, Ace the troll doll. Stan, the tall member, might be in the back.

Her guests had arrived.

She patted herself on the back for shuffling Pam off to Alex's.

How to play this?

Shuggy and his two thugs probably wouldn't try to come in while she was there. They knew she could be armed. Were they waiting for her to leave? Middle of the night? Or just watching her?

Then the Impala started up with a rumble, swerved out onto Vermont. Floated away.

They'd be back. She felt like bait on the hook.

But she was the one who had put herself there.

Now it was time to catch fish.

Come to mama.

CHAPTER FORTY-NINE

Colleen didn't know what time Shuggy and his two cohorts would return, only that they surely would.

She dressed in jeans and denim shirt, pulled on socks and sneaks, left her Bersa and shotgun on the kitchen counter. She got a hard-backed chair, her field glasses, positioned them by the front window. In the kitchen she set up the Moka pot and made herself a large cup full of steaming espresso to stay awake. Stirred in several spoons of brown sugar for good measure, took her coffee into the living room. The only thing missing was a cigarette.

Maybe they'd be back tonight. She'd be ready.

By the time she was halfway through her rocket fuel, she heard a distant rumble coming down Vermont. She set her cup down, pulled the blinds back, peered through the gap with the binos in one hand.

The Impala parked farther down the street this time.

She'd wait. They could all wait.

Even with the coffee in her, she was fighting sleep. That trip to Ecuador was still taking its toll on top of everything else.

Her eyelids drooping, she heard a car door open quietly, and just as softly, shut. Through the glasses she saw a short figure, wearing a dark jacket, strolling toward her building. She focused in. Ace. He crossed over Vermont. She could no longer see him but heard his heels pass under her window. They headed around the corner.

Casing her building.

She got up, went to her office, at the back of the flat. With the light off, she looked out the window.

Here came Ace, hands in jacket pockets, approaching the back lot.

He stopped at the entrance, leaned in to look at her Torino, moved on. Knew she was home.

She thought about calling Matt. If things got any dicier, she would.

Then she heard a car door slam, out front. Light footsteps, heading to the entrance of her building. *What?* Colleen padded to the front window. A shiny black Lincoln Continental, looking familiar, was parked across the street. Colleen craned her neck. The Impala was still parked down the block where it had been, down to one man. Stan, tall and lanky, was coming down the street toward her place now.

Colleen's door buzzer went off. She pressed the button on her watch. Wee hours. Stan wouldn't have had time to make it. Ace was probably still circling the long block. Was it some other ally of Shuggy's? Who'd been in the Lincoln? Reinforcements?

Chest tapping, she got up, grabbed the sawed-off from the kitchen counter, went to the intercom, pressed the button. Didn't speak at first.

"Mom?" she heard Pam say. "It's me. Sorry it's so late. I just wanted to see you."

Her nerves ratcheted into overdrive. Pam? *No!*

Colleen buzzed the door open, shouted: "Pam! Get in here quick! *Now!* And shut that door behind you! Right away! Someone's after—"

She heard a snippet of Pam yelling out in protest before the inter-com cut off. Out on the street, Stan gave a sharp wolf whistle, then shouted: "Hey! *Hurry up!*"

The Impala started up.

They were taking Pam.

Colleen's heart leapt into her throat.

CHAPTER FIFTY

From the hallway, by the intercom, she heard the Impala roaring down the street.

They had Pam.

Run to the living room window? No, couldn't risk shooting from there.

Gun in hand, she charged out into the hall, grabbing the banister for speed as she hurtled down the first flight of stairs.

An apartment door flew open. A neighbor appeared in plaid pajamas, blinking through glasses. She tucked the gun to one side, hopefully out of view. "What on earth is going on, Colleen?"

"Call the police! Someone's got my daughter." Colleen turned down the next flight of stairs. She heard the sounds of a struggle out front, doors slamming, engine gunning, rubber burning.

But by the time she got to the ground floor, out the front door, the Impala was motoring off, the engine fading around the corner.

She stood there, hyperventilating. Mind aflame.

Pam must have come home to keep her company, after all. Of all the times she'd wanted to hear from Pam, see her, Pam had to pick tonight.

And now they had her.

CHAPTER FIFTY-ONE

SFPD came, took a report. Colleen gave the lead officer details on Shuggy Johnston, Stan, and Ace. She didn't have the Impala's license plate but she had the one for Shuggy's Harley. Inspector Ryan had already questioned him, according to Matt Dwight, so he should be easy enough to find. Normally this might be plenty to go on but Shuggy had Pam. The time frame was compressed.

Frantically she called Matt Dwight. She caught him before he went to work. He stopped by, early in the a.m. She'd made a pot of coffee and was drinking it in jittery gulps. Matt declined. His face was drawn.

"You say Pam has a history with Shuggy?"

She told him about Moon Ranch, and Pam's helping deliver drugs.

"This has got to be about your friend Lucky," he said. "They want to shut you up."

Colleen slurped coffee. "Thanks to Inspector Ryan," she said. "That's why Shuggy was staking me out. Waiting for an opportunity. Now he's got the trump card."

"We'll get SFPD to watch the Thunderbird."

"Short term, he won't go back there."

"I'll make sure we're on top of this, Colleen. In the meantime, keep me posted of any updates. You've got my numbers."

She nodded, sipped coffee, spilled some down her shirt. She set the cup on the countertop, thanked him, and showed him out. She checked her answering service. Nothing. She called Alex. Harold the butler told her Alex hadn't come home last night. Colleen assumed that meant she'd stayed at Antonia's. Harold confirmed that Pam had borrowed the Lincoln, told him she was going out for a drive. He was more than concerned when he heard the outcome.

Colleen needed to stay by the phone, in case Shuggy called. She parked on the sofa, the phone on the glass coffee table in front of her.

A day of agonizing crept by. She couldn't eat. Sleep was out of the question. She took a shower just to break the monotony and wake herself up, the phone on the edge of the bathroom sink.

It wasn't until dark that she heard from them.

"Mom?" Pam said, her voice shaky. In the background, Colleen heard traffic. She was outside somewhere.

CHAPTER FIFTY-TWO

Colleen's heart thumped, hearing her daughter's voice on the phone.

"Thank God you're all right, Pam," she said, meaning *alive*. "You *are* all right, aren't you? Where are you? Did you manage to get away?" Maybe she did. Maybe Pam was free.

The phone clattered as it changed hands.

Shuggy's raspy voice broke in.

"Your little girl is fine," he said. "We're having a hell of a time catching up."

Colleen's spirits plummeted. She refrained from uttering threats. This wasn't the time to lose her cool.

"If you're concerned about me making a statement to the police," she said, "I'm not about to do any such thing. You have my word."

"That's good to hear," Shuggy said. "And you have my word that if you say one more thing to the cops, you know what will happen—right?"

"Just tell me what I do next."

"We're down here at the beach: Sloat and the Great Highway."

"What's the deal?"

"You for her."

Colleen sucked in a breath of desperation. She had expected as much. But what choice did she have? She had let Pamela down all her life. Now it was time to pay the price. If she had to sacrifice herself, that's what a mother did. She was prepared.

But she wasn't going to go easily.

And Pam was going to go free.

"I'm on my way," she said.

"Oh—and did I mention not to bring anybody else? Did I mention that? I hope that's not a problem. It would be a real shame for Pam." Shuggy laughed a nasty laugh.

Then he hung up.

Colleen ran a hand through her hair, thinking.

She called Boom. She hadn't wanted to involve him anymore but she was desperate.

"I hope you're not studying," she said.

"No big," Boom said. "What do you need, Chief?"

"I need you to follow someone," she said. "Without being seen."

"And who would that someone be?"

"Me."

After the call, Colleen went and changed her shoes. She had a surprise in store for Shuggy and crew.

CHAPTER FIFTY-THREE

Ocean Beach was deserted when Colleen pulled off the Great Highway past the zoo. Ambient moonlight broke through gusting clouds. Two vehicles were parked in the sand-strewn lot that faced the Pacific Ocean: an old rusting Plymouth on flat tires with a slew of tickets under its wipers, and a Chevy van with a custom paint job booming with rock 'n' roll in the far corner of the lot. Colleen stopped the Torino by the payphone in front of the maintenance building and shut the engine off. Van Halen throbbed from the van.

She tucked her sawed-off in the deep inside pocket of her military surplus parka, a little awkward, and got out of the Torino. She had her Bersa in the back pocket of her Levi's. She suspected she'd be searched and the weapons taken, but you never knew. Her pièce de résistance was the pair of dorky black Dexters she wore, boys size, the right one armed with a spring-loaded shoe knife Boom had fashioned for her. All you had to do was drag your right foot back on a rough surface to eject the switchblade. Ever since her last case, when she had managed to survive thanks to a steak knife taped to her ankle, such footwear was de rigueur on risky assignments.

She strode over to the van. Boisterous young voices in animated conversation discussed the quality of the weed they were partaking of. The sharp acrid smell of pot emanated.

Hand inside her jacket, she approached the rear windows, which were heavily tinted. She peered in.

Saw a couple of teenagers passing a joint, neither one of them Shuggy, Pam, or anyone else she was looking for.

A kid in a headband saw her.

"Holy fuck! Dude! Look! At the window!"

"Don't mind me," Colleen shouted. With a sigh, she walked back to her car.

That's when she heard the payphone ring. She picked up the pace, jogged to answer it.

"And there you are," Shuggy said.

Shuggy wasn't here at the beach. She wasn't too surprised. They were going to run her around. Standard.

"I'm alone," she said.

"Good," Shuggy said. "Good."

"Now what?"

"Mount Davidson," Shuggy said. "The big cross."

"That's where you are," she said.

"Will be."

A lot more remote.

She'd deal with it.

"Just to reclarify," she said. "Pam goes free."

"You got it," Shuggy said darkly.

"Let me talk to her."

"You already did."

"That was before. This is now."

The phone knocked. Pam was put on.

"Don't do it, Mom!" she said, her voice shaking. She'd figured out the situation. In that moment, Colleen was more than proud of her daughter.

"You just stay put, Pam," Colleen said. "Don't do anything that might get you hurt." *Or worse.* "This will be over soon." She hung up.

Looked around. The Great Highway was desolate. All she heard was Van Halen resounding out of the van. "You Really Got Me." The inane lyrics took on a dark forewarning as she got into her Torino, twisted the ignition key. The starter motor ground for a moment, finally fired up.

She eyed herself in the rearview mirror.

She had done nothing but fail Pamela.

No more.

She backed out with a skid, threw the car into gear, headed off towards Mount Davidson.

As she flew up Sloat Boulevard, past the zoo, in the rearview mirror she saw headlights peel out of the darkness and follow her.

CHAPTER FIFTY-FOUR

Mount Davidson was the highest peak in San Francisco and the geographical center of the city. Its shorter sisters, Twin Peaks, to the north, got all the attention with their view of downtown, Ferry Building, Golden Gate Bridge, and Alcatraz, drawing a steady stream of tourists and sightseers, especially at night. Mount Davidson was not so blessed. But on top stood a cement cross over one hundred feet tall, erected with 1500 tons of concrete by the WPA in the 1930s to commemorate Easter Sunrise Service. The rest of the time, Mount Davidson sat in relative isolation.

And the cross, apparently, was where Shuggy waited with Pam. Along with Stan and Ace, no doubt. And who knew who else.

There were several main access points to the forty-five-acre park: a dirt road used by city maintenance vehicles, a set of winding stone steps leading up from the bottom to an even more zigzagged path to the cross, and, on the far side, one other path out in the open. Sutro, a former San Francisco mayor in the late 1800s, had owned half the mountain at one time and planted pine trees on his side, so half of Mount Davidson was forested, the other half left barren, creating a sort of schizophrenic mountain. Colleen opted for the least visible path, the long, twisting one from below, providing the most cover.

She parked near the stone steps at the bottom of Mount David-son. As preoccupied as she was about Pamela, every decision taxed her thinking. This was not the time to lose control. But theory was now becoming reality. The lack of sleep, remaining jet lag, didn't help. She felt jumpy when she needed to be cool and collected.

Fully armed, she headed up the stone stairs, beneath ninety-year-old trees that creaked in the wind and dripped moisture like rain. As she turned into darkness, she heard a car trundling along Juanita below. A big engine. She heard it stop, then park. She breathed a small sigh of relief.

It didn't take long to make her way up to the crooked path above the steps. The wet ground was mucky and slippery underfoot. In her parka, loaded down with the sawed-off shotgun, she was sweating. In the darkness her eyes jumped at any movement. She stayed to one side of the path, in shadow.

Another short set of steps appeared, fashioned out of logs, steep, up to the final ascent. Climbing those, she stood at the bottom, looking up. The side of the huge cement cross appeared through a break in the trees, lit by indirect spotlights.

A flicker of motion.

A flashlight beam shone down.

"S-stop right there," a nasal voice said. Ace with the stutter. The top of his short stocky profile came into view, his frizzy hair catching a scrap of light.

"H-hands up."

She complied.

"C-come."

"I need to see Pam first," she said.

There was some mumbled conversation.

"Don't do it, Mom!" Pam shouted.

Good enough, Colleen told herself. Pam was there, still alive. Although Colleen had thought things through, she couldn't stop her heart from beating wildly. She didn't get scared often, but she was good and scared now. Mostly for Pamela.

"I'm coming, Pam," she said. "Stay calm."

CHAPTER FIFTY-FIVE

"N-nice and slow," Ace said through his nose. "K-keep those h-hands up."

"Turn that damn flashlight away!" Colleen said, ducking into the shadows. "Otherwise it's no deal." It would be too easy to pick her off.

"Do it," she heard Shuggy say.

The flashlight beam shifted to one side.

She took a breath, stumbled up a muddy incline, shrubs blocking part of her ascent, hands up in surrender. Thirty seconds and a lifetime passed before she reached the top. Sweat dripped down the small of her back.

She stopped at a gap in the foliage.

Before her, in shadow, Ace held a short-barreled pistol on her. His flashlight lit up an oval of muddy ground by his small boot. Behind him the hundred-foot-tall cross sat on a raised circular waist-high concrete base about ten yards in diameter.

On the platform, in the misty beam of spotlight, Shuggy shielded himself behind Pam, a big cannon of a gun dangling from one hand. Pam's hands were tied in front of her. On the far side of the platform, standing on the ground, his lower body hidden by the concrete, stood Stan, the barrel of a shotgun visible. He watched Colleen.

Pam wore only a T-shirt and jeans, no jacket, or shoes, just muddy white gym socks. Pam shivered as Colleen boiled with rage.

Her eyes met momentarily with Pam's. Colleen willed herself to send assurance to her daughter, most of all love, love that had so often been unwanted. It seemed to find a place now and for that she drew some small fulfillment.

But to mean anything, love meant that Pam and the life inside her had to stand a chance.

"It's going to be okay, Pam," she said.

Pam responded with a soft, sad, uncertain smile.

"*It's O-OK*," Ace mimicked in a high voice. "*M-mommy's here!*"

Stan and Shuggy laughed.

"Good one, little brother," Stan said.

Ace grinned.

Control, Colleen told herself. *Control*.

"You can let Pam go now, Shuggy," she said.

"You just keep your hands up," Shuggy said from the platform. "Ace—search our guest."

Ace set the flashlight on the edge of the concrete base, partially blinding Colleen as he came in close, the nose of his pistol parting her big jacket. Surreptitiously she eyed the rocks embedded in the mud around her feet. A flat one the size of a plate looked perfect for drawing out her shoe blade.

Ace reached inside her jacket with his free hand, found the sawed-off shotgun in the side pocket.

He pulled it, stood back, held it up for all to see.

"C-check t-this out!" he said, clearly proud of himself.

"Stupid," Shuggy said, standing behind Pam.

Ace threw the sawed-off into the bushes.

"Keep going," Shuggy said.

"T-turn ar-round," Ace instructed Colleen.

She did, positioning her right shoe over the flat rock. If she was going to die, it had to be worth it.

Ace's hands wandered over Colleen's backside, cupping her butt.

"N-nice," he whispered.

"Please be careful, Mom!" Pam shouted.

"I will, honey. You too."

Ace found the Bersa in her back pocket.

"D-dayum!" he said, holding it up.

"Fuck that," Shuggy growled.

"T-turn back around n-now," Ace said to Colleen.

She did, scraping her foot on the rock as she turned. But the blade in her right shoe failed to eject. Colleen's heart twisted.

Ace nodded at the Bersa with admiration, tucked it in the pocket of his biker jacket.

"Let her go now," Colleen said to Shuggy. "Pam won't give you any problems. Neither will I."

"We'll see about that," Shuggy said, "after she watches her mother die."

Colleen froze inside.

"Let her go, Shug!" Pam screamed, trying to pull away. "You promised!"

"*You p-promised!*" Ace whined, laughing.

"Shut up!" Shuggy slapped Pam across the back of the head with his big mitt. She fell forward and he grabbed her by the hair, yanking her back upright. She yelped.

Colleen's vision vibrated with anger. One way or another Shuggy would pay. They all would.

"Time to earn your wings, little brother," Shuggy said to Ace.

"Say w-what, S-shug?" Ace said, mouth open.

"You're overdue, dude. Waste her."

Ace stood back with a frown of indecisiveness, but finally raised the pistol, pointed it at Colleen's chest. His hand was shaking.

"Just do it," Shuggy said.

"Come on, Ace," Colleen said, scraping her right shoe on the stone again while she spoke. "You didn't mind beating Lucky to death."

The switchblade ejected with a ratchet sound. *Yes.*

Ace's eyes were diverted to her foot.

"W-what . . ."

"This is what, asshole." She kicked him in the shin—hard—before his gun went off. The shot went wild as Ace screamed. She kicked him again, sinking the blade into the side of his calf before pulling it out with a scrape of bone.

Ace went down, howling, the gun tumbling away.

She knocked the flashlight off the ledge and went after Ace in the shadows, sinking her foot-blade into his groin. Another scream filled the air.

She fell to the ground, fumbling for his gun while he rolled in agony, clutching himself.

She caught a glimpse of Pam breaking away as Shuggy came charging for her by the edge of the platform. Pam was running down the steps away from the cross, bound hands in front of her. Colleen fumbled the gun into her hands, muddy and slippery. It was a five-shot snub-nosed 38. A quick glance at the rear of the cylinder revealed the gun was most likely fully loaded. Four shots left.

When Shuggy saw Ace on the ground, he retreated for the cover of the cement cross.

"Stan!" he yelled. "Get Pam!"

Ace rolled and whimpered while Colleen snaked around the cement barrier toward the stairs, staying low for cover.

She saw Stan running towards Pam, away from the cross, shotgun up. Colleen fired at him. But you couldn't hit a thing with a snub-nosed revolver from any distance. Stan flinched at the shot, chasing Pam.

Pam loped off in the darkness in her socks. Shuggy was hovering around the edge of the cross, trying to get a bead on Colleen in the dark.

She spun, fired at him. The 38 kicked and Shuggy jumped back, returning fire, the big gun like dynamite. She balked, but the shot went wide, tearing through the bushes. Colleen jumped up, firing again. The shot zinged off the cement. Shuggy flew back behind the far side of the cross.

She saw Pam off a ways. Stan raised his shotgun at her.

Then, out of the bushes to her left, a quiet shot resounded, a *vip* that popped Stan's head like a watermelon. He collapsed mid-run, the gun tumbling to his knees. He tripped over it, a puppet whose strings had been cut.

"What the fuck?" Shuggy shouted from behind the cross.

"Run, Pam!" Colleen shouted, jumping up, bringing up the muddy pistol in both hands. Protected somewhat by the platform, she pointed the gun at where Shuggy hid behind the cross.

"Come on out, Shuggy," she said, squinting with one eye along the short barrel.

"Are you fucking high, bitch?" Shuggy peered around the corner. His gun appeared, flashed before it boomed. Another lead missile splintered cement by her head.

She ducked, panting. Close.

Shuggy's gun appeared again.

But another blast of Boom's high-powered rifle pushed him back.

Boom emerged from the bushes, a long rifle in his hands. He darted over to the platform next to Colleen, positioned himself with arms and rifle supported. Aimed at where Shuggy had been.

"There's two of us," he shouted. "Just one of you. If you move, I got you. If you try to run, man, I got you."

"Fuck you, suntan!" Shuggy shouted from behind the cross, firing another blast.

Boom fired his long rife. A chunk of cement popped off close to where Shuggy's face had been.

"This is a SIG 550 assault rifle," Boom yelled. "Fifty-five millimeter, 300-meter accuracy. I got a thirty-round magazine. When you run out of ammo, I'll come up there and shoot you down like a dog."

Silence. Meaning all they heard was Ace crying on the ground.

"Mom!" they heard Pam shout. "I'm okay!"

Colleen thought about letting Shuggy make a run for it. Pam was safe.

No. She had to make sure this was the end of it.

"I'll go round the other side," she whispered to Boom. "You keep him pinned down here."

"Roger that." Boom was crouched down, the gun on the ledge of the platform, aimed at the section of cross where Shuggy had appeared. His eye was lined up with the sight.

Colleen scooted around the circular base of the cross in darkness. Shuggy was crouching with his pistol. He didn't see her, too busy watching out for Boom.

She stood up, her lower body behind the platform, not ten feet away. She raised the gun.

"Party's over, Shuggy," she said between her teeth.

Shuggy swiveled, mouth dropping. His gun was down.

All Colleen wanted to do was shoot him, then and there. But her daughter had seen her kill. Once was enough. More than enough.

Shuggy's lips drew back in fear when he saw the gun pointed directly at him.

"Give me a reason to pull this trigger, Shuggy," she said. "Any reason will do."

A few seconds crawled by. Glances shot back and forth.

"Fuck it," Shuggy said, tossing the gun. It banged on cement and bounced.

"Hands on top of your head."

He did so.

Colleen motioned him around, out in the open.

Pam emerged from the far shadows.

A flood of relief overcame Colleen.

Boom came around, relaxed his rifle.

"Who are you?" Pam asked Boom.

"A friend of your mother's," he said. "She asked me to follow her." He shifted his gaze to Colleen. "And I did. Down to the beach. Then up here."

"I saw you," Colleen said. "Out by Sloat."

"I lost you for a minute. Good thing I saw your car down there by the stairs."

"That's why I parked under the streetlight," she said. "I was hoping."

"Nothing wrong with that," Boom said. "Nothing wrong with a little hope."

CHAPTER FIFTY-SIX

"Shuggy Johnston has just been charged with the premeditated murder of Herman Waddell," Sergeant Matt Dwight said. "His associate, Bob Bennington—aka 'Ace'—was booked as an accomplice. Charges for abducting Pam to follow."

Colleen let out a sigh of relief. And an overdue smile of satisfaction.

Stan Harrison, the third member of Shuggy's pack, lay in the city morgue.

Colleen and Matt Dwight stood on the ground floor of the Hall of Justice on 850 Bryant by the metal detectors, cops and people coming and going to and from court and various city offices. Voices and shoe heels echoed off the marble floors and walls.

Matt's tie was uncharacteristically an inch below his collar button, which had been undone after he emerged from court. But the rest of his outfit remained immaculate and his hair was freshly styled. It might have been early morning but Colleen knew he'd been burning the midnight oil. For her part she wore a black trouser suit with flared pants and white platform shoes. She was tentatively planning on a celebration.

"That's great news, Matt," she said. "Great news."

"Great *work*—on your part."

She knew he still felt sheepish for what he perceived as dropping the ball on the mayor's shooting.

"I caught a break," she said.

"Your statement and testimony certainly cinched it for nailing those two."

It was the least she could do for Lucky's memory.

"What about Dr. Lange?" she asked.

"Still on our radar," Matt said. "He's a slippery character, hiding his racism behind others, but his day is coming. Someday we'll have a unit that deals specifically with people like him and the hate they spread."

Colleen was relieved to hear it. "With people like you, Matt, I have no doubt."

He gave a modest smile. "SFPD is under the microscope for the Moscone assassination. It got by us, and it shouldn't have. There are going to be some changes. We are all responsible for what happened."

The road to recovery began with a single step.

"What about your associate Boom?" Matt asked.

"He's met with my lawyer," Colleen said. "Boom has a permit for the rifle, but you can be sure there will be plenty of questions about what he was doing with it up on Mount Davidson." And why he shot and killed a man. "Boom is ex-Marine Reconnaissance. Served two tours in Vietnam."

"You're lucky to have him."

"Don't I know it?" Now she just had to make sure a young black man didn't get put through the ringer for shooting a deadbeat like Stan Harrison. Gus Pedersen, her lawyer, would be a good first line of defense.

Matt cleared his throat. "And Pamela?"

"Rocky but better," Colleen said. "She's been through so much recently. Too much. And then this. I'm on my way to pick her up from the doctor's right now, as a matter of fact."

Matt's face fell slightly. "I was hoping you and I could grab a cup of coffee."

"Next time," she said. "And it's *dinner*."

Their eyes met.

"I owe you an apology," he said, clearing his throat. "I should have done more when you filed your complaint."

She had hoped for more. But his hand had been forced by his superiors. And what was done was done. Matt, along with the rest of SFPD, would have to live with the results—a mayor and a district supervisor assassinated by an ex-cop—one of their own.

"I'm arranging a small service for Lucky," she said. "He's still in the morgue. No relatives to claim him. And he deserves better than a county burial."

"I'd be honored to attend."

"Lucky would have appreciated that," she said. "I'll get hold of Owens as well. I'm going to swing by his motel later."

"I'm sure he'll want to pay his respects."

She pressed the button on her Pulsar watch.

"Well, time for me to pick up Pamela."

You couldn't change the past.

But you could atone.

EPILOGUE

"There she is," Colleen said, standing up. She had been sitting in the waiting room of the gynecologist Alex had recommended off Union Square. A view of the Golden Gate Bridge loomed through breaking fog from the corner window. Pamela had just returned from a lengthy visit with the doctor.

Pam wore a pretty orange paisley printed dress, sandals, and a faded denim jacket that was more white than blue. The colors brought out the red in her hair and the blue in her eyes. Her freckles seemed to glow. Just a few days back from that ordeal with Die Kerk, not to mention a night in hell with Shuggy Johnston, and she was already bouncing back. Youth.

And the fact that she wasn't just any ordinary young woman.

There were no other patients in the waiting room, but Colleen still sensed trepidation on Pamela's part. She wasn't smiling. Her face was tense.

Give her time.

"Everything okay?" Colleen asked, quietly.

Pamela nodded. Whatever that meant.

Colleen gave her arm a gentle squeeze. "We can talk on the way home."

They left, took the elevator down to a golden art deco lobby. Leaving the garage, on Sutter Street, Pam staring out the passenger window, not looking at Colleen, Colleen didn't think she could stand it anymore.

"So, what did the doctor say?" Colleen motored toward Van Ness.

"Six to eight weeks pregnant." Pam sighed. "Doc says we're both fine."

Colleen felt that sense of elation. But she tempered it, held it back. This wasn't about her. It was about Pam.

"Well," Colleen said. "That's what we thought—right?"

Pam exhaled a long breath. "Maybe I was hoping somehow I wasn't."

"I can certainly understand that," Colleen said.

"It didn't really hit me until I heard it from the doc."

"I can understand that, too."

"If nothing else, she says the worst of the morning sickness is behind me."

"Good. Hungry?"

"That's all I am anymore. The doc says that's a good sign, too."

"Let's go somewhere special for lunch. We're overdue."

"Deal."

There was silence in the car, then noise as they passed Leavenworth. The twenty-dollar hookers were out early. Colleen recognized one in gold lamé hot pants.

She felt Pam turn and look at her.

"How did you feel when you first knew you were pregnant with me?" she asked.

Bam. Colleen nodded as she drove around a Busvan furniture truck double-parked. "Scared," she said.

"Scared?"

"Good and scared. Sixteen, I knew your father was bad news, but I was going to keep you. Marrying him was my only way to do that."

"It was?"

"It was that or get out of the house." Colleen shrugged as she drove. "Your grandmother wanted me to have an abortion."

"She did? She wanted you to get rid of it—*me*?"

Colleen sighed as she shook her head. "Maybe she sensed what your father was."

"I never knew that."

"Well, now you do."

"But you went ahead with it."

"Not *it*. *You*."

"I always thought Grandma wanted me."

"She did—once she saw you."

"Wow."

"I'm not going to sugarcoat it, Pam. I was full of doubt. I thought about not going through with it, too. But something told me you were going to be worth it."

Pamela looked away, laughed, hard and brittle. "Guess I had you fooled on that one."

"Not by a long shot."

"I'm not so sure."

"Well, I am." Colleen focused on the busy street. "The worst is behind you. I feel it. Just like when I felt you kick that first time. Take my word."

Pamela turned back. "You want me to keep it?"

She had only thought of herself when she killed Pam's father. "My feelings aren't what counts, Pam. Yours are."

"I hate him," Pam said. "That bastard."

Her father. "Oh," Colleen said. "Now there's something *I* didn't know. I always thought . . ."

"Why? Because I was angry at you? For taking him away from me? After what he did to me?"

"What he did was wrong."

"*Wrong* is an understatement, Mom. He was a monster. But even so, there are worse things."

"Like killing him."

"Yes."

"It wasn't your decision."

"I know that, Pam. But I didn't then. I couldn't see anything but anger. And I had to make sure he didn't do it again."

"I know. But you eclipsed me."

Colleen felt her throat catch. "I know I did. *I know.* That's why I'm saying that *this* is your decision. That I'm here to help. Financially. As a mother. Whatever you want. As little or as much as you want. Whatever it takes."

"What if I don't want any of that?"

Colleen felt tears pulling at her eyes. *No. Please. Not this. I can't lose her again.*

She cleared her throat. "Then you need to decide, Pam. I'm done interfering."

"You don't mean that."

"I don't feel it one hundred percent. But I mean it."

"Do you really want a grandson with that madman's genes?"

Colleen shrugged. "Not a granddaughter?"

Pam gave a sad smile. "It feels like a *he*."

"I want what you want, Pam. But I would love to be part of it. If I get in the way, I want you to tell me."

They drove past Polk, Sukkers Likkers. Pre-lunchtime traffic snarling.

"I'm going to keep it," Pam said.

Yes, Colleen thought. *Yes!*

"That's what I would have done," she said.

"No—that's what you *did*."

Yes, she did.

"And I do want you to be part of it," Pam said.

A huge wave of relief washed over her. Who would have thought a sick individual like Adem Lea would bring the two of them together? Like Pam's father, who brought them together in the first place.

"I can't tell you how happy that makes me, Pam," Colleen said, swallowing tears of joy.

"Oh, I think I might."

And then she saw something she did not expect to see.

Mr. Philanderer. With Blondie. Holding hands, if you please, as they turned the corner on Polk. Big stupid grin on his face. Cool bored look on hers.

"Whoa, Nellie!" Colleen said, hitting the brakes right then and there, on Geary; the hazard lights too. A dissonance of horns erupted behind her. She ignored them, popped the trunk lever, hopped out, left the door open. Horns honked. She flipped a hand in dismissal.

"What on earth are you doing, Mom?"

"Back in a jiff, sweetie."

She clattered around to the trunk in her white platforms and black suit. Mr. Philanderer was just across the street, still holding the bimbo's frigging hand. Perfect.

Colleen found her camera bag, rummaged out her Polaroid camera.

She clip-clopped across the street, one arm up to stop traffic, which responded with more honking.

Onto the sidewalk, she maneuvered up in front of Mr. Philanderer. And his squeeze.

Here they came. Looking at her oddly as she raised her camera.

"Say *cheese*," she said.

They didn't.

It didn't matter.

She took the shot.

"You two have a nice day now," she said, stepping back across the street in her heels, arm up to stop traffic again, Pamela looking at her out of the car window like she'd lost her mind.

AUTHOR'S NOTES

November 1978 was a dark month for San Francisco.

Peoples Temple, headquartered in the city, suffered the tragedy of Jonestown when 918 members in Guyana drank Flavor Aid (not Kool Aid as commonly believed) laced with cyanide. And a new phrase entered our vocabulary: "to drink the Kool-Aid."

The shooting of Mayor Moscone and Supervisor Harvey Milk blemished the city's tolerant image. Former Supervisor Dan White received what many thought was a lenient sentence of seven years for two murders after his lawyer pleaded the infamous "Twinkie Defense," citing junk food for White's mood swings. White committed suicide himself shortly after release from prison.

Although *Bad Scene* is a work of fiction, the reader will see the two events mirrored.

Of interest: a 1983 FBI file contains statements that the shootings were part of a larger conspiracy. In addition, the FBI spoke to one individual who claimed he tried to warn the city about Dan White prior to the shootings. Whatever the truth is, San Francisco was forever changed.

ACKNOWLEDGMENTS

Many thanks to my stalwart writing group for shaking out *Bad Scene* over the course of a year. They are, in no particular order: Barbara McHugh, Eric Seder, Dot Edwards, and Heather King; all talented writers whose tolerance of rough drafts and creative typos is more than appreciated.

Special thanks to Stan Kaufman, friend and doc, who helps keep me straight on the medical details.

And John Cadigan for his knowledge of the history of SF's port and the finer points of shipping.

A shout-out to Jeff Guinn's *Road to Jonestown*, a fascinating account of one of the blacker events of 1978 that played a key part in *Bad Scene*. Truth is indeed stranger than fiction.

And thanks, most of all, to you, dear reader, for reading *Bad Scene*. I hope you enjoyed it as much as I did writing it. You are, after all, the reason I do this.

PUBLISHER'S NOTE

Dear Reader,

We hope that you have enjoyed *Bad Scene* and suggest that you read Max Tomlinson's prior Colleen Hayes mystery novels; that is, if you haven't read them already.

In *Vanishing in the Haight*, author Max Tomlinson introduces Colleen Hayes. Colleen is struggling as an off-the-official-radar private investigator, working night security at a warehouse in 1978 San Francisco. She's an ex-con, having spent a decade in prison for killing her husband. Her struggling life changes dramatically when she is hired by a wealthy industrialist, desperate to solve the eleven-year-old murder of his daughter in Golden Gate Park during the "Summer of Love." Colleen has little to go on other than her criminal mind and her fearless approach to search San Francisco's dark underbelly. And during every high and every low point in that search, Colleen never loses sight of her ultimate goal: to find and reunite with her estranged daughter.

Max Tomlinson's second book in the series is *Tie Die*. Colleen is hired by a 1960s rock star to find his kidnapped teenaged daughter. This search takes her to 1970s London, where she discovers a thread that traces to the death of a forgotten fan, connected not only to a music industry rife with corruption and crime, but to the missing teen. The search for another person's missing child is especially poignant for Colleen as she never ceases her search for her own estranged daughter.

We hope that you will read the entire Colleen Hayes Mystery Series and will look forward to more to come.

Oceanview Publishing